THE TYRANNY OF GOOD INTENTIONS

jack stilborn

First Printing: 2025
Chicken House Press

ISBN trade paperback edition: 978-1-990336-97-3

Library and Archives Canada Cataloguing in Publication
CIP data on file with the National Library and Archives

CHICKEN HOUSE PRESS
282906 Normanby/Bentinck Townline
Durham, Ontario, Canada, N0G 1R0
www.chickenhousepress.ca

PRAISE FOR THE TYRANNY OF GOOD INTENTIONS

"Jack Stilborn has written a very funny and thoughtful novel about people, politics, and the never ending quest to do the right thing. The narrator, Andrew Walmer, lurches from one crisis to the next doing his level best to keep his world from spinning right off its axis. I happily joined him for the joyride."

—Terry Fallis, two-time winner of the
Leacock Medal for Humour

"This book is a readable and telling exploration of the 'politics' of contemporary living. For Andrew, the protagonist, life is like counterpoint—musical harmonies that are separate but interdependent—as he attempts to navigate the politics as a member of a condo board, a professor under siege and a partner in 'coupledom'. The wry humour of Jack Stilborn's prose provokes knowing chuckles as we read about the foibles of various human prototypes and of existence itself. Writ large, the book is a timely reminder for all readers of the personal impact of political life as well as a lesson for all would-be politicians of its potential pitfalls."

—Dr. William Young, former Parliamentary Librarian

"Jack Stilborn's debut novel is a delight: funny, poignant and wise. His characters are real, and his writing reads effortlessly."

—Colin Brezicki, author of *Sudden Death*

"*The Tyranny of Good Intentions* is an engaging story of an absent minded political science professor navigating the conundrums of family and the condo board. An interesting cast of characters finds their homespun and humorous way through the shifting sands of one unexpected twist and turn after another. Small things matter in human connections as the condo board struggles portend what can happen in the larger political world. This book is for anyone with an interest in the anomalies of life and humanity."
>—The Hon. Jon Gerrard, former federal cabinet minister
> and longtime Leader of the Manitoba Liberal Party

"Stilborn has a singular author's voice. With subtle wit he leads his characters through hefty issues with a light touch."
>—Arlene Smith, President, Canadian Authors Association
> National Capital Region

TABLE OF CONTENTS

THE TYRANNY OF GOOD INTENTIONS

JACK STILBORN

PART ONE: MAY

Chapter One

My Escape Plan

I was a desperate man. Things just kept getting worse and time was running out.

"I am regretfully resigning from our condominium board of directors, effective immediately," Meena Hamorthy had emailed us that morning.

This left my latest escape strategy in tatters. Meena had been the central player in my two-part plan. First: make sure the board was working well. Second: get off it. Fast.

I was still on the board because I felt I owed it to my neighbours. Someone needed to make sure the board was working well enough to protect our investment in our homes. As a political science lecturer, I knew something about government and decision-making. The board of Britannia Condominium needed all the help it could get.

We also needed a board that could protect us from Sonya, our president, ideally by replacing her with a different president.

Sonya Dietrich, probable cause of the growing crop of For Sale signs. She would never be happy until she could clone herself into 86 Sonyas and shadow every condo resident, peering over their shoulders and giving them daily reminders and scoldings. President Sonya, patrolling the neighbourhood in her pantsuits. Neighbours wondered if they came from army surplus, probably a supplier with soviet era connections.

And then there was the mysterious Britannia Beautification Campaign. Nobody knew when this had started and nobody could say precisely what it was. In practice, the campaign included whatever pet project Sonya wanted it to include. When she invoked it, her board acolytes—the "Sonya-ites" as I thought of them—would show all the independence of hand-puppets. When I dared to raise concerns, I might as well have been talking to hand-puppets too.

I had been trying to activate my escape plan for two

years. But the harder I tried to make sure the board was working well, the worse it seemed to get.

It was already May. My suspension hearing at the university was coming up fast, probably before the end of June. Even if I got lucky and survived, I'd be looking at a full course load starting in the fall. More than likely unfamiliar courses because the department was going to get me, one way or another. Preparing the courses would be a ton of work before classes started in September. If things went badly, I'd be spending my time looking for another job. Either way, I had four months to get off the condo board, probably less.

Meena had been a consistent voice of sanity on the board since I had persuaded her to join last year. For that reason alone, her comments had often been met with apparent incomprehension by other board members. It was as if she came from another planet. The planet of people who talk in complete sentences and say things that have common sense in them. The planet of people who don't have a compulsive need to micromanage their neighbours, including their pets.

Meena had brought the board back up to its normal number of five directors and was a potential replacement for President Sonya. With quiet jubilation, I had begun once again to activate my escape strategy. I had spent two years like a prison camp inmate, secretly digging a tunnel to freedom. Finally, my efforts were working. The only remaining step was to find a replacement for me who would support Meena.

But now Meena would be gone. Her stomach cancer had returned.

Her resignation hit me like a blow to my own stomach. Don't get me wrong. My problem was nothing compared to hers. I was completely sympathetic. But the fact that her problem was bigger didn't make my problem any smaller. Let's be honest. Pain hurts more when it's your own.

I needed a replacement for Meena and I needed one fast. Otherwise, Sonya would find another acolyte. She would then have a majority of acolytes on the board mindlessly voting the way she wanted.

Being Sonya, she would normally have done this already, except this was the week of parent-teacher interviews at the school where she had presided over unlucky students for many years. Given her raging case of undiagnosed obsessive-compulsive disorder, her parent-teacher interviews tended to be long. As a result, her inspection walk-arounds at the condo had not been happening since the beginning of the week. There was even a chance she hadn't read Meena's email yet. But I had. It wasn't often I had an advantage over Sonya in condo politics and I needed to make the most of it.

Barnstad! He was the obvious answer.

Henry Barnstad's name surfaced in my mind as soon as it had stopped being paralyzed by Meena's email. I didn't know many of my neighbours well enough to try and recruit them for the condo board, but based on occasional driveway chats, Henry seemed to check off all the board director boxes. Starting with the most important box, which was not taking flight whenever I mentioned the condo board.

I had cultivated Barnstad over several months when I still hoped I was looking for my own replacement. The picture just seemed to get brighter and brighter. He was an affable man whose approach to life was captured by what seemed to be his favourite phrase: "no problem." He was also interested in the condominium, especially some of its long-standing maintenance issues. *Interested in building maintenance,* I remember thinking. *The man is probably sick. Next he's going to say his hobby is accounting.* But this was the kind of sick Britannia Condominium needed. Not to mention the kind of sick I needed for my exit plan.

Barnstad was the right kind of interested, curious but far from eager. Not one of the people who craved to be directors, invariably the last people who should be. When I had found out he worked as a manager of capital projects for the local school board before his retirement, I had gotten that special vibration I imagined a hunter would get when, after long hours of waiting, the perfect stag strolls into the clearing and pauses, just in range. Henry was a potential condo president, not a stag, but for me, the feeling was the same.

I headed down the Crestview Court laneway towards the townhouse where Barnstad lived with his wife, Jane. With luck, I might catch him before he departed on Saturday morning errands and we could talk, person to person. As I made my way, I was thinking hard about how to tailor my pitch for him to join the board. With a last name like Barnstad, Henry had to have a Swedish background, maybe raised by parents from one of the Swedish immigrant communities in Northern Ontario. Likely, on some deep unconscious level, he would be missing the community-mindedness and modest lifestyles that still continued, although their roots in early Lutheran farming communities had largely become a thing of the past.

As I approached, Barnstad was strolling down his walkway, headed for the Subaru in his driveway.

"Good morning, Henry," I said. "I'm sorry to disturb you on a beautiful spring day like this. I bet we both have a long list of things to do, but an opening on the condo board has just come up and I want to make sure you have a chance to consider it. I think you would be perfect for it. Do you have a couple of minutes?"

"Morning, Andrew," he said. "Funny you should be asking that. I was—"

I hated to interrupt the man but I needed to get my pitch in to frame the conversation. "Yes, you probably weren't expecting this but, as I don't have to tell you, we're all in this, working together," I said, infusing my voice with a lilting Swedish cadence, and softly blending a slight "v" sound into the "working." We were all part of a community, building a life with our neighbours, talking in little phrases, phrases that could be strung together, spoken in melodic sentences, just like they did in those Swedish movies. I was reaching out to the man on a deep, subconscious level.

Local theatre is my hobby and this is the kind of thing I can do. Some people call me a bit of a ham, but they underestimate me. It's all about tapping into the emotions. This is where decisions actually get made anyway. Faced with a decision, people have been trained to think they need to start by thinking. They might even be thinking that all they are doing is thinking, and making a rational decision. But that isn't the way it works. For most people, thinking might be going on, but mostly as a way of fabricating justifications for shifting feelings. The feelings would be following their own mysterious path.

This is a life lesson I never tire of sharing with my political science students. Even if they never set foot on a stage, they need drama skills. Many of them imagine they will be going into politics and I make sure they know that for this, drama skills are essential. They are also essential in political science itself, for understanding the people who go into politics and why the others vote for them. My students never get that from my departmental colleagues and they need to know it.

Drama skills are definitely needed for anything involving sales, and almost everything involves sales one way or another. To be honest, more than a few political science students end up in sales, assuming they avoid careers in fast food.

Henry was looking at me with a puzzled expression, but there seemed to be a kind of happiness in his eyes. This told me he was on his way to wanting to be a board director, maybe even amused to recognize that this was something he'd been wanting all along. He just might not be quite ready to admit it.

This was a delicate moment.

If somebody is not quite ready to say they want something and you make them feel pressured, then they're going to say they don't want it. And once they've said they don't want it, their conscious mind is going to go into overdrive thinking up the reasons why they don't want it and never did. If that happens, you're basically done. Your best strategy is to quickly get them to agree to another discussion, so they don't lock themselves in. But I didn't have time for another discussion. Sonya would be making her rounds, if she wasn't already. I needed to find a way to close the deal.

"Vee haff even a plan for a community 'gordon,'" I heard myself saying. I couldn't believe I was doing this. Where did this come from? I saw his expression waver as soon as the words left my mouth because they were so completely wrong. They came out of a B-grade movie about Nazi prisoner of war camps, maybe, or about Swedish villagers sitting around half drunk from aquavit.

Besides, it wasn't true. We didn't have a plan for a community garden. Or a community 'gordon' either. This issue had been batting around our community for years. A series of well-meaning people had taken it on. Then they would get busy with something else. This seems to be the way things go in condos.

It was the performer in me, I just couldn't resist responding to an audience and taking it to the next level. I had always been like this and it was one of the reasons I had ended up where I was. In a mess, frankly, with my teaching career hanging in the balance. In a mess with Francine too. My wife, or I guess that would be "former wife." We had been separated for going on three years and guilt about this was part of my daily life.

However, standing in Henry Barnstad's driveway, I needed to focus.

"A new board director would be perfect to help us make a fresh start on this," I continued, attempting to expunge all traces of Sweden from my voice. "Of course, I would stay on and support you in any possible way. Especially while you are getting up to speed."

This was absolutely the last thing I had been planning to say. I only said it because I sensed his enthusiasm faltering. Now, if Barnstad said "yes," I would need to put my exit plans on hold. He would be very unusual if he could get on top of everything the board was doing quickly. So I was basically signing on for months. Maybe more, because before I left I'd still need to find a replacement for me. For Barnstad's sake, it would need to be somebody who wasn't another Sonya-ite.

Barnstad was smiling.

"Well, Andrew, that was quite a speech. I've been feeling a bit guilty about not having stepped forward before this, but the contract work I was doing made this impossible. So no problem."

Guilty. The word hit me. It was such a big part of my own life. This was my chance to reach him on a personal level and form a bond with the man.

"I totally hear you," I said. "Guilt is a toxic emotion; and really, you shouldn't feel that way. Your experience as an owner, observant and knowledgeable but not tied to decisions of the past, could actually help you to make a real contribution. So please don't feel guilty. I just hope you will be willing to agree to step up now, when the community really needs you."

"But that's what I'm saying," he said. "I'm saying no problem, I'm willing. But I really need to run. I'm due to pick up Jane at the mall in ten minutes, so thanks for this, and I look forward to working with you, Andrew. Here's my card and let's chat again soon, okay?"

He was pulling out of the driveway almost before his answer had sunk in.

The man had said yes.

I had someone! I had found a new director. I was actually implementing my plan. It felt terrific.

This was a moment to be savoured. I returned to my own driveway and stood there, leaning against my Jeep and savouring. There was new warmth in the air, the special warmth that comes each spring as the sun moves higher in the sky. I could even feel it coming from the Jeep. A sun-warmed fender against my left buttock, one of the unexpected pleasures of the season.

All traces of snow were now gone. The flower bed by the front steps of my townhouse was coming alive. The rose bush I had put in last year had survived the winter and new leaves were emerging.

It was almost as if Barnstad had been ready with his card to give me, even before he knew what I'd be asking him. *This man is organized,* I thought, *just what is needed on our condo board.*

Idly, I turned the card over in my hand. "Henry Barnstead, Retired," it said. Barnstead. Not Barnstad. Barnstead wasn't a Swedish name. More likely English. The man probably wasn't Swedish after all. My effort to find his wavelength had done no harm, but likely made no difference.

Life, I thought. Was it only my imagination, or had his answer to my offer had the slightest echo of an accent? It could have been a Swedish accent even, or at least the cadence that a departing Swedish accent might have left. Maybe the man was an unconscious mimic. This would be an unexpected quirk in a manager of capital projects, but in this life, who knew? Or maybe he had thought I was Swedish. Maybe he'd even been reaching out, thinking he was helping a neighbour who might be uncomfortable about having an accent...

Whitish cardboard in the flower bed caught my eye. "Urban Farm Girls" was stamped on it, in big mauve letters. Vaguely familiar. I realized it was the name of a nearby bakery where I had bought some delicious scones in the fall. I bent over to remove what was left of the box, catching a mild whiff of the manure I'd spread around the flowers before winter. *Ah, the smells of spring,* I thought. New life. New pungent life.

"Shit!" It was 1:30 already! This was my day with little Andy and Francine would have my hide if I was late. Again.

I dashed into the kitchen and grabbed an apple. That would have to do for lunch until later. I ran to the Jeep. Little Andy was now 11, relentlessly approaching puberty and soon never to be little again. I needed to make good use of the time I had left before he became a teenager. I also needed to not be late again.

Chapter Two

Late for Little Andy. Again.

The grey Jeep in my driveway was hardly needed for my lifestyle as a condo townhouse dweller and lecturer in political science. Maybe that was why I had wanted it.

My excuse was that I needed something that could take me and Andy on camping adventures. The Grand Cherokee was Jeep's heftiest model, with plenty of storage space. Mine had over-size wheels that raised it to a commanding position on the road and would be more than equal to the wilderness camping I had been promising. I had only been able to afford it because of its age and apparent history of backwoods abuse, judging from an abundance of scrapes and small dents. To me, these added to its rugged appeal.

Even so, I had been conflicted when I thought about the politics of future campus visits. A vehicle called the Cherokee seemed problematic on a campus newly sensitive to issues of reconciliation with Indigenous peoples. It also consumed large amounts of gas and was quite flagrant about this appetite. You could smell gas even when it was stationary in the faculty parking lot. This did nothing to bolster my reputation among colleagues who favoured self-righteous gas-sipping hybrids or electrics.

The Jeep started on the first try. It also began to move when I put it into Reverse instead of emitting the grinding noise I had been hearing occasionally. In the Crestview Court laneway, I headed for the exit, around the circle of forty-three Britannia Condominium townhouses where I had lived since Francine and I separated.

The first year after our split had been difficult, a time of emptiness. For me, it hadn't gotten easier since then, just difficult in a different way. The first year had been a period of stiff and fragile truce that we maintained for the sake of our son. More recently, however, I had been getting the feeling that Francine had crossed a private threshold and I was seeing the old liveliness in her eyes, free of hurt. I had graduated from bringing Andy back after our days together to bringing him back with pizza for the three of us. When we had time, home-cooked meals were sometimes replacing the pizza, and Francine and I had been collaborating on some of them.

I treasured my time with Francine as much as the outings with Andy. At times, especially as we chatted and worked so easily together in the kitchen, I felt that she might be beginning to feel the same. However, I didn't want to risk whatever feeling might be developing by trying to put things into words too soon. The thought of losing even the hope of being together again terrified me. With each visit, the time to leave would inevitably arrive, with the strain of not letting the sadness show. Instinctively, I would conceal this with jokes. I was living the soap opera cliché: laughing on the outside, crying on the inside. It was a cliché, but that didn't make it less painful.

Our break-up had been my fault. I had only been trying to be helpful, I kept trying to tell her. Monique had been so troubled, so needing a kind arm around her. Her shoulders so small and fragile. That was how it had started, innocently and unexpectedly, right there in Monique's apartment where I had dropped by to take a look at a failing dishwasher during a week when Francine was away at one of her women's rights conferences. I felt the wrongness of what had happened right away, but I couldn't just drop it immediately and add to Monique's pain. She had lost

Peter, her husband of ten years and an old friend of mine, eight months before to metastasizing melanoma. We saw each other off and on for about four months. My hope had been to try and get her thinking about the rest of her life and accept the reality that I couldn't continue with the part I was playing.

As time went by, she returned to her pottery at the arts collective and signed up for tennis lessons. Men she was meeting began to be mentioned. When I told her, as gently as I could, that I couldn't continue seeing her, I was surprised at how well she took the news. She almost seemed relieved. "We can't ever tell her," she had whispered. As if Francine might be listening. We both seemed to be thinking about Francine. Finally.

That was how we left it, but it didn't stay that way for long. Honesty has always been fundamental to me, part of who I am, at least for the important things. It's just that there aren't that many important things, so normally this isn't a problem. But the longer the affair went on, the more guilty I felt. After Monique and I stopped seeing each other, the feeling of dishonesty did not go away. So one evening, after Andy had been put to bed, I blurted it out. I told Francine, again and again, about how accidental it had been, how a moment of compassion had unexpectedly turned physical.

With her uncompromising ethics, her law professor's mind, her passion about the rights of marginalized minorities and women, her despair about where her principles would take her, and her absolute determination to follow them, Francine had responded exactly the way I should have known she'd respond.

"We can't be together anymore, Andrew," she had said, her voice expressionless. "It would be such a betrayal of the women I've worked with over the years. Such a betrayal of myself. I've been so committed to zero tolerance. I just can't..."

By this time, she was weeping. So was I.

That was how it ended. I got to keep my honesty, she got to keep her principles, and we lost each other.

We had worked on the details together. Each of us with our private sadness about what we were doing concealed by attention to practical arrangements. I had agreed that I should be the one to move. Everything else she proposed was immaculately fair. All I wanted was to make it less painful and get it done with.

That was also how I had found myself living in Britannia Condominium and, in a moment of weak-minded helpfulness, on the condominium's board of directors. I had agreed to be appointed in response to President Sonya's urgent pleadings after she found out I taught about governments at the university. Her plea was that I would fill an important gap on the board.

"We've had problems with conflict in the past," she

had said. "We really need somebody who knows about procedure and legal advice and all that kind of thing."

I knew that small volunteer organizations often struggle although everyone is well-intentioned. I felt an obligation to help out. After all, if we can't work successfully together in small groups, what hope is there for the big ones?

I pulled into the traffic circle in front of Francine's ten minutes late. I'm a strong believer in punctuality, but unfortunately, I'm also not that well organized. For me, ten minutes late was actually on time, or even a bit early. I felt guilt about this, but people who knew me seemed to deal with it. Sometimes, Francine and Andy stayed with clock time, but lately they seemed to be getting more flexible, especially Andy. I liked it when they used what I think of as human time or maybe a unique kind of family time, something just for us.

Francine and Andy waited on the doorstep. She wore something simple and red. It was a great colour against her dark skin, and as usual, she looked effortlessly smashing.

"How's it going?" I said, as Andy headed around to the passenger door. "Hope you're not too swamped these days."

Francine's research and teaching workload made her a busy person. With her women's and minority rights advocacy and work on the anti-discrimination cases that had drawn her to law in the first place, she was often pressed for time. This was typical Francine. I would not have wanted her to be any different.

"Not swamped," she said with a grin. My question

would not have distracted her from my lateness unless she had wanted that. I was being given a break.

"One day, I hope the minority rights business won't be so good," I said. Another grin.

"I have a litigation deadline, so you guys get out of here. Go and have some fun!"

On our way to the park where Andy and I go to practice, I asked him the usual questions: how's school, how's life, what's up? And he gave me the usual 11-year-old boy answers: basically "okay," "okay," and "the usual." He would soon be a teenager, I told myself, and these answers would be memories of precious moments of father-son communication. I had been a teenager. I knew.

As we drove, he got more talkative, especially when I got around to the Bears, his Little League summer baseball team. He was obsessed with being the pitcher, even though the team was dominated by 12-year-olds who had an extra year of growth going for them. I got the impression that the main importance of school was that it provided opportunities for him to measure his progress against other kids who would also be Bears in the summer.

"Me and Anwar pitched yesterday after school," he said. "He's not that big but he's wicked. He can do curveballs, Dad." I heard a distinct note of reproach in his voice.

"Okay," I said. "You're getting there. Let's focus on that today. You just have to work on the basics until they're automatic. Key fingers! What are they?"

"Thumb, index, and middle," he answered. "Thumb isn't a finger. You messed up, Dad."

"Are we teaching English or learning baseball here?" I said. This was how we talked. Friendly banter. *He'll be a good companion,* I thought, *for the fishing and camping trips that have remained trapped in a permanent planning stage so far.*

We had been working steadily on his pitching, starting last fall and picking up as soon as the spring weather let us out. He was surprisingly strong for an 11-year-old. He could really burn them in. On our last outing, when my mind had wandered to vague anxieties about the condo board, he had burned one into my solar plexus that gave me a sharp reminder of mortality.

At the park, we picked up our standard routine. It started with warm-ups, then consolidating strengths like his fastball, then working on additions. The park was a good place to be on a Saturday in May. The steady rhythm of catch and throw, catch and throw, was just enough activity to keep me in the moment. My dilapidated Rawlings had served me since my early twenties and fit my hand like, well, a glove. There wasn't a better feeling than the crisp smack of a ball arriving in a good baseball glove, right dead centre where you want it, on a sunny spring day, warm enough to take the stiffness out of the leather and bring out the special smell that seems to be a permanent aura of baseball gloves.

Our routine, after practice, was to adjourn to a Dairy

Queen where Andy always ordered the same thing, a giant chocolate milkshake. An 11-year-old after two hours of baseball practice could make a milkshake disappear with amazing speed. As usual, I was still sipping my smaller one when the snorkelling sound of satisfied completion resounded across the table.

"Yaaahh!" he said. "I'm living my dream! Baseball and milkshakes. Thanks, Dad."

This was new. Another sign. Andy was growing up.

At Francine's, we were greeted by the mouth-watering smell of her magic pasta sauce, slowly bubbling towards the succulent readiness that she insisted on before serving. Andy headed off to his room and video game land, where he and his friends seemed to spend most of their time. Francine brought a bottle of Valpolicella and glasses to the counter where I had settled.

"Wine," she said. "It will help with any solar plexus issues."

After pleasantries about her day and Andy's progress as a pitcher, Francine shifted to my suspension hearing. As the only Black professor in the law faculty, and a long-standing minority rights advocate on campus, she was following the complaint process closely and providing a lot of advice. I liked to think her interest wasn't just academic. Maybe it had something to do with what I still thought of as our family.

"Andrew, your hearing is coming up next month. Bring

me up to date with how things are going. Have you had a chance to talk to Colwyn yet?"

Colwyn was a biology prof who had successfully fought a suspension last year, after his remarks about frog gender had allegedly made several students in the class feel unsafe.

"Well, I've been working on my arguments. But things have gone off the rails at the condo board with another resignation so I've been kind of distracted lately."

"Andrew, you're telling me that a condo board that you've been trying to get off for several years is distracting you from the possible end of your career in the political science department. Am I hearing you right?"

"Well, I..."

"I don't think you understand your position, given the way things are on campus right now. You think of yourself as Andrew, everybody's friend, the lecturer who gets the laughs, right? But there are students these days who only see you as a middle-aged white man, end of story."

I poured us more wine, but Francine was not easily deflected.

"You will never convince some of them that white male privilege isn't the basic reason why you're at the front of the classroom, getting paid what they see as a rich salary while they sit there in little desks and have to pay money to be there. And the power to award them grades puts you squarely into the patriarchy. So you have a bullseye on your back, Andrew. I'm just saying. You are going to need to fight for your rights, here. You're already feeling guilty about what you said, and you should be, but you can't let that paralyze you. You have responsibilities to yourself as well as to Gina. If you ignore them, I worry that you are going to pay a completely disproportionate price for what was essentially an ill-considered and foolish joke."

"Yes, you know I get it," I said.

The informal investigation triggered by my department head following Gina's complaint had made the new atmosphere apparent. Gina and her cause had been taken up by the Trans Person Feminist Action Caucus, an on-campus advocacy group determined to pursue the issue to a formal hearing and, I suspected, some form of public execution. My immediate future had been left in the hands of a series of informal committees and appeal committees composed of unhappy-looking colleagues. Serving on these committees had become newly important, as was avoiding recommendations that might be awkward for what every-body was calling "the university brand."

Multiple appeal procedures didn't make the process more effective. They just gave each stage an incentive to pass the buck to higher levels. Most of this complexity was a recent creation, reflecting the highly political mind of Michael Mossman, the Dean of Arts and Sciences. The creation of an expanding universe of committees and pro-cesses, declared to be taking the university to the cutting edge of social justice and inclusiveness, had been a hall-mark of what more and more people were already refer-ring to as "the Mossman era." It had already gotten media attention and approving comments from the Minister of Education. Faculty members could be heard speculating about Mossman as the next university president.

"Look, Andrew, we're your colleagues, so of course we're on your side in this," Jasmine Murray, my depart-ment head, had explained. "Your attempt at humour was well-intentioned, but you now realize how inappropriate it was, and we need to make sure students and the communi-ty are aware that Gina is being supported by our depart-ment. This is especially important for a political science department because, as you know, many of our potential students are passionate about these issues."

Jasmine looked at me sympathetically. Then her gaze slid away.

"Fortunately, the university has robust appeal proce-dures that will ultimately deliver a fair outcome. I hope you share my confidence in that. What we need to do is protect the department's reputation by recommending strong mea-sures and then let the appeal procedures do their work. Of course, I can't know what our investigation will recom-mend before it has taken place, but I'm hoping you under-stand the lay of the land we're dealing with here. Our de-partment can't be useful to students if it isn't credible to them."

So, basically, they were going through the motions and covering their butts. With the best of intentions, of course. They would look good to any students who found out about it, and leave it to higher levels to sort things out. I had agreed to what we called a "voluntary suspension" pending the results of the informal inquiry. Apart from this, the predictable outcome of the buck-passing was the formal suspension hearing I was now facing, likely before the end of June.

"But Francine," I said. "Gina, like many trans people, is a wounded person. Our culture is full of messages telling her she is different and doesn't belong. I don't think the rest of us have any idea how wounding that is, especially to a young person. That's where the anger comes from. I don't think that fighting for my rights is going to respond to that, or bring the trans community into the university in a healthy way. I think I need to reach out and communicate understanding."

Gina was the student who had stood up in my class, in a state of almost incoherent rage, and screamed at me before stomping out. I had been vaguely aware that she had started out the year as Gene, a young man, but had transitioned to women's clothing and requested that her name be Gina. Her words that day were branded on my memory, partly because she was one of my best students and they had been so out of character for her:

"Fuck you! We're not taking this kind of shit anymore!

You're singling us out and targeting me! I'm reporting this!"

I had been explaining floor-crossing to the class. This is when a sitting M.P. literally relocates across the House of Commons chamber, moving from Government to Opposition benches or the reverse. While this sometimes reflects an individual's opportunistic choice, more often it is the result of an agonizing period of reflection. Party membership is something tribal, much deeper than attachment to party policy positions that come and go.

"For activists, party affiliation is a basic part of personal identity," I had said. "Changing parties can be an extremely wrenching experience."

I had groped for something unexpected that might lock my somewhat abstract comments into student brains, and added: "A little bit like being a trans person, except without the reconstructive surgery."

There had been several muted chuckles at this but I had a queasy feeling in my stomach as soon as the words left my mouth. And then Gina stood up.

My first reaction was to wonder why there wasn't more reaction. But when I saw how angry Gina was, the feeling in my stomach took over. It was shame, and I felt sick with it. How could I have been so oblivious? The fact that my first thought had been all about me and my teaching performance instead of Gina made me feel even worse.

After the classroom door slammed shut, I tried to turn

what had happened into a learning experience for my students. I spoke to them as honestly as I could. However, the discussion fell flat and then died completely after a blue-haired young man, normally quiet, stood up and told me that I was the one in need of education. Some trans people needed gender affirmation surgery, but reconstructive surgery was completely unrelated. I could see that the students just wanted out of the room and I didn't blame them. I thanked the young man and said I could see that he was right. After ending the class early, I headed to the department to tell my Chair what had happened. I wanted to find Gina and apologize directly to her but that wasn't an option. It would just make me a power figure interfering in a complaint.

"I work with activists and several of them are in my classes," Francine was saying. "As very young and idealistic people, they respond to injustice with instinctive anger. That makes them want to annihilate the opponent. But mutual understanding, and rights within a context of recognizing the rights of others, is what will get us where we need to go. We need that to make sure our progress is sustainable. I work for this within our movement and it's part of why I'm helping you here. Even though there is a kind of conflict of interest in it for me."

"Thank you," I said. "I can't tell you how much I appreciate it."

It was true. I really couldn't tell her. I like to think I'm pretty good at acting, which is expressing the emotions of others, but I'm not so good at expressing my own. The problem with emotions is I always get emotional about them. So I keep away from that stuff. As far away as possible.

"I'm going to see what I can find out about the formal hearing," she said. "If we know who will be on the panel and who will be representing Gina, we will have a pretty good idea where this is going."

By then the pasta sauce was ready, so Andy was summoned and we sat down to dinner. It was the kind of dinner that makes good memories. Succulent food and lots of teasing. Andy has always been teasable. He has a great sense of humour. Lately he's starting to tease us back, which is delightful.

Before I knew it, it was time to go.

"Time to go for my solar plexus training," I said. "Can't face that Andy without this."

They were still smiling as I headed out the door.

I was soon pointing the Jeep back home. Back to the condo. Back to my life alone.

As I drove, my thoughts went back to my suspension hearing and my job. Francine was right, I should be taking it all more seriously. After all, what does a 38-year-old man who has been teaching political science, mostly introductory courses, do if he loses that job? We live in an era of ridiculous specialization. Once you have a label stuck on you, you simply don't get considered for anything else. You're always competing with people who have experience and how many job ads for people my age do you see that say "no experience needed?" What was puzzling me, however, was that I didn't seem to be panicking about this. At least, not yet. Maybe I deserved what might be coming to me.

Instead, my anxiety dreams all seemed to be about the condo board, almost as if my subconscious were trying to distract me.

Chapter Three
Alexandra's Lilac

I could only see her feet. Well, feet and lower legs actually. Her feet were clad in pink ankle socks and new-looking white Nikes, going past me up the walkway towards my front door. First one and then the other, along with the bottom 24 inches or so of each shapely leg. It could only be Alexandra. There was no mistaking her sinuous athletic stride, even when you only see the bottom twenty-four inches of it.

I couldn't see more because I was lying under the Jeep

in my driveway. It was the second time that week. An unfamiliar rattle had begun to emanate from somewhere beneath the middle of the vehicle and I was trying to figure out where it was coming from.

I debated briefly about calling out hello to the disappearing legs but I would have had to follow up by emerging to chat. It isn't that easy for a 38-year-old man to get out from under a Jeep. It hadn't been easy to get down there. It would be even harder to get out. The wiggling, straining, grunting, and head-banging on low-hanging parts would have to be repeated in reverse. Each injury would be a reminder of an injury sustained on the way in, a danger that should have been remembered. A danger that would have been remembered by somebody more attentive.

Besides, I kind of liked it under there. There was a quietness about it, surrounding sounds muted by the bulk of the Jeep. Once you were under it, you could enjoy the unique combination of smells that older vehicles create: used oil mingled with dirt, a whiff of gasoline and exhaust, rubber—especially if it is warm—and the pungent heavy grease from the differentials and the transfer case. There was also a special feeling of security. Two tons of Jeep engineering is good protection, and my Britannia neighbours were unlikely to be looking under a Jeep for a board director.

During my early months as a newly separated man in my new condominium, Alexandra Varga had been hard to ignore. Her dusky skin and cascading auburn hair, the luminous green eyes and spectacular curves, her languid journeys to and from the Mercedes in the parking area; always so unhurried, so self-possessed.

Before I had even met her, I had harboured ambitions. However, it was soon obvious that they would have to stay in the harbour. Her exotic career as a curator at the National Gallery, specializing in prewar European art, attracted periodic media attention, and the people who came and went from her doorway included local celebrities in the world of art. Each visitor radiated self-confidence and sported what the fashion magazines would call a unique "look." I didn't have a look. I dimly realized that I would never have one.

Besides, there was Francine. I had begun to hope that I had not lost her permanently. Alexandra had drifted out of my mind except when the issue of her lilac made one of its periodic appearances on the board agenda. Apparently, boards had been discussing it for close to eight years. During this time, several board members had been driven into early retirement in a state of emotional exhaustion. Charges for legal advice had been accumulating.

The dispute was over who owned the large lilac bush in Alexandra's back yard. Yards are condominium property but designated for exclusive use by the owner and, over the years, many owners planted trees, sometimes with the consent of the condominium and sometimes without it.

The lilac had become an imposing specimen, occupying a significant portion of the small yard and advancing, every year, further onto the common space behind the yard that was maintained by the condo. Initially, the dispute had been over who was responsible for annual maintenance, mainly bills for trimming the tree. However, a healthy lilac produces offshoots, and Alexandra's lilac was unusually prolific. The dispute had escalated to include the cost of removing invasive baby lilacs that emerged on the common area each year. These incursions impeded landscaping and created a risk of falls and insurance claims. The condo had been removing them and billing Alexandra. However, Alexandra emphatically denied that she had ever installed the lilac and only paid condo charges for this work under protest.

The lid of my mailbox creaked open, then closed. The Nikes retreated past me, heading in the direction of Alexandra's house. Evidently, she had dropped something off in my mailbox. It had to be about the lilac. Alexandra was a very busy person and there had been lengthy intervals of silence; however, she was also tenacious and, after eight years, clearly not giving up. Our property manager would have told her about the board's most recent meeting. Alexandra must have found out that the condominium board was meeting later that week.

Last month, the board had considered an email from Alexandra to Sonya indicating that she would be consulting a lawyer. My attention had drifted during much of that discussion, journeying along what had become my personal Britannia-related version of the stations of the cross: a familiar list of reasons why I hated being on the condo board and needed to get off it.

A prominent reason had been sitting across the table from me: President Sonya. Her gaunt and humourless face rarely showed any sign of animation, except in conversations about the condominium rules and our duty to enforce them. Sonya's approach to her fellow board members, notably me, strongly suggested that she had missed her calling as a parade ground sergeant barking orders or, perhaps, a prison guard.

A second reason was the meeting agenda. This was Sonya's work. It listed twenty-three items, most of them about the condition of the flower bed in front of the office or other utterly boring minutiae. However, on the Britannia board, even a weedy flower bed could produce lengthy discussion, and length was no guarantee that there would be a conclusion.

Item #13 was titled *Sharon Meyer's Cat*. The presence of a cat on our agenda provided me with the latest explanation of the damage to my tooth enamel that my dentist had been warning me about, along with advice about teeth grinding. Escalating dental bills: another reason why I needed to get off the condo board.

Like most agenda items, number 13 came with no

written proposal or information that would allow people to do homework ahead of time and come to the meeting prepared. This approach to meetings had been causing me frustration since I arrived on the board. However, my calls for a more organized approach seemed to have no impact. Sonya had her ways of doing things.

"We've had a complaint about Donald," she had said, introducing the item. "As I'm sure you know, Donald is Sheila Meyer's cat. Kristin Wigglesworth's Doberman charged right through her screen door trying to get at Donald in her backyard last week."

"Kristin told me she recognized the cat and it was Donald," Sonya continued, adding with evident satisfaction: "So Donald was in her yard in violation of Rule 12(a). As you know, Rule 12(a) prohibits cats from being outside an owner's yard unless they are leashed. We need to enforce our rules. We have been advised, again and again, that if we don't enforce them, we are failing to perform our duty as a board of directors."

Kristin was demanding compensation. A rambling discussion ensued. Were we responsible for costs created by people breaking our rules? How could we recover costs from Mrs. Meyer if we paid for the door repair? How could we confirm that the cat had actually been Donald?

I had been distracted by a text message from Andy about our next pitching practice session and I didn't know what the conclusion was, if there was one. I only knew that, during intervals of attentiveness, I kept thinking about how I needed to get off the condo board.

Sonya proceeded to Item #14, Alexandra Varga's email, her pen beating a tattoo of impatience on the board table. "We all have the email from that woman," she said. "We have been over this again and again and I hope we can avoid spending precious board time on it again this evening. We have important decisions waiting for us tonight. Can we agree that we just have the Property Manager send her an update of the email we sent last time, stating our position and notifying her that the cost will be added to her fee?"

Discussions of the board's position on Alexandra's lilac always foundered on the same basic problem. There were no condo records clearly establishing ownership of the lilac. Most of the dispute had unfolded during the period when Henrietta MacKenzie had been the board director serving as secretary and records keeper. Henrietta's legacy had consisted of a substantial box containing records. However, I had been the first board member to actually look in the box for records applying to the lilac. To me, the aversion of board members to the box had been inexplicable. However, on a volunteer condo board, where any offended person can easily just stomp out the door, this kind of thing called for delicacy. I was the one who wanted to stomp out the door. If others stomped first, I would be left holding the bag.

When I had opened the box, it was packed with hand-labelled file folders. *Finally*, I thought, *we can solve the tree dilemma once and for all.* However, to my dismay, I found that the files were all labelled "Mackenzie" in the same spidery handwriting apparent on the side of the box. Seventy-two files labelled "Mackenzie." Many appeared to be Mackenzie household files, including Bell Canada invoices and monthly credit card bills mixed in with condominium records in some folders. The Mackenzie enjoyment of products from the local liquor store was conspicuous. None of the files had anything to do with lilacs, condominium-owned or otherwise.

"I don't mean to repeat discussions we've had several times," I had said, hoping for an advantage by responding to Sonya's proposal ahead of other directors. "We're all now aware that Henrietta's files have nothing about the lilac in them. If we can't prove ownership then I think we have to concede the issue. We need to let Alexandra know before she goes to her lawyer and we end up generating even more expenses over this."

My comment had been met with blank stares and looks of vague discomfort. Silence in response to my comments was an all too familiar part of my experience at board meetings. I would make an obvious point, entirely sensible and clear at least to me. However, it would be greeted with a kind of blankness, even suspicion, as if I were an interloper in the boardroom, speaking an incomprehensible foreign language.

Sonya had broken the silence. "We have been advised, again and again, to stand our ground on this," she said.

"Alexandra Varga has been a problem here from day one," was Doreen's contribution. "She went straight to that lawyer friend of hers at the beginning of this instead of trying to work with us about it, and her fancy friends keep parking their cars in front of her house instead of in the Visitors' Parking."

Philippe, our fourth board member, had delivered a flowery speech about his dedication to community service. It morphed into an impassioned continuation of his latest obsession: the need for expensive business cards embossed with the title *Condominium Director.*

Board discussions were often like this, consisting of unrelated monologues randomly interrupting one another.

For reasons that had since become clear, Meena, our fifth, had been absent.

My concerns had not been shared by other board members, leaving Sonya free to go ahead with her direction to Bill, our property manager. Alexandra's visit to my mailbox was the predictable outcome.

I completed my examination of the Jeep's underpinnings. Most of the drive-train seemed to be losing lubricant and almost anything could be the problem. A journey to the mechanic would have to be scheduled.

Levering myself out from under the Jeep, I retreated to my house in defeat. Absentmindedly, I had been wearing a new white shirt. The shirt was no longer white. A large black grease stain had also appeared on my arm. I would get whatever was in my mailbox on my way to the shower and the laundry hamper.

The envelope in the mailbox bore the return address of Binks, Stratton, Eale LLP. No surprise there. Richard Eale had already provided two of the terse and formal letters that had now become the means of communication between Alexandra and the board about the lilac. There was also a hand-written note on the envelope:

Hi Andrew. I'm hoping you can make sure this letter gets immediate attention from the board. We're all neighbours so we don't want this to escalate further. Thanks so much!
Alexandra

This was a new twist. I seemed to have been designated as her emissary.

The letter outlined Alexandra's familiar position. However, the closing paragraph upped the ante significantly:

Please be advised that, in view of the repeated failure of Britannia Condominium to produce evidence demonstrating my client's ownership of the lilac on the condominium property known as her back yard, my client has directed me to prepare a court filing. However, she is prepared to allow an interval of 21 days from the date of this letter, in order to provide Britannia Condominium with a final opportunity to reconsider its position, do the right thing for an owner who has always fulfilled her obligations to the condominium, and avoid the distraction and expense of litigation. I am requesting on her behalf your statement within 21 days affirming that Britannia Condominium is the sole owner of the lilac in Alexandra Varga's back yard and will now assume full responsibility for all maintenance costs relating to this tree.

The issue would have to go to the board. Again.

Freshly showered, and with the evidence of my foray under the Jeep removed, I made copies of the letter for distribution to board members. There was now the possibility that things might finally go my way. With Barnstead as my ally at next week's meeting, all that was needed was a change of heart by Philippe, our most unpredictable board member. Barnstead's influence could bring him onside. As a retired manager of capital projects, Barnstead would have special credibility with Philippe, who often professed special (if vaguely defined) experience with building infrastructure. Philippe would also want to be one of the guys. If this wasn't enough, Philippe could always be moved by flattery. I would be ready to supply copious amounts.

It was time to take on Sonya. Barnstead and I could do it! The board meeting next week would be a real turning point. Sonya would have to recognize that she no longer controlled the board. Predictably, this would lead to a return of what she referred to as her "digestive issues." *Who knows,* I thought, *she might even expire of a laxative overdose and that would solve my problem right there.*

In this newly hopeful mood, I turned to my evening's work: grading a set of essays that I had agreed to take care of for Marina Kerr, a colleague who had been burdened with two of my courses.

Chapter Four
Try-Outs

I'm not a hater, except for Michael Mossman. Even with Mossman, I would never do anything personally. But I wouldn't have been grief-stricken with him dying on his own, preferably after some form of public humiliation.

Not surprisingly, when I arrived at Andy's try-out game I felt a surge of adrenalin when I saw Mossman already installed on the bench beside coach Greb. He was there because he was always on time, always conspicuously well-organized. He was talking to Greb with unusual ani-mation. Greb was stolidly chewing the wad of gum that seemed to be essential when he was coaching.

Mossman is the Dean of Arts and Sciences, so there had been an edge to our relationship since news of my blunder about floor-crossing filtered through the university. Before becoming distracted by the deanship, Mossman had been a cognitive psychologist producing a steady stream of articles documenting human irrationality and funded by prestigious research grants. During my ten years at the university, his star has risen rapidly, most recently to his position as Dean. My star has not risen. In fact, I don't think I actually have a star. I am at best an unremarkable moon in the academic universe, or possibly a minor asteroid.

The root of my dislike of Mossman was not just envy. His posture and deportment were what triggered it. The way he walked, especially. I couldn't help seeing the man as a product of thousands of years of Mossman family evolution, genetically tailored for walking at a stately pace in academic processions and wearing a robe. It wasn't just his posture or regal gaze, there was something about the way he moved that made me imagine an invisible brass band escorting him, marching in tandem as a solemn honour guard for Michael P. Mossman, Dean of Arts and Sciences and probable future president. People on campus pathways spontaneously cleared the way for Mossman, as if he were some kind of potentate. They even allowed room for the invisible band. If entitlement could have a body and walk down a sidewalk, that would have been Mossman. He barely deigned to acknowledge greetings from the hoi polloi, altering his pace only for vice-presidents or above.

It didn't help that his son, Marcus, also wanted to be a pitcher for the Bears. As of last year, Marcus had showed no sign of talent or any serious interest in pitching, but there he was. Fitted out with high-end equipment and looking every inch like a budding star of the Little League. He was a smaller, thinner and more acne-marked version of his father; although, in fairness, I had to recognize that he moved like other boys, not an emperor-in-training.

By the time I got to the baseball field, the try-out game was close to over. The game had conflicted with the final rehearsal of the theatre group I was directing, which appeared to be headed for a truly catastrophic performance of Oscar Wilde's *The Importance of Being Ernest*. I had no choice but to ask Francine to drop Andy off on her way to an evening seminar, so I could make a last-ditch desperate effort to infuse even a small amount of drama into what was, ostensibly, a drama.

Marcus was pitching as I arrived, a soggy throw that barely stayed aloft across the plate. The batter, a husky girl at least a head taller than any of the boys, walloped the ball into left field and charged around the bases.

"Go Amanda!" her team yelled, "Go!"

Amanda went. With unexpected speed for a somewhat

overweight 12-year-old girl. It was a home-run, putting the Reds two up on the scoreboard. Greb signalled Marcus off the mound and put Andy on for the next pitch.

Andy looked confident as he walked to the mound. My kid, but now he was on his own. There was nothing left I could do for him, a bittersweet moment for any parent. He took his time, wound up, and smoked a fastball across the plate. The batter, who seemed to be a second Amanda, swung wildly and missed. Strike one!

The fastball was Andy's strongest pitch but I hoped he had been showing coach some versatility. He wound up and made his second pitch, deceptively low but rising as it reached the plate. Amanda didn't swing. Strike two!

Alright! My kid! I spontaneously rose to my feet and was about to cheer. Then I remembered I was at a practice game for 11 and 12-year-olds. For all I knew, the second Amanda's parents might be right in front of me.

I sat down.

Andy went back to his fastball for the clincher. It was definitely fast, but also high and wild, drifting out of the strike zone and hitting the second Amanda on the shoulder. She went down and her coach ran over to her. Coach Greb arrived on the scene and knelt beside them, his mouthful of gum apparently intact. The coaches conferred.

"Folks!" Greb announced. "We've had a great game here tonight. Lots of great playing and congratulations to the Reds, I'm sure you'll have a great season. You can all expect to hear from us in the next couple days on starting positions. So, thanks for turning out, everybody, and have a good night."

I met a dejected-looking Andy as he retrieved his gym bag.

"I'll catch Greb," I said. "He needs to know that your fastball almost never goes wild."

"Nooooo, Dad," he wailed. "Puhleeze. He hates it when parents do that. Let's just get out of here. I don't know what happened. I think it was in my wrist."

"Okay," I said. "You're right. He's already seen lots of your pitching in practice."

Besides, Greb had already gone back to his place on the bench and Mossman was talking to him again. I needed to have more confidence in Greb than I felt. He had coached the Bears for two seasons, moving them steadily up in the league standings. He was a longtime presence in local adult baseball and something of an athlete in his youth. However, the passage of time appeared to have brought a gradual reduction of extraneous motion. He now sat, Zen-like, beside Mossman. His only activity was his steadily moving jaw, the wad of chewing gum still in place. His weathered face, at least the part of it visible beneath the bill of the brown Bears baseball cap, remained impassive. From time to time, the pace of the gum-chewing slackened momentarily, which may have indicated that messages from Mossman were being processed.

I needed to have confidence in the coach. I also needed to still the paranoid voice in my head that was wondering if Mossman was poisoning Greb's mind against Andy, just because of his scandal-tainted father. There was no question that Mossman had an ulterior motive. He always did. However, there was no way of telling what it was. I also needed to have confidence in Andy, who knew the coach.

"Dairy Queen?" I said to Andy, as we walked to the Jeep. He brightened visibly. Any concerns about his future career in baseball seemed to be addressed by the prospect of a chocolate milkshake.

We repeated our standard visit to the Dairy Queen and then headed for dinner at Francine's.

After dinner, with Andy once again online with friends in a complex game that appeared to involve some sort of interplanetary invasion, Francine and I picked up our on-going conversation about my suspension hearing.

"You're not going to like this," she said.

Right, I thought. *What a surprise that was, the way things had been going lately.*

"The College Trans Feminist Action Caucus sees this as a potentially break-through case. I got this from Marion Philbert. She's part of the Caucus leadership collective and I know her pretty well.

"Marion told me the Caucus sees this case as symbolic

because Gina is recent in her transition and especially fragile. For them, you are symbolic of an entrenched patriarchy that is tone deaf to the struggles of oppressed minorities. So they have already hired a lawyer and are working right now on the case they will present at the hearing. And the lawyer is Sophia Landsdorf. You've heard of her, I assume?"

Sophia Lansdorf. Yes, I had heard of her. Several of her recent cases had put her in the news and she knew how to use public attention. She was a pro. She did what she needed to do in order to get high profile organizations and people to take her clients seriously.

"Francine, I'm starting to get very worried about what you're doing to your credibility by being involved in this," I said. "This isn't just about your place in social justice on campus, although I know that is important to you. It's about the influence you have within the movement, and your ability to moderate some of its excesses, which I believe is helping the movement to actually accomplish things. I would feel terrible to see that compromised."

"Don't worry," she said. "And don't patronize. I know how to take care of myself."

"Of course," I said. "I hope you know me well enough to know that I would never doubt you that way. It's just that—"

I admired Francine for what she does, but my feelings for her went well beyond that. Being separated hadn't changed them. It was just that I didn't know how to say this without putting her on the spot and getting into complex emotional waters.

"We're going to have to do something to reframe the case, Andrew," Francine said. "I'm going to be with your lawyer at the table. You need allies outside the patriarchy. A Black woman with established social justice cred on your side is going to help. You may not like this, but there's at least a little bit of politics in almost everything. You're also going to need more than this. We need to think about how to make sure you're not perceived as just a typical middle-aged white male power-figure."

"I don't deserve what you're doing," I said. "You're throwing away your credibility on something that doesn't deserve it either."

"I'm not throwing anything away," she countered. "I work for justice and I often disagree with my sisters in the movement. They know what my motives are and I'm not shy about explaining my views. The people whose opinions I value respect me for what I am. When Marion and I talked, I was entirely frank with her about what I'm doing and why, and I hope it provokes some thinking. Marion knew about our separation and said she couldn't understand how I could do this, since I have 'lived the struggle against patriarchal oppression' in my own life." But she's an intelligent woman. She will think.

"So getting back to my question, we need to make the

hearing, and Gina herself, see you as a human being, not just a symbol."

"How do we do that?" I asked. "How do I not look like a power-figure? And besides, what about using this case to reach out to the trans community and communicate some real understanding? I think that is what I need to do. I could reach out and maybe help the process of making them feel genuinely accepted."

"Andrew, what you've just said is exactly your problem! You have a vague abstract idea about how things should work, but you aren't seeing what is right under your nose. The university community doesn't work that way yet! Some day, I hope it will. What is happening right now is that you, one person, are in danger of being punished far out of proportion to any harm that was done by your joke. Your joke was insensitive, but you already know that. You don't feel any hostility to trans people and your joke didn't express any. We have to get that message across. The university can't afford to lose people like you. Seriously!"

"But, what I think I need to—"

"Andrew, I have to interrupt here. It just hit me: your thinking here is exactly the same as your thinking about the condo board. Really! You have a vague idea about how the board should work and you let it stop you from doing what you obviously need to do, which is get off it. You seem to seek out opportunities to suffer for the sake of others! I wonder if this is your Catholic upbringing coming out here."

"Francine, if people can't run a condo board properly, what hope is there for solving problems like the Middle East? Or anything really?"

Francine had been smiling as she interrupted, but I could see she wasn't entirely joking. And there might be something to what she was saying. Francine is clever, more clever than I am. She was outflanking me and I couldn't deal with me and the condo board in the middle of me in the suspension hearing.

I punctuated the conversation by pouring us more wine.

I needed her to understand that I was on the condo board for solid reasons. Besides, I also wanted the wine.

"Andrew, how would you feel about wearing a dress to the hearing?"

This was the Francine I knew. She saw my thoughts going to the condo board and the state of the world and she was preempting me. Her face was expressionless.

"I... I... What about Andy? How could we ever explain to him what was going on?"

"If you could see your face!" she said, starting to laugh uncontrollably. Francine had ambushed me, punctuating the conversation in her own way. The condo board was no longer in my thoughts.

"Okay, I'll go for it, but only if I get to wear panties too. I've always wanted to wear them to a faculty hearing."

By now we were both laughing hysterically. Andy came out of his room to see what was going on, smiling expectantly but also looking distinctly puzzled. I wondered if he had heard the "panties at a faculty hearing" part.

"Gotta go. Mom will explain," I said as I stood up. "You guys have early mornings tomorrow, so I'm out of here for now." Francine and I were still laughing as I headed out the door. I was already looking forward to hearing how she would explain Dad's clothing tastes to Andy.

I felt a sweetness as I left them. It wasn't just the joke. Francine's irreverent sense of humour had been missing since we separated, her wicked teasing that had always given me such joy. Missing until tonight. *Was it possible her feelings for me were coming back?* I hastily pushed the thought away in case the answer might be 'no.'

As I drove home, I distracted myself by returning to Francine's apprehensions about the hearing and wondered why I wasn't more anxious than I seemed to be. I wondered if my heart was really in my job. Since Francine and I had separated, it sometimes felt as if my heart wasn't really in anything.

I had been teaching for ten years, mostly the same familiar introductory political science courses along with my specialty, a seminar on parliamentary government. I had drifted into this after a lengthy period of graduate studies largely devoted to student drama productions and baseball. The thought of Adam Ferguson, an obscure eighteenth-century Scottish historian and political theorist suggested to me by my PhD supervisor, had been my dissertation subject. I felt that my studies had confirmed history's verdict: the man deserved to remain obscure. My dissertation efforts had slowly expired, leaving me with an ABD (All But Dissertation) degree that made a future academic career unlikely. I sometimes wondered if Ferguson's obscurity might have been contagious.

However, since the alternative was unemployment, obscurity had its attractions. The political science department was trying to fill a leave replacement position in legislative studies as my doctoral work petered out. The field had been one of my doctoral course work subjects and, somewhat to my surprise, I found it interesting. This had led to some modest publishing and occasional teaching that had garnered enthusiastic reviews. The appointment was an obvious solution for them and for me too, as I tried to figure out my future.

When the professor I was replacing unexpectedly left the department, that future had effortlessly fallen into place. Teaching provided an opportunity for me to activate my love of drama, including imitations of political speeches. Students accustomed to grim endurance in classes on political institutions responded gratefully, and my classes rapidly developed attendance numbers that made me an asset to the department. So, for ten years, I had been helping the department at budget time and teaching students a little bit about how government works as well.

On the whole, it was a good life and it had left me plenty of time to devote to amateur theatre. This remained my real love, at least in theory. It would have been in practice too except for the people I had been working with lately. The last couple of years had brought an uninterrupted stream of enthusiastic but completely talentless performers. I had always felt that amateur theatre should be for people who started out as amateurs, not for people who struggled to rise to that level. Directing plays at the Community Theatre was giving me new empathy for the mythical character Sisyphus, endlessly pushing a stone up the mountain only to have it roll back down.

Francine's warning about the prospect of losing my little sinecure had not sent me into a panic. On some level, it almost seemed to be welcome. It promised uncertainty after ten years of predictability. This was strangely exciting.

She was right, of course, that there were good practical reasons for pleading my case and defending my rights. However, I found myself thinking that, perhaps, this was an opportunity to grow. I was only 38. Did I really want to go on for possibly twenty-five or thirty years, doing what I had been doing for the last ten?

As I steered the Jeep into its parking space, I realized that I needed to do some serious thinking about my future, regardless of what might happen in the suspension hearing. Since Francine and I had separated, I had been going through the motions in my life in a state of near numbness. What was left to care about? And why was getting off the condo board what I kept obsessively thinking about?

Chapter Five
Let My People Go! Now!

Go down, Moses,
Way down to Egypt's land;

The deep, sad, resonant voice was mine, it felt like the essence of me, singing the powerful words over a chorus so gentle it was a soft rain of harmonizing sound.

Tell old Pharaoh
To let my people go!

I was not just singing the words, I was feeling the

words and their wonderful music. They were coming from somewhere deep in my being, as if I were the song itself; as if I only existed as the wonderful voice and the sweet feeling of its sadness…

But even as this was happening, it all began to fade away. I was not that magnificent bass singer, standing in front of a massive weeping audience, carried along by the voice and words. There was a vague feeling of pressure along my spine, and also on the back of my head. The feeling of singing was disappearing. I began to see the outlines of a familiar room, early sunlight streaming from behind what was supposed to be a light-proof blind. I was lying in my familiar bed, emerging by gradual degrees from an unexpected nap into familiar reality.

"Let my people go!" The phrase lingered, echoing in my mind as I came more fully awake. It spoke to me. Somehow, it crossed the multiple barriers of culture, race, and history, emerging from a depth of experience I would never have. But still, it spoke to me.

Let me go, was the feeling. Off the condominium board. Let my people go, especially me! It was past time for me to be out of there and getting on with my life. I only needed to build my escape route and, with Henry's agreement to join fresh in my mind, I felt optimistic that I would find a way. Henry was my first step, my first brick in the wall. Previous walls had fallen down, but this one would surely stand. I only needed to build out the bridge and then move across it. Well, something like that anyway.

Time, however, to return to reality. I faced a day of uninspiring chores followed by our regular condo board meeting. Before I knew it, I would be scrambling to get ready so I could stop by Barnstead's door on my way to the condo office. Tonight was the night when he would be appointed to the board. A friendly gesture would help solidify the alliance that he and I were forming.

Later that day, I finished a hasty dinner and jogged to Henry's. The doorbell was answered by Jane, his wife. I could never look at Jane without thinking the phrase "a woman of indeterminate age." If anything, it was an understatement. She was indeterminate in every possible way. She wore a housecoat that was either very old or deliberately mottled in a combination of colours, none of which prevailed. I could not remember any occasion when I had seen her face betray even the slightest emotion. The sight of me at her door produced none.

"Hi, Andrew," she said, in her familiar monotone. "Henry thought you might be coming. He needed to talk to Sonya before the meeting so he's already left."

This was a surprise, but it made sense. Henry would be getting to know the president before committing to the board. I thanked Jane and headed across the parking area to the office, which was a small building beside the pool. It contained the boardroom, largely occupied by a government surplus table. Its brown laminate surface bore scars testifying to the frustrations of public servants at some earlier time. The plastic storage box containing the Mackenzie files reposed where I had left it months ago.

I entered the boardroom, only slightly late according to the large wall clock Sonya had installed, making sure it was positioned to be visible to all board members. Everyone was at the table except for Philippe. Philippe Gibbon was always late. However, to avoid angry protests and accusations, meetings never started before he was settled at the table. This meant that, for practical purposes, I was early.

"...never go there for chicken." The words were distinctly audible even though everyone seemed to be talking at once.

As usual, Sonya was prevailing. Although not conspicuously loud, her school teacher's voice cut through background noise like a surgical knife. Her role as the board's resident authority about everything included chicken, apparently.

Sonya made me think of the raptors in bird books I had read to Andy when he was younger. Or hawk exhibits at the Museum of Nature. Her gaze had the same intentness that detected helpless prey from astonishing heights. It followed me as I made my way to my chair. I sat down with a feeling of relief that I had escaped her talons.

Predictably, Doreen was nodding in agreement with Sonya. A large and somewhat garish hair clip amplified her enthusiasm. Doreen Nicol had volunteered for the board a year after Sonya, and her motives remained a mystery to me. She possibly wanted a more sociable alternative to her computer screen after a day in her home office. Doreen's round, expressionless face and thick-lensed glasses made her hard to read. Aside from venomous comments about some of her neighbours, she had little to say during meetings, her knitting needles clicking steadily away on brightly coloured sweaters for grandchildren.

Henry looked on with genial amusement. He sat to the right of Sonya, who was flanked on her left by Bill, our property manager, and Charlene, our recording secretary. Henry seemed completely at ease, almost as if he were already a long-standing board member.

Philippe arrived. With a theatrical flourish, he hung up the over-sized and blindingly white Panama hat that always accompanied him to board meetings. The hat could hardly be more obvious as a symbol of Philippe's deep-seated craving for attention and need to feel important, not to mention providing subconscious compensation for his diminutive height.

Sonya got the meeting underway. "We have two late-breaking agenda items," she said. "Henry Barnstead has volunteered to join the board, so I will nominate him as a director. And we have the lawyer's letter about the lilac bush at number 23 that Andrew circulated last week. Are there other additions?"

There were none. The meeting moved to routine business, rapidly passing the minutes of the previous meeting before coming to rest on the monthly financial report.

"I'd like to call on our treasurer for an overview," Sonya said.

This was a routine step at every meeting, regularly producing the same utterly predictable result. Each month, in his capacity as treasurer, Philippe responded to Sonya's invitation by staring fixedly into the middle distance and saying nothing. It was almost as if he could put himself into a trance.

Bill was ready to step in. He assured board members that there were no issues of concern. Sonya invited questions. There were none. The financial report was declared received and approved.

"Now, I'd like to dispose of our two items of new business before we continue with the other agenda items," Sonya said.

"First, I know we are all very sorry about Meena Hamorthy's news. On behalf of the board and our community, I would like to express our thanks to Meena for her work as a director. I am sure we all wish her well as she deals with the health challenge that has required her to step away from the board."

"I am very pleased to be able to nominate Henry Barnstead as a director. Until recently, demands of the contract work he's been doing since he retired have prevented him from joining us. However, he has been a wonderful help to me in recent years, especially with our infrastructure issues. He has agreed to be nominated, so I'd like to call for your vote to appoint him."

Like the others, I voted yes. However, the apprehensive feeling in my stomach was probably mine alone. Could Henry be another Sonya-ite? If he was, my prospect of freedom was going down the toilet. Yet again. There was no way I could leave our condominium in the hands of that woman without a board that could keep her under control.

"...by Andrew." It was Sonya. The sound of my name drew my attention back to the meeting.

"I am sure people have heard enough about this issue," she continued. "But Andrew, do you feel you need to add anything?"

"Well," I said. "I think we need to recognize that the lawyer's letter takes things to a new level. If this goes to court, it will be up to us to prove she owns the tree. As we all know, we simply don't have solid proof—"

Philippe interrupted. Sonya let him.

"Andrew, we are here to serve the whole community, and sometimes that means we have to make the tough decisions. And then we have to stick to them. Alexandra knows what's involved in going to court and there's no way she's going to do that. She has to be bluffing."

"Sonya has given me the background on this," Henry

said. "I agree with Philippe that we shouldn't just cave. It sets a bad precedent and it just encourages owners to go to lawyers. I've also had friendly mailbox chats with Alexandra and, as a new board member, I think she would see me as more objective. So I'd be willing to reach out to her and see if there might be compromise solutions to this."

Philippe was nodding. Sonya was nodding. Doreen was nodding in support of Sonya's nodding. I could see where this was going. I would not be able to visit Alexandra in triumph. However, Henry's offer was only a postponement. At least I could quietly let Alexandra know that I had tried and that her cause was not lost.

Sonya summarized our agreement to Henry's offer for Charlene to record for the minutes and the meeting turned to other business. The main business on the agenda was "Potted Plants," with Sonya's name beside it.

Sonya had spotted potted plants on the second floor balconies during what she called her "weekly president's patrol." "I do apologize for not having given you a proposal in advance, but I've been run off my feet with parent-teacher meetings over the last two weeks.

"These plants are becoming a terrible eyesore," she continued. "We need to remember the Britannia Beautification Campaign, and this is the kind of thing we can't just let slide."

"I can see them from my balcony," Doreen interjected. "I bet they're from big box stores that have spring promotions going. Those plants always look half dead and I don't think people should be buying them."

"The plants are a plain violation of Britannia Condominium Corporation Rule 38," Sonya resumed, opening her dog-eared copy of our rules. "Balconies shall be kept in presentable condition at all times, they shall not be used for storage of bicycles, kitchen items extending beyond the exteriors of the standard barbecues (see Rule 27), gardening items, or any other items or clutter."

"Our balconies are key to our curb appeal," Philippe broke in, adding that Rule 38 was central to what he called "balcony management by the Corporation."

"As Philippe always reminds us, we're all here to serve our community." Sonya was reaching for Philippe's support. "We need to keep moving forward on the Britannia Beautification Campaign and Rule 38 is part of Philippe's wonderful contribution to this with our legislation and protocols."

Characteristically, Philippe glowed at even a hint of positive recognition. Sonya's comments brought him to full incandescence.

Sonya called for a notice requiring the removal of all potted plants from balconies within forty-eight hours, with provision for their removal by the condominium if owners failed to act. Access to balconies would be achieved by our window-washing contractor, using the small, automated lift normally employed for his work.

Doreen was nodding. Emphatically. Not for the first time, I wondered if Doreen's support for Sonya ever resulted in physiotherapy bills.

The proposal seemed ridiculous. Impossibly draconian and completely out of proportion to the problem, if there even was a problem.

"We need to think carefully about this," I said. "We shouldn't be forcing people to get rid of plants just because we happen not to like them. We need to think about how these owners would be affected, and how it will make them feel about living here.

"As you know, I teach about these issues, and finding the right balance between individual freedom and the needs of the community is a fundamental issue at all levels of government. Intruding on people's choices is always a serious decision. Toleration is a central principle in democratic societies. The philosopher John Stuart Mill gave us an important rule of thumb: restrictions should focus on direct impacts that actions have on others and leave people free to make their own choices outside of that. So, really, what are the direct impacts of the plants on us?

"And the second issue is proportionality," I continued hastily, preempting interruptions. "is requiring the plants to be removed proportional to the seriousness of the problem, if there even is a problem? We shouldn't be using a hammer to swat a fly. I don't think people even see these plants unless they are looking for them, and nobody has been telling me they are bothered by them. If we intervene at all, our intervention needs to be proportional to the problem."

My comments were met by silence. Board members regarded me with sober expressions. It was hard to tell what they might be thinking.

"Have you seen those three big red pots at the Zalewski's?" Sonya said. "One of the plants is already dead. They directly affect me because I hate the look of them and I don't see how they can be in proportion when they are just completely ugly."

I looked at Henry hopefully.

"I'd like to thank you for this, Sonya," he said, dashing what remained of my belief that I had found an ally. "We are responsible for how our condominium looks, and poor quality plants from chain retailers have been a problem here for many years. By the middle of summer, they are often dead and they make our whole property look like it's not being looked after—"

"Yes, I completely support Henry's point," Philippe burst out, although Henry had only been pausing for breath. "These plants might be okay for people in social housing or something, but they don't belong in Britannia Condominium! And there's another issue here too. What about legal liability? We're the board of directors of a corporation here, and if children get on the balconies and throw one of those pots down and hit somebody, we could be looking at a lawsuit."

"I don't mean to interrupt," Doreen interrupted, with unusual fervour, "but your point goes beyond the plants and I'm not going to be shy about naming names. The Jacobsens, in number 36, they have two cats that seem to spend virtually all their time out on the balcony as soon as the weather permits. And you know what that means! There is no cat-box out there, so they use the plants! Unless there's a breeze, I can smell it! I might as well be living beside a cat box, and that certainly isn't what I need after a day in my office! So we need to do something about this. And I completely support what Philippe is saying. We need to do it now!"

Doreen's jowls trembled with fury and her face was flushed as she finished her tirade. Something about the Jacobsens, or possibly the cats, was tapping into the current of free-floating hatred that flowed in Doreen's personality, transforming opinions into dogmatic convictions. *How do I argue against this?* I wondered. How do we get rational decisions out of this?

"I have said many times that we should ban cats from the balconies," Sonya reminded them, cementing her alliance with Doreen.

"Look, folks," I said, hoping to bring them back to the basic issue. "I—"

However, Philippe could never let a digression go by without claiming a position at the forefront. "I've said again and again that we need to start taking a holistic approach to these issues," he declared. "We all have! Sonya is completely right! This is about serving our whole community, so Bill? What can we do about these cats?"

Our property manager had been sitting stolidly through the discussion. His face maintained the expression of respectful attention habitually deployed at board meetings.

"If the board agrees, I will do some work on this and come back with a proposal. I need to look into the ramifications to make sure we come up with something workable. A ban on cats might have some legal implications because, as you know, we do advertise Britannia as a pet-friendly condo. So let me take the time to make sure about this and then I'll come back to the board with something."

Bill could be quite clever, tactically. He avoided direct questions to any individual who might create awkwardness by answering them. Instead, he sought a response from an abstraction called "the board." Normally, the abstraction remained silent. This allowed him to go ahead and do what he thought was needed.

Adjournment time came and went.

There was something different about Sonya. I realized it was her hair. It made me think of the bird book again. There were ducks that looked like that. Her hair looked like it had been done by a taxidermist.

When my attention returned to the meeting, directors had created a specialized balcony coordination committee so they could save time and be efficient. They looked immensely pleased with themselves. The committee was mandated to develop a list of permitted balcony plants, rules about pets and noise, and a clear enforcement plan.

Directors all volunteered immediately. Except me. I tried to ignore offended looks coming in my direction.

"Before we wrap up," Sonya said. "The balcony plants are urgent so we need an action plan. Can you agree to authorize me to work with Bill to get them dealt with?"

Heads nodded. Except mine. Sonya studiously avoided looking in my direction as she instructed Charlene to record board agreement.

Should I prolong this? I asked myself. Before I could object, Sonya raised an unexpected item.

"One more thing before we go. I just received this letter from our auditor today," she said. As Sonya passed out copies, she explained the letter while board members stared blankly at it.

"It warns us that one of our investments involves levels of risk that the Condominium Act doesn't permit," she said. "The letter recommends immediate cancellation, which would involve a significant cancellation fee."

An awkward silence descended. Philippe, our treasurer, had recommended the investment. The rest of the board had gone along. Philippe did not take well to anything suggesting he might ever have made a mistake.

"As I don't need to remind everybody, this was agreed

upon unanimously by all board members," Philippe said. "It pays a better return than the traditional GICs that previous traditional boards have always used. I think we should get a second opinion before we make any decisions on this."

"I've had a chance to look at this," said Henry.

Sonya eyed him with a knowing expression. Obviously, they had arranged something.

"I've had quite a bit of experience with auditors over the years. Generally, on this kind of thing, they give you options if there are any. If the board would be agreeable, I could contact the auditor and explore this further with a second opinion if necessary."

"Thank you, Henry," Sonya said. "I think this is a great idea. Unless someone objects, let's call this unanimous."

No one objected. Philippe's mouth opened, but then the reality appeared to dawn that Henry's proposal avoided a potentially embarrassing board decision.

"I think we should take advantage of Henry's experience by appointing him as treasurer," Sonya continued. "That would avoid confusion for the auditor to be able to work with him. I've had a chance to chat with Henry, and I think we should all be grateful that he is willing to take this on."

"Philippe, now that we have someone else on the board with treasurer's qualifications, this would allow us to make the best use of everybody. It would free you up to focus on the wonderful work you have been doing on rules and enforcement issues, which we all agree is so important.

"I think we need to recognize this work with a new position that would communicate it better to owners," Sonya continued. "What about Director: Policy, Legislation, Protocols, and Enforcement?"

Sonya braced for Philippe's response. The rest of us watched expectantly. However, moments passed. "Excuse me," Philippe said, intently keying something into his phone.

More time passed. Philippe looked preoccupied and I imagined a primitive scale working behind that youthful forehead. On the one side: an apparent loss of status, although the new title seemed impressive, much longer than "Treasurer." More clearly on the positive side: a graceful exit from the treasurer position, which had been producing awkward moments on a monthly basis and focused on boring numbers. Adding further weight to this positive side were Sonya's intoxicating compliments about his very important work on our rules. But still, there was the loss of the treasurer position...

Sonya brought the suspense to an end by quickly thanking everyone for their cooperation.

"Let's have this recorded as a unanimous agreement to give this new division of labour a try," she said. "It's getting very late so, if you're agreeable, I can provide

Charlene with wording. We're all here for the right reasons, to serve our community, so if this doesn't work out we can always work together to find something better."

And with that, and in the absence of other business, she quickly adjourned the meeting.

Henry and Sonya left the office together.

I left alone.

My dream of freedom tangibly receded with every step they took. Britannia still needed a board that could control Sonya. Ideally, a board with a different president.

How, I wondered, *will I ever get out of this?*

How? And when?

PART TWO: JUNE

Chapter Six

Mrs. Svensson for Director?

Would I eat a bowl of rotting fish in order to get somebody to join the condo board?

Stripped down to its essence, this was the question I faced. I didn't have time to think about it deeply because there I was, sitting at Ingrid Svensson's kitchen table. The bowl of rotting fish was right in front of me. It seemed to be a china bowl, adorned with a pink floral pattern. It reminded me of the bowls of my childhood, carefully arranged in my mother's kitchen cupboard. The smell was overpowering.

Ingrid sat across the table, watching me expectantly. Bobbi, her small white dog, was sitting on his mat by the kitchen door. He was watching me intently, maybe expectantly also. It is hard to tell with a dog.

The week had begun with no sign that a visit with Ingrid Svensson might await me. However, one thing had led to another in the days following our last board meeting. The meeting had started a train of events that unfolded rapidly, leading straight to the bowl in front of me on Ingrid's table.

It had started on Monday when I arrived home after a long evening with my theatre group. I had spent most of the evening trying to inspire amateur actors to stop talking as if they were early readers, awkwardly sounding out words on the back of a cereal box. A letter had been waiting in my mailbox. It was from Philippe, addressed to all board members.

The internal struggle that had paralyzed Philippe at the board meeting had apparently continued through the weekend. Pleasure, created by Sonya's flattery about his vitally important contribution to condominium rules, had competed with pain, in the form of indignation about the loss of his position as treasurer. The letter made the outcome clear. Indignation had triumphed. By Sunday evening it had banished pleasure and risen to towering heights, finding expression in impassioned words:

Letter of Resignation

Fellow Directors of Britannia Condominium, CCC 032:

After deep reflection, I have concluded that I have no choice except to resign from the position of Director on the non-profit volunteer board of Britannia Condominium, effective immediately.

I joined the board two years ago as a result of my passion for serving our community. However, in recent months, I have found my efforts and role diminished and actively undermined. My participation on this board and my reputation in this community have been maliciously acted against by this board, led by President Sonya Dietrich. I have completely lost confidence that my work on behalf of my fellow owners will receive impartial or fair treatment by this board. I do not believe recent decisions by this board operate within the boundaries of law or good governance. The decision to remove me as treasurer was made without advance notice, without fulsome or fair debate, and without a recorded vote. It is an attack on the financial management of this corporation, and therefore, it violates the fiduciary duties of this board.

I am resigning so that I can pursue my concerns against

this board with the community and in court if necessary. As a courtesy, I am serving notice that I will now be contacting Britannia Condominium owners to bring about the reforms that I have been working for as a director. These reforms are long overdue.

Regards,
Philippe R. Gibbon

I had been expecting Philippe to come to terms with his demotion from treasurer and stay on the board, especially given Sonya's flattery and the grandeur of the new title she had offered. In all walks of life, there are people who compulsively need to be the director of something, which generally means they shouldn't be. Along with Sonya, Philippe had been the Britannia board's conspicuous example. His recent fixation on the need for personalized Condominium Director business cards had been only the latest illustration of his ego investment in the board. However, evidently, I had misjudged the depth of the wounds inflicted at the last board meeting.

Philippe's resignation was the last thing I needed. My hopes for Henry Barnstead had already taken a beating and now another vacancy needed to be filled. Sonya would already be busy filling it. Philippe had been unpredictable, but at least he hadn't been an automatic Sonya-ite. I was going to end up a minority of one unless I acted fast.

But who to recruit? That was the question. Britannia Condominium was a large community, eighty-six townhouses arranged around two circular courts separated by a ravine on six acres. Modern life is impersonal. I knew a handful of immediate neighbours and they had already made it clear that board work was not for them. Beyond that, I only knew a scattering of people well enough to say 'Hi' to at the mailbox and chat about the weather. Interest in the weather is an admirable human trait, very Canadian. However, it is a questionable qualification for appointment to a board of directors.

I needed somebody and I needed them now. The image of Mrs. Svensson drifted into my mind, perhaps because as I had arrived home I had seen her walking in the laneway accompanied by her dog, Bobbi. As always, Ingrid's rotund figure bounced along with animation, her face radiating its familiar expression of cheerful optimism. Bobbi bounced along beside her, also with animation but at a somewhat lower altitude.

What about Ingrid Svensson for director? She seemed to be a genuinely decent person and, unlike Barnstead, she really did have a Swedish background. An appeal to her community-mindedness was bound to find a receptive audience. Before retiring, she had been an office administrator at an insurance company. People liked her. She was the closest thing to a neighbourhood social butterfly on Crestview Court, the cluster of homes where we both lived.

Before I had moved to Britannia, there apparently had been a Mr. Svensson. According to neighbours, after his retirement he had taken up weight-lifting and begun to appear, with immaculate timing, doing crunches on the Svensson lawn in a tiny bathing suit just as the teenage daughters of his neighbour were arriving home from high school. After several months of this, there was no longer a Mr. Svensson. Instead, Bobbi had become Ingrid Svensson's constant companion. The neighbourhood consensus was that Bobbi was a definite improvement.

This was, of course, an appallingly bad way to compose a board of directors. As a professor of political science, I felt shame. However, it seemed to be the way things worked at Britannia condominium. Based on stories from friends, and conversations at several conferences of condominium directors, I had slowly learned the truth about condominiums. They were corporations on paper, governed by the Condominium Act, but in reality, many of them hovered in a kind of limbo, halfway between serious organizations and groups of neighbours chatting over the back fence. And those were the good boards. The bad boards resembled menageries in zoos.

In any case, my problem was practical, not about organization theory. I needed an ally on the board and I needed one fast. Mrs. Svensson was bound to be better than whoever Sonya would come up with. Sonya would find an acolyte unless she could be preempted.

At this point in my reveries, I heard a gentle tapping at my door. On my doorstep was Ingrid Svensson, with an especially big smile for me as I opened the door. She must have been heading to my house when I had seen her walking.

"Hi," she said. "I just saw you driving in. I never knew you were Swedish, Andrew. Karen told me that Henry told her. Why didn't you tell me? You must come over, if you have a minute, I have a special treat for you."

Reflexively, I was about to declare my lack of connection to Sweden. But then I realized this was my opening. It hadn't done any harm with Henry even though he wasn't Swedish, so why would I give this away with Ingrid? And besides, I didn't know for certain that there was no Swedish in my background. My ancestors had lived in various parts of Britain and the Vikings had been all over the place there, impregnating anything they could get their hands on. Strike while the iron is hot, the saying goes, and so I did.

"Hi, Ingrid. You just caught me coming back after working with my theatre group. But okay, sure. How can I say no to a special treat?"

"Surströmming," she said, with obvious pride as we walked back to her place.

"Ahh!" I said, striving for enthusiasm although I had no idea what she was talking about. It could be a noun, but then again, it could be a verb. I didn't know. From the sound of it, it was plainly something Swedish. Since I hadn't denied my Swedishness, I needed to play along.

"Just today it came. From my cousin Henrik in Gotheburg. He always sends me, every year. He gets the good nine month stuff, so I get it here in June usually."

I nodded enthusiastically. "Excellent!" I said. "How nice of you to think of me. My connection to Sweden has become very distant," I ventured. "So I really appreciate this as a way to get back in touch with it. And speaking of getting back in touch," I segued, "I was planning to get in touch with you about some things that have been happening in our condominium."

It was clumsy but it served the purpose. As we headed towards her door, I gave her a compressed version of what had been happening, and how we really needed some new people on the board. Community-minded people. Working together. Building a community with our neighbours. I didn't torque it up the way I had with Henry and stayed completely away from any mention of community gardens, or "gordons" either.

"I could think about it," she said. "Climbing onto this thing you are calling a board."

I couldn't tell if this was her idea of a joke. I didn't want to know.

"Oh, that's good to hear," I said, with a gentle chuckle that could have been at a joke, if there was one. Or she could have seen it as happiness at her agreement. "We can talk more, if you have any questions and, of course, I'll be on the board to help you get a handle on things."

The conversation was interrupted as we arrived at her house. Then, as we proceeded to the kitchen, it was interrupted by the smell.

It was, without question, the most putrid smell I have ever experienced. It vaguely called to mind memories of childhood vacations and decaying fish on beaches, somehow combined with the sulphurous smell of rotten eggs. In Ingrid's kitchen the smell was in an enclosed space and vastly more powerful. If I had managed as a child to fall face-first onto one of those putrefying corpses, perhaps the intensity would have been similar.

"So!" Mrs. Svensson's beaming face was turned to me. "Here we go. Just sit down and enjoy, and there is your knäckebröd on the plate there, and the boiled potatoes if you want. You just don't get the chance to have something like this here in Canada and I don't want to distract you."

As she said this, she poured clear liquid from a bottle into a tumbler in front of me. *Akvavit*, the label said. Like the one already in front of her, the tumbler was not small.

All of this on an empty stomach, I thought. But really, what choice was there? I raised the tumbler and took a good belt, seized a piece of what appeared to be a disk of rye crisp to have at the ready, and forked a helping of what looked like disintegrating sardine corpses from the bowl in front of me.

In my mouth, it felt like a soft room-temperature paste.

The smell was so intense that it was impossible to determine if it had a taste, beyond a slight sourness. I chewed and swallowed, following with a vigorous bite of the rye crisp and a shot of the aquavit to speed that on its way.

"Yes," I choked out. "This is special."

"Don't talk," she said. "Just eat and enjoy!"

I did as I was told. My stomach began to feel queasy, more so with each bite, so I opted for a bomb-the-bridges approach and worked my way through the bowl as fast as possible, sluicing down flaccid herring with gulps of aquavit in the hopes of controlling my heaving innards.

"Amazing!" I croaked, as I disposed of the last bite. Raising my glass, I managed: "Let's drink a toast to your coming onto the condo board, Ingrid, and of course, a toast to Sweden!"

With the drinking of the toast, I rose urgently to my feet and explained that I had work to finish that evening and needed to run.

"But thank you again, Ingrid, for sharing this with me. And thank you so much for being willing to join our board! I will be in touch as soon as I tell Sonya the good news!"

I really did have to run. My stomach churned ominously. There also seemed to be an unevenness in the laneway that had not been there before I drank the aquavit. By the time I reached my door, the only thought in my brain was whether I would make it to the toilet in time.

I did. But only just.

After emerging, I brewed some strong coffee to settle my stomach. Then I went to my desk to check emails. There at the top of the inbox, less than an hour ago, was the email from Sonya. My stomach lurched again as I read the title:

"New Director!" it said.

Dear Andrew,

We are fortunate indeed that Letty Bishop has agreed to step up again for our board, as a replacement for Philippe.

Summer work season is now upon us, with its need for special attention to compliance issues around our community. We will need all hands on deck, so Letty's help will be very timely. As you know, she is a former president of the board so she will have valuable knowledge and experience to share with us in the months ahead.

I have already received responses from Doreen and Henry so a majority has approved this appointment. I'm hoping we can give her the welcome she deserves, Andrew, and you will add your Yes vote and make this appointment unanimous.

Regards
Sonya

Letty Bishop! Of course I had heard of her. She had been the president who mentored Sonya. From what neighbours had told me, this basically meant they had competed with each other to see who could find the most ingenious ways to irritate owners. The woman was now 92 years old.

I am not an ageist. But 92? We were going to need to stock the condo office with absorbent bibs for board meetings.

There was no way I could leave the board now. I was the only voice of sanity left. The only voice who could at least tell owners what was going on and somehow, eventually, find people who would join the board and help me protect my investment. It was ridiculous but there it was.

There it was and there I was.

Stuck again.

Chapter Seven

How to Not Get Ready For a Suspension Hearing

"**I** just got the call, Dad! I'm pitching! Coach Greb says I'm for sure one of the best three!"

It was Andy on the phone. He was ecstatic.

"Congratulations, Andy! That is wonderful news. To be honest, I'm not surprised based on how you've been pitching lately. But it's great that Coach Greb agrees. You should feel real proud of yourself because you made this happen with the effort you've been putting in."

"Thanks for the practice work-outs, Dad," he said. "I couldn't have done it without them."

"Maybe," I said. "But don't undersell yourself. You made this happen by choosing a goal, figuring out what you needed to do, and then staying focused and doing the work. I bet you would have found a way to do that anyhow."

"That's a lesson you can take forward in life," I almost said. But I caught myself just in time. I had grown up bombarded with life lessons at every turn from my teacher parents and look how I had turned out. I felt a tinge of awkwardness. I was applauding him for doing what I had chronically avoided. The great thing about 11-year-olds is that they aren't making those connections yet.

"Hey, what about a celebration this weekend? I could book us into Krazy Karts for Saturday afternoon. You could invite a friend if you want, maybe you could even work out a strategy to beat Dad."

"Awesome!" he responded. "I can't believe how good this summer is turning out to be, and it's not even summer holidays yet! I'm going to ask Anwar. He's in the pitching group too and him and me are doing drills after school."

Krazy Karts, a go-kart rental track on the edge of town, was where Andy and I had started going last year to vent our accumulated need for aggression and generally have some fun. I'm not a competitive person by nature, but there was something about the immediacy of the go-karts, the raucous sound of small engines straining against weight, and the feel of tires at the limit of adhesion. It brought out an urge to win, by fair means or foul. So far, Andy seemed to think this was funny, but I realized that I was going to have to start curbing myself and let him get some wins. After all, I was a 38-year-old man trying to be a good parent, not some kind of hormone-addled teenager.

By the time Saturday arrived, I was definitely ready for some kart action. Earlier in the week, I had endured a lengthy interview with Elwood Doidge, the Faculty Association lawyer who would represent me in the suspension hearing later that month.

Francine had prepared me for the interview. My role was to make sure he had the full facts, she said. His role was to protect my rights, not serve as a vehicle for my high-minded thoughts about inclusiveness and the university. She was right, of course, but focusing exclusively on the protection of my rights still felt wrong to me. What about Gina? Did thinking about my rights mean not thinking about hers?

"Andrew," Francine had said. "You need to recognize the game you're in and cooperate. If your suspension is lifted, you will have endless opportunities to be idealistic once you're back in the classroom. Obviously, if it goes the other way, you won't."

I took an instant dislike to Doidge when he greeted me without a trace of eye contact or a smile at the university office he was using. Decked out in a grey three-piece suit and the kind of garish tie chosen by people trying to proclaim that they aren't just boring people in suits, he was completely out of place on a university campus. His voice, initially noting that I was seven minutes late for the interview, was a nasal complaintive whine. The voice went on to lament the humidity and heat for early June, which I had been enjoying as a harbinger of summer. Then it moved on to the substance of the case.

It soon became clear that undermining Gina's credibility was central to his plan for the hearing. He would contrast her outburst in the class with my established reputation as a popular and respected lecturer.

"But this feels like bullying," I had objected. "Gina's anger is the measure of her fragility and I'm not comfortable just taking advantage of that."

"It's all very well for you to be uncomfortable," Doidge said. "But we have to use the facts that we have; otherwise, we have no basis to protect your rights."

It became clear, as well, that he was carefully constructing an argument that my joke had been an educational stratagem intended to help everyone in the class recognize that Gina was like everybody else, in the sense that identity issues were a ubiquitous part of the human experience.

"This isn't really the truth," I objected. "I've been telling the department, and the investigating committee, that my joke wasn't hostile because I know I didn't feel hostile to Gina. But I can't honestly say it was part of a deliberate educational strategy either. It was basically a thoughtless comment that came to me on the spur of the moment. The fact that Gina experienced it as targeting can't just be ignored, it is part of a reality that we all live in."

"You're being too subtle for a suspension hearing," Doidge responded. "And also, it is up to the hearing to weigh the importance of Gina's perceptions, not us. Your joke may not have reflected a deliberate educational strategy at that instant, but surely it was consistent with the broad character of your teaching.

"And besides," he added as he closed a file folder decisively and put it aside, "we have extensive corroboration concerning your character and the values apparent in your teaching. That is a powerful argument that we cannot afford to ignore.

"I need you to take the rest of this week and go over the details of your account to the investigation committee very carefully and prepare talking points," he said. "If there is anything you can add, or any corroborative witness that I haven't talked to, please let me know. If not, during the hearing I will need you to stick consistently to what you have said. These cases often stand or fall on consistency and I'm confident I can find a few weaknesses in Gina's story. I will be in touch before the hearing to make sure you are ready."

The meeting left me feeling trapped in a legalistic process cranking along according to its own adversarial dynamic and mysterious rules, represented by a man who was tone-deaf to my concerns. However, there wasn't anything obvious I could do to change the game or, probably, the outcome. I was still seething about it as I picked up the boys at Francine's, only slightly late, and headed for Krazy Karts.

Krazy Karts had a wicked dog-leg corner, my favourite. That corner often resulted in journeys into the protective tires that lined the track for hapless go-kart pilots who tried to follow me and didn't stay on the perfect line. Alternatively, there were those who tried to stay ahead of me, with the same result, sometimes abetted with a little nudge to their inside rear wheel at the apex of the corner. With thoughts of Doidge and the hearing still hovering in my mind, I was already planning to make good use of that corner. I was sick to death of thinking about the hearing and his patronizing instructions had only added to my resentment of the man.

The kart track was rarely busy, even on a Saturday, and we seemed to be the only customers apart from a squad of girls who looked to be about 12. With solemn faces, they were droning steadily around the track, showing no ambition to pass anyone, much less sideswipe each other into spin-outs. No shrieking. No laughing. No fun. They could have been driving hearses in a funeral procession.

They are missing what karting is all about, I thought. The competition, the spin-outs, and journeys into the tires. That was what the tires were there for: to catch spinning karts!

Andy set off with Anwar close behind him and I was soon in hot pursuit. It took me three laps to catch up with them and another one to get alongside when Anwar, who was now ahead, went wide in a corner. A sharp side-swipe and off he went, into the tires.

"Dad!" I could hear Andy yelling. But he was also laughing.

Another two laps and I was right behind them again. This time, Andy went wide on the dog-leg and I nailed him on the back wheel and sent him off backwards, shrieking "Daaaaaaad!" as he went. Anwar had been right behind me, and he couldn't react fast enough. Off he went too. This was fun! Exactly what I needed.

The side-swiping had slowed me down, and as I left the corner, two of the girls got past me. I had noticed glances in our direction as the shrieks of the boys rose above the noise of the karts and now the two were plainly intent on catching the boys. Since the boys were slowing themselves down by continuously cutting each other off, the girls caught them within a lap and the leading girl sent Andy into the tires with a well-placed bunt. "Daaad!" he shrieked. Then he realized it wasn't Dad.

The battle was now plainly on and I needed to get into it. I got the second girl at the corner where I had side-swiped Anwar, and off she went. Into the tires. I heard a satisfying squeal and, as I headed onto the backstretch, I could see Andy gaining on the girl who had caused his excursion into the tires. A third girl had gotten separated from her friends but she was now in my sights, half-way around a corner. Positioning the kart for maximum speed as I exited, I gained on her rapidly and, at the next corner, got to the inside and managed a gentle lateral side-swipe, running her off the cornering line so she lost speed and would be a sitting target for the boys. In minutes, I heard more excited shrieking.

In the distance, half-way around another corner, I could see the fourth girl, a more cautious driver than her friends, and maintaining a steady, moderate pace. I came rapidly up behind her and gave her kart a good bunt, sending her erratically off the course and into the tires.

She needs driving lessons, I thought. As I glimpsed her on my way past, she seemed somewhat larger than the others, and she had gone into the tires without any shrieking. However, I didn't have time to process this because I was now focused on catching Andy and Anwar. They were visible, heading into the next corner, in close competition with two of the girls who had quickly acclimatized to the karts and were now going at a good clip. Their lighter weights were helping them to stay ahead of me. We went around and around, for three laps at least, before I had what was now a tight cluster of very intent kart pilots squarely in my sights, and I began looking for the right corner to make my move. However, before I could close the gap, a figure in white overalls jumped onto the track and waved me vigorously to the side.

"Sir, I'll have to ask you to leave the track," he said, as he motioned me to the pit lane.

"Is there a problem?" I asked, as I slowed to a stop. "We still have half-an-hour based on our start time."

"We've had a complaint," he said. "We saw you bump that lady who has her girls here for a birthday party. I'm sorry, but I have to enforce the posted rules."

I didn't want to involve the boys in an embarrassing scene, so I meekly complied and slunk back to the Jeep.

The boys were now completely absorbed in a battle with the girls that was producing plenty of excited shrieking. It was plain my presence would not be missed. From the Jeep, I could watch and enjoy vicariously. The girls were definitely holding their own. One of them even gave the mother a very professional side-swipe in the corner nearest to where I was parked, allowing me to savour that journey into the tires in full detail.

After another fifteen minutes or so, the mother shepherded the girls off the track and Andy and Anwar had it to themselves. They were having a blast. Closely matched, they swapped the lead numerous times on each lap and would have been going even faster if they hadn't felt the need to give themselves a thumbs up each time they managed a pass.

When the boys finished their time and arrived at the car, they knew what had happened with me because they had seen the mother stop and conduct her arm-waving conversation with the attendant. The boys seemed to be viewing this drama as part of a special addition to the day's entertainment by Dad.

We headed for the Dairy Queen. On the way, they talked non-stop when they weren't laughing and I got the impression that some of the conversation was subversive. "...Totally backwards," I heard, and "...got himself kicked out," along with "cool," and "awesome."

"It's them!" Andy yelled as we pulled into the parking lot.

It was. Now equipped with ice cream cones, the three girls were following their mother out the door of the Dairy Queen. Their faces were solemn with concentration on the cones. Once again, they were following each other in single file.

There was something about the way the mother marched at the head of the little column that seemed vaguely familiar, but I couldn't quite place it. They advanced across the parking lot, arriving at a large grey Mercedes SUV.

MOSS*MAN, the licence plate said.

I felt this immediately in my stomach. I'm bad at recognizing people in unfamiliar circumstances but, with the aid of the vanity plate, the identity of the biggest girl was unmistakable. It was Angela Mossman. I had met her briefly at several faculty gatherings when the Mossmans had deigned to socialize with the academic proletariat.

"Hey guys," I said. "Let's do the drive-thru and get something for Mom. It's late enough in the day that she should get a Saturday break."

I didn't take time for consultation and piloted the Jeep around the building to the drive-thru, where we would be safely out of sight of the Mercedes. Anwar went for the same giant chocolate shake that Andy always ordered and I got mediums for me and Francine.

It seemed unlikely that Mossman's wife would have recognized me, especially in the heat of action on the track. The faculty population was large and, besides, I was not even a regular at the annual receptions and other formal events where Dean Mossman and his wife administered ritual welcomes to a throng of faculty members who must have remained largely indistinguishable to them.

Although the milkshakes had temporarily distracted the boys, the sight of the girls set them going again on the duels that had occurred at the track. They had reached an age where revulsion of girls was beginning to give way to other feelings, but whatever feelings were beginning to emerge were kept out of the guy talk, which was emphatically contemptuous.

"That one with the blue shirt," Anwar was saying. "She kept trying to look back and then she'd lose control before I even did anything. And then all she'd do was keep screaming."

"Yeah," Andy responded. "You'd think she would have learned. But that one with the yellow jacket, she was a lot tougher, she almost got me a couple of times."

"Yeah, she was pretty good after her mom left," Anwar said. "For a girl, I mean."

There was also more of the mumbled talk involving snatches of "Did you see when he…" and "your dad, he…" typically followed by snickers. I was going to need a strategy for handling this when we got to Francine's. Nothing came to me as I drove.

What did come was an alarmingly detailed memory of the office at the kart track. Specifically, of the reservation/sign-in list that had been waiting on the counter and that I had signed in haste, for all to see. What if Angela Mossman had been curious about who her on-track assailant might have been? Mine would have been the only other name in the 2 p.m. box on the list. What if she remembered it? What if she asked her husband about it? My reputation on campus did not need this story. Mossman, I knew, would be only too happy to make sure it got spread around to the right people.

What if, what if…

I didn't need another distraction just when I was supposed to be honing my story for the suspension hearing, canvassing my memory for forgotten evidence of my sterling character and high-minded dedication to educating the young.

At Francine's, I had barely pulled to a stop when the boys were out of the Jeep and running to the front door. They already had Francine's ear by the time I got there.

"Yes, Mom, we had an awesome time," Andy was saying. "And you should have seen Dad on the track! He was a total wild man!"

Both boys began talking over each other and laughing delightedly.

"You should have seen… he went after these… this lady… he got thrown out," was what I heard.

Francine's expression took me back to my grade-school years, when I had been prominent in a pack of errant boys provoking teachers.

"What were you thinking, Andrew?" she said. "Are you familiar with the concept of self-sabotage?"

"Yes," I said. "I guess that sometimes doesn't stop me from doing it. But you should have seen them. When they all got going, they were completely in the moment and really having fun. The girls too! Probably most of all. It gave them a day-pass to get away from that suffocating Mossman propriety. I'm not sure which of them was the birthday girl, but I bet this is one birthday she won't forget in a hurry."

Francine didn't say anything. She didn't need to.

"You're right, of course," I continued. "Angela Mossman probably hasn't laughed since she married Michael, except as spousal support when he does his imitation of somebody with a sense of humour at faculty receptions. She wasn't laughing at the track either. So I can't argue with you, I might have given myself a problem here. Another problem, I guess."

After the boys had been fed at a riotous dinner and a tired Anwar was collected by his dad, Francine and I returned to the subject of my hearing. Her advice about my problems with Doidge's approach was typical Francine:

"Just tell the truth, Andrew," she said. "He will ask the questions he needs to ask, in the way he needs to ask them. All you have to do is answer honestly and not insert digressions or interpretations. The same will happen when you are questioned by Sophia Lansdorf. You need to tell the truth because it's the only way to be 100% consistent under cross-examination. If there's any inconsistency, Sophia will be on it in a heartbeat, and she's an expert at using that kind of thing to full effect. I know you would do this anyway because that's who you are. I'm just saying, don't try to be anyone else. It's your lawyer's job to marshal the facts and make the arguments. Just leave that part to him."

"Yes, I hear you," I said. "I'm just not happy about how this whole thing is going. The more I think about it, Gina's issues are personal and, beyond that, cultural and political. I don't see much progress coming out of a debate between lawyers."

"I'm sure you're right," Francine said. "But this is where you need to stop thinking like a political scientist and deal with reality. You're not going to be reaching out to Gina on a personal level in the middle of a suspension hearing where your job is at stake. If you did, it would look completely contrived. You're also not reshaping the university, Andrew, or resolving the tragedy of the Middle East, or other problems around the world. At least not this week. You're just trying to make sure justice gets done in this hearing."

"Yes, I can't argue with you," I said. "Of course I'll do what I need to do. And I'm grateful for your help in this, Francine. Really grateful. Not to mention, more than a little curious to see how Gina and her team react when they see you sitting beside Doidge at the hearing. That could be interesting."

"I hope they find it interesting," she said. "I'm thinking there will be some discussions after the hearing and that will be my opening to try and do a little educating."

"But coming back to the practical issues, Doidge will have been working with you on the factual narrative you will need. Have you put together your speaking points for the hearing? I could take a look at them and point out potential trouble spots if you like before you get Doidge's feedback."

"Thanks, I'll try to get them to you, And yes, Doidge

has me working on that. In fact, I was trying to work on my notes this morning, but then I had a neighbour at my door in the middle of it, and another on the phone. Sonya is on the warpath again, and apparently she was out walking the property with Bill and supervising the latest folly she's talked the board into, which is removing plants from the balconies. So now people are getting notices, saying they have forty-eight hours to remove them or else the condo will do it. She's turning Britannia into the condo equivalent of one of those South American countries where people are being disappeared, except with us, it's plants, Francine! I don't know why she was even out there since managing contractors is the property manager's job."

"Andrew, you're not serious."

"I wish I were joking. This is a long story, but basically the board passed a motion that plants in pots on balconies are a violation of our storage rules, and if people don't remove them, they would be confiscated by the end of the week. This morning, Cynthia Williams, who lives three doors down from me, was livid because she had just gotten a notice about the pots of what she calls her breeding stock, which apparently need to be outside. And then I had a woman from the west side on the phone asking me what I was going to do about this, and I couldn't seem to get it across to her that I am only one board member and the board had already voted to do this, so—"

"I wasn't talking about the plants. It's you I'm worried

about. You and your career. You're wound up in condo politics and not answering my question. Your talking points. Have you done them?"

"Well, no," I had to say. "I've also been distracted by trying to get a good person onto the board, who would help to deal with Sonya. It hasn't been going very well."

"Andrew, you really need to get off that board! And you especially need to make sure it doesn't take you away from doing what you need to do for the hearing. I admire your commitment to volunteer work and your neighbours, but right now you need to make sure the hearing doesn't make you the latest victim of political correctness."

"Yes, I promise," I said. "I'll focus on my prep work. It shouldn't be that difficult. The details of that day aren't hard to remember. I've never had a student so enraged at me before."

"We'll get you through this," she said.

I didn't know if she was as confident as she sounded, but I could feel my mood improving just from the sound of her voice.

"I can't tell you how important it is to me that you are really on my side for this," I said. "But now I see that the clock is telling me to be on my way. Thanks for feeding us tonight. I think Andy has made a new friend and Anwar is going to be excellent for him."

"Yes, that was a lovely evening. It's wonderful to see Andy so happy. But really, Andrew, you don't have to side-swipe the dean's wife and girls at the karting track to be a good dad, you know," she said, with a mischievous gleam in her eye.

"Now you tell me," I said. "Next you're going to take away my panties."

She was still smiling as I went out the door.

Chapter Eight

The Horticultural Disappeared of Britannia

"**M**r. Walmer? What the hell is going on?"

"Hello? I'm afraid I don't really know… uh… who is this, please?"

It was Henk Van Vliet on the phone, calling from the other side of the complex. He was one of the many residents who were never heard from unless they were unhappy about something. I was hearing from him. He definitely was not happy.

"They just took the plants off my balcony, and I saw Sonya out there directing everything! Why is the board letting her get away with this?"

"Well, Henk, I'm afraid the board passed a motion about this. You should have gotten a notice at the beginning of the week, so—"

"What notice? I didn't get any goddamn notice! This is what I'm always told, whenever Sonya is up to something! Jeez, I can't believe how that woman gets my dandruff up."

"Well, Henk, I can certainly understand that you're upset, and I'm very sorry about that. But there isn't much I can do. The board did authorize the removal of plants that owners didn't take off the balconies after they got the notice."

"I didn't get any notice! Or at least I never saw it. This is oppression, Andrew. It's what you'd get in North Korea or something! My wife had her daffodils waiting in six pots and I was going to transfer them to the flowerbed. You're a board member, Andrew. You have to do something about this!"

"Henk, I will certainly do what I can. But once the board passes a motion, I'm only one board member, so I can't just somehow veto it. I will certainly tell Sonya but, really, it's far more effective if you email the property manager and ask him to forward your message to the whole board. That way, you communicate directly. Otherwise, they don't know whether I'm giving them accurate information about what you think. But I'll certainly track Sonya down and make sure she knows..."

This is the absolute last thing I need, I thought as I hung up. *There's always something!*

It was Friday and it began as a beautiful sun-drenched morning filled with promise. Until the phone rang.

Even though I was not a captive of the weekly round of lectures and other duties on campus, there was still something special about Fridays. It was the feeling of freedom that weekends brought. Not to mention, these days, my time with Andy and Francine. And this Friday, I was feeling extra energized. We had staged the final performance of *The Importance of Being Ernest* Thursday evening, and the play had been a success, at least by standards appropriate for amateur theatre. Nobody had forgotten their lines except for Merriman, the butler. We all knew this would happen and I had made sure the rest of the cast was well-prepared. Oswald Pfeiffer, or Ossie as we called him, was the oldest member of the cast and ideal for playing Merriman, apart from his problem with lines. It was almost as if his memory actively repelled them. But Ossie loved our little theatre and he loved acting. We had come to see him as a kind of mascot. So I had modified the script by adding little prompts from other characters like "Merriman, you always say you have to get the papers about now..." and Ossie had made it through to the curtain call in triumph along with the rest of us.

The final performance had been to a small but enthusiastic crowd. Actually, it may not have been all that enthusiastic, but it was unquestionably small. Largely composed, I suspected, of relatives. Afterwards, the cast had surprised me with a bottle of Glenfiddich and my 'Ernest,' a computer salesperson named Trent Skolnik, had made a speech thanking me for my patience. It left me feeling that at least part of what I had been trying to teach them had actually gotten through.

My inner voice had been whispering that I was also responsible for the crime against drama that had just been perpetrated on the stage but, for once, I just smiled and remained gracious. After all, the players had devoted hard-earned leisure time to learning their lines and turning out for practices. Who could tell what doors this experience might open for them. Trent said that even if he didn't perform again, when he went to a play he would be seeing it with a new understanding of what he called "the whole programming side of acting." He didn't say what this was and I didn't ask him. He plainly felt that the experience had given him something.

Apart from needing to run a batch of graded term papers up to a colleague on campus, I was free from distractions through the morning. I was thus poised to focus, finally, on getting ready for the suspension hearing and preparing my speaking points. Then Francine could look them over on the weekend.

The main problem I was wrestling with was the one I had discussed with her: support Doidge's determination to portray my joke as part of a deliberate teaching strategy to foster inclusiveness, or tell the truth. The more I thought about it, telling the truth—that it had been a spontaneous joke—was the easy part. The harder part was that this didn't seem to be enough. No matter what happened, Gina's challenges would remain the same, and official action by the university, up to and including terminating me, wouldn't really change the past or the present. Nothing official would. Official action was necessarily impersonal, an administration of justice. However Gina needed to feel understood and accepted, most importantly by real people, especially her peers—the other students—but also by the rest of us, including me. But Francine had been right, reaching out to her on a personal level in the middle of a suspension hearing would inevitably seem opportunistic. It wouldn't be credible, so it couldn't be helpful.

So there I sat. Stalled. And now distracted by Van Vliet's phone call and wondering whether it was worth it to go out and find Sonya immediately, in the middle of her Friday morning assault on our plants.

My eyes strayed to my study window, as they often do in order to escape from something on my desk. My study faced the court and my neighbour's homes, each with the distinctive front-facing balcony often highlighted in realtors' brochures. Crestview Court lay peacefully under the morning sun, a traffic circle surrounding an island occupied by four stately oak trees. Facing the circle were forty-three mid-century modern townhouses. The court appeared to have largely escaped the scourge of invasive plants that had inspired Sonya's board proposal; although, as I looked more closely, signs of floral non-compliance were visible on several balconies.

It was too late to warn people. No sooner had I thought to do this when a small, indomitable figure appeared in the laneway leading into our court. Sonya. She walked at about half her usual speed, hobbling actually, and relying heavily on a cane. The neighbourhood grapevine had been buzzing for several days about the cane. Apparently it was needed because of an ankle strain Sonya had sustained when she toppled off the stool that she had ascended for the purpose of inspecting toys in part of a neighbour's yard that could not be seen from outside the fence. Condo rules prevented directors from entering yards without notice. "Exclusive use common elements" the Condo Act called them. But the Act didn't prevent Sonya from toting her light-weight step stool around as she made her weekly tours, using it to peer over fences.

The cane and hobbling only served to emphasize Sonya's determination. For the discharge of her balcony-clearing responsibilities, she had donned one of her distinctive pantsuits. It was brown but at least avoided any sign of camouflage. Sonya was staring intently at the balconies. Her ability to spot infractions of condo rules from great distances had been honed, I imagined, by years of vigilance in her primary school classrooms. It was uncanny, bordering on clairvoyance.

Behind Sonya, at a deferential distance, our property manager consulted papers on a clipboard when he wasn't looking stolidly at his feet.

Following Bill in the procession advancing around the court was the mobile lift used by Ottawa GlassKleen, our window-washing contractor. It was fluorescent orange, and its extremely gradual progress involved a droning assault of engine noise. Astride the lift was Bert Hallowell, Glass-Kleen's owner. He was driving instead of one of his assistants, I assumed, because of the fine motor coordination that might be involved in approaching balconies with Bill in the bucket.

I had not expected additional participants in the procession, but there she was: our newly-minted board member, Letty Bishop, the nonagenarian clone of Sonya. She was thin to the point of emaciation and her narrow face reminded me of a hatchet—a hatchet bearing sharp, combative little eyes, and a thin-lipped unsmiling mouth. Letty's fragile form was clothed in a dark blue pantsuit that appeared to be from the same source as Sonya's. She kept pace with Sonya despite her reliance on a walker that vibrated visibly with her efforts.

At regular intervals, Letty stopped and directed

emphatic hand signals to the court and the laneway entering it. Traffic management. The court slumbered under a morning sun and there was no traffic to be seen, but the opportunity to manage something would have been irresistible. Sonya and Letty were going to be like body doubles on the board, mutually reinforcing their obsession with non-existent problems and maintaining a level of regimentation that would have done credit to a maximum security prison. Not for the first time, my involvement with the condo board descended on me as a kind of claustrophobia. As far as my neighbours could see, I was complicit.

Sonya's progress halted. She and Bill conferred, both pointing to the balcony of number 23, across the court. I couldn't see flowers but, undoubtedly, there were some. However, after further conferring, which largely seemed to involve Sonya talking to Bill, the signal was given and the procession moved on. The stop had prompted a round of especially vigorous hand signals from Letty and, no doubt to her satisfaction, the procession had been unaffected by the non-existent traffic.

In all likelihood, there was an "arrangement" with number 23. Sonya had her friends. Flexibility could be granted to those whose support for Sonya and her works was unconditional. Or, in fairness, there might have been a definite removal commitment from the owner. I could always raise questions at the board table about these incidents, but Sonya would have her stock answers at the ready.

"Andrew, if you want us to be completely rigid about things, all you need to do is propose that for a vote," she would say. Or there would be an explanation: "The Duckworths have a contractor on order," she might say. "But he is dealing with illness in the family."

Or something. There was no way to know, without devoting time to forensic investigation. Given Sonya's response to anything that suggested criticism, this would turn a possible owner compliance problem into an entirely definite problem with Sonya.

At number 21, Sonya came to a full stop, rigid with concentration as if poised to pounce. Then she visibly relaxed, gave a satisfied nod, and spoke to Bill. Bill retreated to the lift. The metallic vibration of Letty's walker was briefly audible through my open window before she also halted. Letty continued her signalling as Bill gave instructions to the contractor.

The lift lurched into motion, entering the driveway of number 21, and swivelling to face the balcony. Bill climbed into the bucket and, with Bert concentrating intently on the controls, the bucket rose. Slowly it approached the balcony and stopped with mere inches of clearance. Bill swung a leg over the railing, stepped to a row of four potted plants, seized two of them, and transferred them to the lift bucket. Then came the remaining two, this time with

Bill accompanying them into the bucket. The bucket descended. The lift exited from the driveway. Bill deposited the plants into a small trailer behind the lift.

It was over in minutes. The procession resumed.

They advanced towards my side of the court. If I were going to tackle Sonya, this was the moment. I had explained to Van Vliet why this would be futile, but then I had promised. Abandoning my desk, I headed downstairs to my front door.

In the laneway, in defiance of hand signals from Letty that appeared to be directed at me specifically, I stepped in front of Sonya. She greeted me with an expression I suspected had evolved over the years in her primary school classrooms, reserved for hapless students who had failed to complete assignments or developed sudden problems of bowel control. I had to make a conscious effort not to apologize for something.

"Good morning, Sonya," I said, striving for a friendly note. "I think you should know that I just got off the telephone with Henk Van Vliet and he's furious about this. I'm concerned you're going to offend more owners by taking plants and we'll end up getting deluged with complaints."

"Our notice outlined our procedure, Andrew," she said. "We've been advised that we need to treat owners the same. Some of them aren't home, and we can't afford to pay Bert for multiple trips."

"But Sonya, personal contact would let you explain what is happening, and owners could move their plants and keep them, or at least arrange to recover them later."

"Andrew, as you know, the board agreed to this. We don't have any arrangement for holding plants, and that would just set a precedent. If we leave them by the office, we could have people stealing them, and then we'd have to deal with that."

"But, Sonya, surely..."

"Andrew, you tend to be soft-hearted, and on a condo board, you can't be. Rules are rules and we have been advised that we have a duty to enforce them. Anyway, please bring your issues to the board table where we can all discuss them. I really need to keep moving here. I'm only free this morning."

She resumed her progress around the traffic circle. Bill, with an apologetic look to me, followed her. The lift, its motor returning to full volume, discouraged conversation as well as any loitering in its path. At the foot of the procession, Letty Bishop marched proudly past, nodding to me with a look of ill-concealed triumph.

I had little choice but to retreat, defeated, to my office.

Soft-hearted, she had said. The phrase nagged at me. There was probably some truth to it. They likely thought of me that way on the board. I often seemed to be the only one resisting Sonya's forays into rules and wrist-slapping.

Of course, wherever you have people, you need rules.

But across the world of government, including the small-scale government you have in a condo, we often ignore the reality that formal written rules are clumsy instruments. In a world where things go wrong so often because people feel powerless and ignored, rules are impersonal. We all live mostly in our heads, in private worlds. Most of the time, you never know what is going on inside the other person, or how they might be experiencing the things you see. You can't just assume you know. What seems trivial to you might be very important to them, and if they get the feeling you don't understand them or care, the scene is set for conflict.

Van Vliet, this morning, was a case in point. Who would have expected it in a retired construction worker? Those flower pots were special to them, part of their love of plants and gardening. And only on the balcony temporarily, so really not a problem. But Sonya had marched ahead with her mantra of "rules are rules." The condo was making the plants into a problem.

Predictably, the problem would end up being a distraction for the board. It was already a distraction for me, just when I was supposed to be devoting the morning to the suspension hearing and my talking points. It was now after 11:00 and I had accomplished nothing. I had half an hour, at most, before I would need to head for the campus to drop off my marking early enough to catch people who would be leaving to enjoy their Friday afternoons.

Talking points, talking points, talking points. My heart wasn't in them.

There wasn't any way to square the circle between what I needed to say and what Doidge was trying to get me to say. Talking points would only smoke this out into the open and bring more pressure on me to play the suspension hearing game. Francine was sympathetic, but she was also advising me about how to avoid being a victim at the hearing. Wouldn't my concerns just draw her further into something I already felt guilty about her being involved in at all?

I was stalled. Walking to the campus might clear my head. I grabbed the papers and headed out the door.

Sonya and her troops were now stationed in front of number 18. Cora Voitovich had been home and was now standing in her driveway in a pink housecoat. She was hard to miss—partly because of the housecoat, which was a very large one, and partly because of her hair. It was a vivid pink, closely matching the housecoat. Cora's head jerked emphatically as she spoke and waved her arms at Sonya.

Cora was like that. Demonstrative.

This wasn't Cora's first confrontation with Sonya over her yard. There had been removals before, but Cora's garden was resilient. It was like the WWII cities that tenaciously emerged even after carpet bombing. Each emergence illustrated, yet again, that she had highly individualized tastes in the area of flowerbed decor. Along with flowers, Cora's front garden periodically blossomed with installations that implied a very creative interpretation of the condominium rule about plantings, which permitted authorized flowerbeds only. The rule was silent about ceramic toads and imitation castles, reflective twirling wind chimes, garish imitation palm trees, plump little garden gnomes, and Cora's unique innovation: multi-coloured flashing lights, apparently connected to a timer.

Sonya, however, stood her ground. Her jaw was thrust forward, her lips were moving, and her head was jerking emphatically. It could have been a kind of pugnacious duet except Sonya and Cora were not singing.

I already knew what Sonya would be saying. I didn't need another confrontation with her, or the challenge of trying to referee Sonya and Cora. I hastened around the other side of the circle and out the Crestview Court laneway. This took me to Richmond Street and the elegant red brick heritage homes in the neighbourhood surrounding the condominium. Originally planned for a location near Ottawa's Britannia beach, Britannia Condominium had retained its name while morphing into an inner city urban renewal project in the mid-seventies, to the vocal distress of existing residents. For me, however, the neighbourhood—with its massive trees arching over roadways, and quaint homes with their carved lintels and elaborate wooden gingerbread—was a place for soothing walks, including treks to the campus.

I hadn't had the pleasure of making the acquaintance of neighbourhood residents and didn't regret it. They ran to two types. The original cohort of pioneers were now elderly retired public servants and teachers who had arrived in the neighbourhood to raise families in more humble times. They maintained what they proudly believed was a bohemian vibe by accumulating expensive crafts from local boutiques. They were joined, and increasingly displaced, by doctors, lawyers, and business executives whose affluence was displayed in driveways populated by Audis and Mercedes Benzes. Busy lives meant they were rarely seen in the neighbourhood. Both groups conspicuously avoided the periodic Britannia Condominium garage sales.

My walk to the campus took me along streets whose names harkened back to the Scottish and English upper class that had developed the city: Roseberry and Strathcona, Elgin and Somerset. A pedestrian bridge took me across the canal to the campus boundary and, from there, it was an easy stroll across the campus commons to the Arts and Sciences building.

As I neared the campus, the quiet of the streets gave way to increasing traffic as converging streams of students headed to classes. A vaguely familiar figure caught my eye, sitting on one of the benches in a scenic look-out area by the bridge. Recognition didn't hit me until I had continued onto the bridge. It was Gina. She was sitting by herself, hunched over and looking miserable. I paused my steps and cautiously observed more closely. Her shoulders were shuddering slightly. She dabbed at her eyes with a tissue. Crying by herself, alone on a bench while throngs of students passed her by, chatting, self-absorbed in their simpler and happier world.

What to do? Communicating with Gina was strictly forbidden by the suspension hearing protocols. This had been true since the complaint had triggered the department's informal investigation, and now that the hearing was only weeks away, it would be even worse. Leaving protocols aside, contact was obviously improper, given my status as a lecturer in the department and, in relation to any student, a power figure.

On the other hand, Gina's distress was obvious. She looked terribly alone, sitting on that bench, ignored by the stream of students and, I imagined, consumed by the special loneliness dictated by her circumstances.

I had to do something. I was at risk of being conspicuous standing there and potentially compounding the trouble I was already in. I needed to move along. Now!

But my feet weren't moving. There was something about the sight of her sitting there. Walking away didn't seem like the right thing to do.

Chapter Nine
Hearing Day

I hadn't told anyone what I had done after I saw Gina by the bridge. Not even Francine. She would have understood, but her lawyer's ethic and dedication to due process would have obliged her to disclose it, putting me in serious trouble and, potentially, Gina too.

I also couldn't tell anyone what I was going to do. That was because, with the beginning of the hearing minutes away, I still didn't know. There seemed to be no acceptable option left.

In my heart, I wanted to acknowledge that my joke had been wrong and apologize. And why not leave it up to Gina to decide what the remedy should be? Let's give power to the powerless for once, I had imagined myself saying. However, there was no way the panel would hand that decision to a student. And a spontaneous apology could even be seen as a cynical strategy to impress the hearing panel and mitigate sanctions.

Unless I could think of something, I was going to end up sitting there looking stoically at my hands and doing nothing. But after my conversation with Gina by the bridge, doing nothing was not a tolerable option. It would merely be another form of complicity in what the university was doing to her, with everybody blindly convinced they were acting in her best interests.

When I had approached Gina by the bridge, I had fumbled for what to say.

"Gina, are you okay?" I asked, although it was obvious she wasn't.

She looked at me, hesitating for a moment, and then said the words I couldn't forget.

"Professor Walmer, I don't want to be somebody's issue. I'm just trying to be a human being, like everybody else. It's all I've ever wanted."

"I think I understand," I said. I couldn't claim to understand her experience, but I shared her unhappiness with the hearing process. "I'm afraid that in the hearing process, we both end up being issues. It's just the way these things work. Anything I'm saying to you could be inappropriate influence. So I can't stay here. Is there anything I can do to help?"

"I feel so horrible because I had just been put on new meds that day in your class and I really don't know what came over me. I'm just so sorry about everything, I..." Her voice trembled.

"Gina, please don't apologize," I said. "Please don't feel that you have to. What I said was insensitive and I'm the one who should be apologizing. And the university teaching culture needs to recognize the realities you are talking about."

I wanted to tell her how ashamed I felt and apologize fully, right there, but even pausing to talk to her was inappropriate. I needed to stop the conversation.

"Would it be helpful if you could talk to somebody completely detached from this whole thing, but sympathetic?" It was the only thought that came to me.

She looked hopeful.

"It wouldn't be proper for me to recommend somebody," I said. "But Francine Antoine, of the Law Faculty, happens to be my wife. You may have heard of her and her work. I'm sure she could help you. She is advising me about the hearing so she can't be advising you, but she knows people. I'm pretty sure she could suggest someone. The only thing is, she can't know we've been talking..." I trailed off.

How could Gina go to Francine for help but then explain why Francine couldn't directly advise her without telling her about our meeting? I suggested that all Gina needed to say was that she was aware of Francine's work. As I was departing, I tried to reassure Gina about what she was doing, that the hearing would contribute to progress on campus.

Heading into the hearing room, I was technically on time although Doidge had asked me to arrive at least ten minutes early. Doidge and Francine were already at one of the tables that had been arranged for complainant and defence, facing an elongated table where the hearing panel would sit. They were chatting and the chatting appeared to be friendly.

"Hi, folks," I said.

"Andrew." Doidge's gaze remained on his papers.

My last meeting with him had not gone well. I told him that I wanted to apologize to Gina at the very beginning of the hearing, so she might feel it was sincere instead of merely responding to demands from her lawyer or the panel. However, Doidge was emphatic that his role was to defend my rights, and a spontaneous apology would only give her lawyer ammunition.

"Hi, Andrew," Francine said. "How are you doing?" She was keeping things impersonal, since we were being watched from the complainant's table.

"Fine," I said.

I could see that I wasn't fooling her. She resumed her conversation with Doidge, but her eyes kept straying to mine.

The chair at the centre of the table reserved for Gina and her support team was unoccupied, but I recognized several of the campus activists that Francine worked with from time to time, including her friend, Marion Philbert. They were watching Francine closely. Marion was talking to an older woman whose face appeared to be etched with a permanent scowl. Who knew what they might be saying.

Whatever it was, the conversation suddenly stopped and Doidge also went silent.

I hadn't previously seen Sophia Lansdorf in person, but there was no doubt about who she was, commanding attention just by walking into the room. She could have stepped out of the pages of a fashion magazine, with her immaculate navy blue suit, white blouse, and jewelry discreetly showing gold. Her assistant reinforced her status, walking several steps behind her and carrying two large briefcases.

Lawyers have a bag of tricks to gain the psychological upper hand before a legal proceeding even begins, and Sophia was a virtuoso. She strolled to the complainant's table, taking in the room with the relaxed attentiveness of a powerful carnivore, immune to fear. Sharks in documentaries came to mind, inspecting and selecting prey. Her gaze had the same deadness in it, the same relentless measuring of strength and weakness, the predator's calm alertness.

Settled at her table, in the power position at its centre, she began an unhurried inspection of ours. I rated an indifferent glance and Francine received a quizzical nod. Her attention focused on Doidge. It was methodical, systematic, calculating. I imagined a detached weighing of competing strategies for humiliating the man, and possibly sending him off for some kind of vocational rehab as punishment for daring to defend a pathetic free-rider on male privilege like me. I didn't know how much of this was apparent to Doidge, but he was beginning to fidget.

A side door opened. The suspension review panelists filed into the room, led by C.M. Waseau, the university provost who had convened the hearing. A diminutive figure almost hidden by an ill-fitting black gown, Waseau walked quickly ahead of the panelists as if he feared being trampled.

Malicious tongues at the faculty club, typically fuelled by drink, dismissed Waseau as a walking illustration of the Peter Principle, the tendency of people in organizations to rise to their level of incompetence. The tongues did not pursue the theory to conclusions that might relate to their owners, but permanent tenure and the freedom from mandatory retirement created an expanding population accumulating at senior levels in the university, allowing the Peter Principle to operate to full effect. Over the years, this population had been accommodated with an expanding range of impressive-sounding offices involving limited responsibilities.

However, the provost's responsibility for disciplinary matters was becoming increasingly significant. I had the impression that Waseau tried to be fair, dealing with colleagues whose high-minded rhetoric about education was not infrequently aligned with personal advantage.

"Good morning, everyone," Waseau said, as the panelists seated themselves. "It is now 10 a.m., our scheduled time of commencement. If our recording secretary is ready, I would like to open proceedings by calling for a statement of the charges against Andrew Walmer, lecturer in the Department of Political Science."

"Mr. Chair?" Sophia rose. "With apologies, I would like to ask for a brief suspension of proceedings. Gina Di-Novi, whom I am representing today, has not yet appeared in the hearing room."

"Are you able to indicate when she is expected?" Waseau asked. "I am sure we would want her to be present for the statement, although I expect she is familiar with her own complaint."

"Mr. Chair?" Doidge was on his feet. "I submit that it is not respectful to my client or to other participants in this proceeding to demand a delay before proceedings have even been properly begun. And furthermore, I..."

"Mr. Chair," Sophia overrode Doidge's voice. "We are not aware of the explanation of Ms. DiNovi's failure to appear, and therefore, it would be premature to interpret it as a lack of respect. I support your preference for her presence."

"Furthermore," Doidge continued, "I submit that her failure to appear continues the erratic behaviour Ms. Di-Novi displayed in Andrew Walmer's class, which is at the root of this frivolous complaint."

"Mr. Chair," Sophia had remained on her feet. "The only frivolous complaint before this panel is Mr. Doidge's intervention. It is a defamatory attack on my client and an attempt to bias the hearing against her before proceedings have even begun. I request that you advise the panel to ignore Mr. Doidge's intervention."

"Your request is granted, Ms. Lansdorf," Waseau responded. "Mr. Doidge, please be seated and refrain from further interventions of this kind."

"Thank you, Mr. Chair," Sophia said. "In response to your original question, my assistant is attempting to contact Ms. DiNovi. We expect to have further information shortly. I am requesting that the hearing suspend until we can determine when Ms. DiNovi can be present. She may need to provide instructions based on our proceedings, including reactions of the defence to anything I may say. For this reason, the hearing should not proceed until she is present."

"Request granted," Waseau said. "Let us see if the complainant can be contacted."

Gina. Not there!

For the lawyers, this was just another opportunity for legal argument and points scoring. None of them—not the lawyers, or her so-called support people, or the panelists sitting there comfortably awaiting developments—had been with Gina by the bridge that day. None of them had seen her anguish. None of them had heard her words. "I'm just trying to be a human being, like everybody else." I couldn't forget what she had said. The sadness in her voice. It pierced my heart.

What was keeping her from the hearing? What was she going through at this very moment? Nobody seemed concerned. Insulated by professional roles, the process, and its familiar rules, the causes they thought they were serving, and their easy confidence that they were doing the right thing, they almost seemed prepared to go ahead without her.

Gina's empty chair was the loudest sound in the room. It was screaming something. Why weren't they hearing? Why weren't they even listening?

And Doidge was plainly determined to use his lawyer's tricks to shame the victim, to eviscerate her in front of a roomful of people, and damn the human consequences!

I am not a violent man, but the urge to grab Elwood Doidge by the lapels of his pretentious suit and throttle him, right there in the hearing room, was hard to resist. However, I did resist, but I found myself rising to my feet.

Doidge reached out a hand to stop me, but I had him by at least fifty pounds and I had momentum. Francine eyed me from beside Doidge. She looked worried.

"Okay," said Waseau. "Our staff is trying to contact the complainant as well. And now..." he directed a puzzled look at me. "Mr. Walmer, can I help you?"

I took a deep breath. My mouth opened. Then I was talking.

"Mr. Chair," I said. "I have decided to defend myself in this hearing and I am releasing my counsel as of right now."

"Mr. Walmer, this is quite unprecedented," said Waseau, looking at me resentfully. "I will need to consult with the panelists. However, I believe it is your right."

Doidge finally looked at me, his expression venomous.

I returned his gaze. We shared a moment of non-verbal communication that left no uncertainty. We felt contempt for each other. Deep contempt. Each of us wanted the other one gone.

However, I was the client and Waseau had recognized I was within my rights. Doidge shifted his gaze to his papers, efficiently packed them into his attaché case, rose, and silently departed.

Waseau conferred with his panelists. Several of them regarded me with newfound respect. Others looked indignant. Mme. Barbeau from the French Languages department was gesticulating in a way that threatened to cross the border into assault. Waseau was flinching. He seemed to be seeking the shelter of his oversized academic gown.

At Gina's table, her advisors regarded me avidly. I was the hunted, unaccountably breaking cover and now vulnerable. Sophia Lansdorf's gaze was harder to read. It mingled disappointment, perhaps at the disappearance of a professional challenge, with something that looked like amusement.

Francine slid into the chair of the now departed Doidge. She touched my arm.

"Andrew?" she said. "Do you know what you are doing?"

"No," I said. "I don't. I only know that I wanted that appalling man out of the room before Gina had to listen to him."

Now, at least, he was gone.

"Andrew, unless you want to defend yourself without having prepared a defence, you appear to need legal representation. As far as I can see, I'm the only legal representative available. What do you say?"

It seemed like the intervention of a guardian angel.

"Yes," I said. "Oh, god, yes! Please just get me out of here. You have carte blanche."

She stood up.

"Mr. Chair?" she said. Waseau looked at her distractedly. "Ms… um… I'm sorry." He shushed three panelists simultaneously talking at him. "Could we have order, please?"

"Mr. Chairman, I am Francine Antoine of the Law Faculty and am a member of the Ontario Bar, although I do not currently practice. Mr. Walmer has requested that I serve as his representative, at least on an interim basis. If this is acceptable to the panel, it would allow the hearing to proceed today without concerns about the entitlement of participants to legal representation."

Waseau looked expectantly at me. I nodded agreement.

Sophia rose to address the chair, but before she could speak, there was a commotion behind Waseau with a cellphone chiming. The administrative assistant who had accompanied him into the room swiftly arrived at his elbow, thrusting forward the phone.

"It's her!" she announced.

"How did she..." Waseau muttered as he reached for the phone. Waseau's complexion was normally tinged with grey, which I had noticed was a standard shade for middle-level executives at the university. Those above displayed a healthy tan, from the golf course perhaps.

As the conversation proceeded, the grey became more prominent and also seemed to whiten. Waseau turned away from the panel table and emphatic gestures appeared to be occurring beneath the folds of his gown. Then he was nodding. He talked to his assistant, who had returned to his side with a sheet of paper. He was back on the phone. As he turned toward the room, we heard him say, "I understand, of course."

"I have just spoken to our complainant," he announced. "Apparently, she has been trying to reach us this morning with a message she felt should be provided to the hearing by me, not by her representative. Ms. DiNovi wishes to withdraw her complaint and requests that this hearing be terminated. She has emailed my staff a prepared a statement that will be distributed shortly. It reads as follows:

"Provost Waseau, panelists and participants in the hearing about my complaint:

"I have decided to withdraw my complaint relating to Professor Walmer's joke in his class on parliamentary governance. I am hoping that his suspension from teaching will be terminated and that no other sanctions be applied because he is an excellent professor.

"I have concluded that the university's complaint procedure is not the remedy I need for what happened in that class. However, I recognize that the process provides students with important protections and I am grateful that it exists. I would like to thank everyone who has been involved in preparing for this hearing. I also hope that you will consider, today, a proposal that I believe would make an extremely important contribution to the university.

"I am asking the hearing panel to recommend that the university provide mandatory sensitivity training to all professors. The university should consult with the College Trans Feminist Acton Caucus about the details. Education and understanding are the way forward for Professor Walmer and everybody else, and the university should lead the way.

"I do not want this request to be seen as part of any bargaining about my complaint. This is why I have withdrawn my complaint regardless of how the panel responds. However, I hope that the panel will take this opportunity for action that would really mean a lot to me and my community.

"Thank you for your attention."

For the second time that morning, stunned silence descended on the room.

Sophia rose.

"In order to discharge my obligations as her representative, I believe I need to speak with her directly," Sophia said. "I need to be entirely confident that she has not been subject to inappropriate influence. Would you agree to call her back, Mr. Chair?"

Francine rose.

"Mr. Chair, I believe it is in the interest of all parties to confirm Ms. DiNovi's intention at this point. Her message leaves some ambiguity as to whether Ms. Lansdorf remains her representative at this moment or has already been released. My client needs to have certainty with respect to this matter because it may affect our response to any further participation by Ms. Lansdorf. Therefore, if Ms. Lansdorf agrees, I propose that you, Mr. Chair, Ms.

Lansdorf, and I hold a conference call with Ms. DiNovi immediately. This would allow us all to satisfy ourselves that any obligations we may have are being met."

"I believe Ms. Antoine's request is reasonable, Mr. Chair," said Sophia.

Waseau's face expressed relief, tinged, perhaps, with incredulity that two lawyers for opposing sides could spontaneously agree about something.

"I am suspending this hearing while we conduct the conference call," he declared. Ms. Lansdorf and Ms. Antoine, please join me in my office across the hall."

Waseau and the two lawyers exited the room and conversation at two of the three tables resumed at heightened volume. At the panel table, relief appeared to prevail and I had the impression that academic gossip was rapidly replacing discord about the hearing. After all, they were about to be let off the hook.

At Gina's table, her advocates were clearly chagrined and Marion Philbert suddenly looked very tired. A vigorous but extremely short discussion had occurred with Sophia before she left the room. I had heard "...can't allow this," from one of the advocates, and from Sophia, very distinctly, "...represent my client, not the sisterhood." The women at the table spoke quietly with each other while glaring fiercely in my direction. Obviously, I had to be responsible. After all, I was the embodiment of male privilege and the patriarchy and was plainly up to something, although how it could be connected to Gina's decision was a mystery.

At our table, there wasn't much conversation. I was the only person left. I sat quietly and tried to arrange my face into an expression that might mollify Gina's advocates. This was challenging. They were idealists, at their core, and saw the world through a political lens and the purity of their cause. I was the enemy. They were courageous and I had to admire that. I didn't support some of their tactics, but I supported their cause. However, I wondered if Gina felt there was room for her, the living person, in the world of their intentions, or if she felt they saw her only as a card to play in their larger game.

Waseau, Ms. Lansdorf, and Francine returned to the room.

"Ladies and gentlemen," Waseau began. "Ms. DiNovi has confirmed that she will not be participating in any further proceedings related to her complaint. We are satisfied that this decision is hers alone and does not reflect any outside pressure. She has also released her lawyer from further duties. Unless I hear an objection from our hearing panel, I am prepared to terminate this suspension hearing."

The panelists eyed one another. There was no objection.

"Thank you to everyone for your participation on this unusual day," Waseau declared. "The panel will now convene in camera to discuss its report and recommendations.

Mr. Walmer, I expect your departmental chair will be in contact with you in the near future concerning your current suspension, which I understand was an informal one arranged at the departmental level."

"Thank you, Mr. Chair," I said. "I believe everyone in this room would agree that the university, and many of us as individuals, have work to do in order to make our university a truly inclusive place of learning. I strongly support the recommendation for sensitivity training. I believe it might have helped me avoid the classroom comment that I now deeply regret. I am volunteering to provide any assistance that may be helpful, if the university proceeds with this recommendation. Perhaps I could be the example of what needs to be changed," I added, eyeing the caucus people as I spoke.

They regarded me stonily; however, I glimpsed a tentative nod from Marion Philbert.

The room began to empty. Francine and I sat at our table, looking at each other.

"There is something I have to tell you," I said. She was smiling.

"And there is something I have to tell you, Andrew. But not here."

Ms. Lansdorf approached our table while her assistant packed away files.

"Well, that was interesting," she said, eyeing Francine. "Quite theatrical. Which one of you came up with it?"

She was smiling too and seemed unusually friendly for a lawyer who had just lost a client.

"Actually, I did," I said. "Francine wasn't involved and I guess I caught you both by surprise. But that's what you thrive on, right? Professional challenges?"

"Well, as always, there were some procedural counter-arguments I could have made but, in working with Gina, I've come to trust her judgment. Her decision was surprising, I have to admit that. It was certainly a recent one. I wonder if there might be things I'm glad I don't know, Mr. Walmer."

She gave me a penetrating look.

"I guess there are always things we don't know when we're dealing with human beings," I said. "Before the hearing, the panel had the power and Gina didn't. But she took it. She took it in her own way. I'm proud of her, and I think she will feel good about what she did. I hope so, anyway."

"I'm familiar with you as an expert witness, of course," Sophia said, turning to Francine. "You do some excellent work. But this is the first time we've met on opposing sides. I hope we can avoid that in the future."

"I'm sure we can," Francine replied. "I use several of your litigation strategies in my classes and I think you're a terrific model for young women."

"Thank you," she said, as her assistant approached, carrying their cases. "Mr. Walmer, you may not to be an entirely lost cause. I wish I could say the same for some of your colleagues. Take care," she said, as she headed for the door.

In person, Sophia Lansdorf was entirely gracious. The predator's gaze was gone, replaced with friendly and very intelligent eyes. She even had a sense of humour. This was something I had noticed about lawyers. When they weren't competing with other lawyers in a courtroom, they could be quite human.

"I absolutely have to dash," Francine said. "I need to make sure Andy and I are ready for our trip." She and Andy were booked on a flight for London, where they would spend two weeks visiting with Francine's parents in their charming Hampstead rowhouse. "I'll call you when we get there."

"Let's celebrate with a dinner somewhere nice as soon as you get back," I responded. "And I hope you and Andy have a terrific trip!"

I felt a pang as I said this. Of course I wanted them to have a great time with her parents. They were amazing people and they doted on Andy. I just wished I was going with them. I hoped it wasn't showing. I didn't want to put emotional complexities into Francine's much-deserved vacation.

"Hey!" Francine was smiling. "I guess it's back to the classroom for you. Congratulations!" And then she was walking away. "You and Doidge," she said over her shoulder, a glint of mischief in her eyes. "This could be the beginning of a beautiful friendship for you, Andrew."

I had news for the department. Heading for the Arts and Sciences building, I wondered how it would be received.

Chapter Ten
Uprising!

“I s she...?” Sonya’s voice trailed off.

Letty Bishop’s head had sagged forward mere minutes after the board turned to the main item on its agenda. Letty had sagged before even voicing an opinion. Very uncharacteristic.

“She might just be sleeping,” Doreen said, eyeing Letty. And then, after a moment: “She seems awfully... still.”

“Surely she couldn’t be...” The possibility that Letty Bishop might have expired, mere moments after her appointment had been recorded for our minutes, was too shocking for Sonya to acknowledge out loud. After all, Letty was Sonya's hand-picked director, her appointment engineered by email before I could propose anyone else.

Letty's diminutive form slumped in her chair, head canted downwards onto her chest. I was sitting beside her.

"Could you give her a nudge, Andrew?" Barnstead suggested. "Or maybe check her vital signs?"

I gave her a hesitant nudge.

There was no response.

"Letty?" I said. And then more loudly: "Letty?"

It was all very well for Barnstead to call for vital signs to be checked. He was sitting on the other side of the board table. I was the one who had to do it and I didn't know how to check for vital signs on a 92-year-old. I wondered if a 92-year-old would even have any.

"She must be sleeping," Sonya said. "At her age, they sometimes have sudden naps."

I wondered why Bill had been on his phone instead of doing something. If Letty was experiencing a medical emergency, then surely a property manager would have a procedure to deal with it. Or if she had actually died, then, strictly speaking, she was no longer a board member, so it shouldn't fall to board members to deal with her.

"I don't think she's sleeping," I said. "I think we need to call 911."

Bill stepped to Letty's side and gently applied a finger

to her neck. "I'm not finding a pulse," he said. "I've already called 911."

"We need to give Bill some space," Sonya said as a distant siren became audible. "Actually, we need to clear the room so the paramedics will be able to get their equipment in. Let's shift to the storage room."

We had met in the storage room once before, when unfinished maintenance work made the board room unusable. Equipment and repair materials occupied most of the room. A stack of folding chairs was available for use when guests came to board meetings and there was enough space for us to sit with laptops or papers on our knees.

"I'll wait here with Bill," Sonya said. "Poor Letty. It's the least I can do."

We vacated our chairs and began to move towards the storage room.

"Henry?" Sonya avoided my glance. "Could you get them started on the letter? We really need to deal with that."

Before we had tumbled into a condo board equivalent of the classic Monty Python dead parrot sketch, the board had been about to consider the letter hand-delivered to our mailboxes the previous day. I had spotted mine as I returned after meeting with my department head in the aftermath of my suspension hearing.

Jasmine had told me how my teaching career would be resuming and the news was not pleasant. She outlined my heavy load of introductory courses and told me that a graduate student would be presenting the fourth-year seminar on parliamentary government. This was my favourite course, about issues that increasingly preoccupied me.

"I'm sure you're not surprised that we had to ensure arrangements for this important course before we knew your hearing outcome," Jasmine had said.

I had braced for punishment if I emerged unscathed from my suspension hearing. However, I had not anticipated that half my teaching time would be devoted to bringing enlightenment to engineering students, a group congenitally hostile to anything related to political science. I was being sent to the department's equivalent of the Gulag, no doubt about it.

Returning home, I had almost walked past the envelope protruding from my letterbox. Envelopes in the letterbox were rare, and if one came from an owner, it usually meant trouble.

I had the letter in front of me once I got settled in the storeroom. Its flamboyant style was unmistakably Philippe's. The fact that it had been distributed to all condominium owners reflected his chronic need to make as big a splash as possible:

"Demand for a Special Meeting of Owners," was how it started.

After extensive consultation of members of our community on behalf of the owners of Britannia

Condominium CCC 032, we the undersigned have reluctantly been forced to conclude that a special meeting of owners is necessary to clear the air and establish a way forward for our condominium. Our fundamental purpose is to serve the interests of our community. We need a Board of Directors that maintains good governance at all times. It must respond to the will of the community and the needs of owners.

Someone had done their homework, probably Philippe. His contribution as treasurer had been invisible, but his command of entitlements created by the Condominium Act had always been impressive. The Act gave owners the right to a special meeting if it was requested by at least fifteen percent of them.

The letter devoted lengthy attention to the impressive qualifications of its signatories. Eventually, it got around to specific demands:

(1) An immediate stop to oppression by the Board of Directors, including actions to remove potted plants from balconies;

(2) A community referendum on all aspects of the implementation of Rule 38, relating to balcony management by the Corporation. We believe this rule is a far-sighted contribution to our quality of life and property

values that is being brought into disrepute by this Board;

(3) The creation of a Britannia Condominium Owners Advisory Committee (BCOAC). This Committee should consist of up to 6 resident volunteers to be identified at the meeting we are requesting. The Committee would be mandated to provide advice to the Board on all aspects of the implementation of Rule 38 and other related matters to be identified by the Committee based on community consultation;

(4) Owner Consultation Meetings. The Board should hold monthly owner consultation meetings, open to all owners, for the purpose of building a stronger sense of community in our condominium and ensuring that owner feedback is heard. This Board needs to be accountable to owners on a regular basis; and

(4) Stop redacting minutes so that owners cannot see what was in them. Owners have no way of determining if the information should have been confidential or not. Also, we want a commitment that the Board will review its overall approach to minute-taking to find a better way to deal with confidential information.

The letter skated around the Condo Act requirement that owners who wanted to replace a director needed to identify the person, state a reason, and identify the replacement who would be nominated. Instead, it declared that a slate of nominees was being prepared by Philippe, but it would only be used if, in the course of discussion, consensus could not be reached and existing directors decided to resign.

It seemed obvious that the plan was to rely on public humiliation to clear the way for changes to the board, no doubt involving the glorious return of our local champion of community service and his supporters.

Included in the letter were the signatures of 16 owners, with *Philippe M. Gibbon* heading the list, inscribed with his familiar expansive flourish. Apparently, none of them had found the time to check the numbering of their list of demands.

"...wakes me up after eleven at night every week!" intruded on my consciousness, distracting me from the letter.

Doreen was declaiming about a tenant's truck, a very loud and very red one.

Henry nodded sympathetically. "He does burn-outs going past my place," he interjected. "I don't know what he's doing leaving it in visitors' parking in the first place."

"Shouldn't we be thinking of Letty?" I interrupted. "She wasn't moving at all..."

"Have you seen his girlfriend?" Doreen continued. "She looks like about 18 and she has this giant dragon tattoo on her shoulder. I saw it when she was sunbathing in his front yard and she just looks like a little slut."

Sonya came into the room and seemed to know instantly who they were talking about.

"This is the kind of riff-raff we don't need," she said. "We already have enough of them, with those two units getting sold to landlords last year."

How do I talk to people about stereotyping, I wondered, *when their entire thinking is composed of stereotypes? How do I talk to these people at all?*

"Sonya, what about Letty?" I said. "What is happening?"

While Henry and Doreen had been preoccupied with the truck, I heard people moving about in the boardroom. Doors were opening and closing. There didn't seem to be much talking.

Bill had followed Sonya into the boardroom. As they came in, the outside door was closing behind the paramedics.

"They were very efficient," she said. "Letty is in good hands. All we can do is hope and pray."

As she spoke, I heard the ambulance moving away. There was no siren. I didn't see any sign of flashing lights.

"I know we all hope she's okay," Sonya continued. "She's a wonderfully resilient person and a real trooper for stepping onto our board again."

"Sonya, I actually think..." Bill began. He looked distinctly uncomfortable.

"We need to hope and pray," Sonya interrupted firmly,

glaring in Bill's direction. "Poor Letty! I'm sure we'd all just like to go home and reflect at this point, but we really do need to deal with that letter."

"Yes," said Barnstead. "Let's hope the best for Letty. I suggest we keep strictly mum about this. I'm sure neighbours will have seen the ambulance and the rumour mill will be flying, especially with Gibbon's hi-jinks going on. We shouldn't be saying anything about a board vacancy until we're ready to fill it."

"Absolutely," said Sonya. "And thanks for that, Henry. I know this has been very disturbing to everybody, but we are here tonight on an emergency basis. We have ten days under the Condo Act to respond to this letter. I think we should try and focus on that before we leave."

"Yes," said Doreen. "Poor Letty! She was really mad about that letter and I'm sure she would have wanted us to go ahead."

"Correct me if I'm wrong, Bill," I said, "but I don't think we have much choice here unless we have reason to believe that the letter is somehow fraudulent."

"No," Bill responded. "The Condo Act is pretty clear that they have a right to a response if the required number of owners requisition a meeting. If the Board says 'no,' that will just feed the problem unless there is a very good reason."

"What if they want new directors?" Sonya's congenital frown was even deeper than usual. "Don't they have to state who they are going to propose, so owners can think ahead of time?"

"They do if they are proposing this," said Bill. "But that part works like elections at our regular Annual General Meetings. People can get nominated ahead of time and circulate information about themselves, or they can get nominated from the floor at the meeting."

"I've never liked that nomination from the floor part," said Barnstead. "It just opens the door to sudden board take-overs."

"Maybe so," said Bill. "But it is what it is."

"I think it's there to try and make sure that condos have elected boards," I said. "As we all know, it's often a struggle to find volunteers to do this. So nominations from the floor allows for filling the positions when people are together at the AGM and face the reality of vacant positions."

"Fine," said Sonya. "But Philippe's behaviour here is completely shameful. He was at the board meeting where we decided to do something about the balconies. He was even the person who came up with that rule in the first place. He didn't utter a peep of objection. He supported everything and he should be ashamed of himself!"

"In fairness," I said, "I'm not sure he supported how it was done. There were some very angry owners out there and maybe they bent his ear."

"Andrew, it was completely based on the board decision," Sonya snapped. "Everyone had an opportunity to raise objections. Including you, and nobody did."

"Yes," Henry said. "We all had an opportunity and I think we can all agree that Philippe is letting his ambition get out of control here. He looks like he thinks he's some kind of emperor, the way he goes strutting around. We don't know what he's been telling people. He could have been getting them all stirred up about his removal as treasurer and who knows what else."

"I completely agree!" Doreen interjected. "Philippe is just being a disgusting little traitor. Board members are supposed to have some loyalty and he's just going around stirring people up. And look at how he takes care of his yard! He has his winter tires sitting by his garage door and they've been there since he took them off at least two months ago."

"Exactly!" Sonya declared. "I'd like to hear him explain how he thinks that contributes to the community service he's always talking about, not to mention our resale values."

"Bill?" Doreen resumed. "Why are those tires still there? This is completely against our rules and they make our neighbourhood look like a junkyard."

"I wouldn't advise going after him right now," said Bill. "It would just give him an excuse to complain about being singled out because of his letter and make things more difficult."

"I think we all agree about Philippe," I said. "This has

been a difficult meeting, very stressful for everybody. And I think we need to remember our property manager's advice here. We really don't have many options. So—"

"Yes, let's get a meeting date," Henry interrupted. "I move that we direct Bill to confirm our agreement to a special meeting and propose a date. Bill, I believe the Condo Act has some timelines, so could you suggest something?"

"How about Thursday the 12th next month," said Bill, who evidently had worked out the logistics ahead of our meeting.

"So, all in favour of Henry's motion?" Sonya said. Barely pausing for breath she announced, as was her habit: "Agreed. Please record unanimous agreement for that one, Charlene."

The meeting was speedily adjourned.

Directors headed for the door.

Sonya and Doreen left together. Henry said "Good night" and quickly made his exit as well. The directors seemed to have an appetite for my company similar to mine for theirs. I departed alone, leaving Bill to close down the office once Charlene had gathered her laptop and other equipment.

Henry's lack of eagerness for my company had been concealed with social skills. I wondered if it had anything to do with what I had seen the evening of my suspension hearing.

That evening, I had returned home late after my weekly tennis game and a few drinks, probably around 11 p.m. As I pulled into my laneway, I spotted Henry scuttling away from Alexandra's front door and then strolling along the lane. His leisurely pace looked exaggerated, as if he wanted to be seen. Out for an innocent evening stroll, glancing about here and there at the condominium as a conscientious board member might. But I had noticed the scuttling. Middle-aged men don't scuttle gracefully.

Eleven p.m. was, to say the least, an unusual hour to be concluding a meeting with Alexandra. She had agreed, several weeks ago, to call her lawyer off as long as negotiations about the tree issue were moving forward. There was no longer any urgency.

PART THREE: JULY

Chapter Eleven

Coup d'etat Britannia-Style

L ife, I was thinking—you're either bored or over-whelmed. Why does it always have to be that way? So much had happened between the last board meeting and tonight. I was still struggling to process it all. However, there I sat in Hall B of the Community Centre, waiting for the hastily organized special meeting of owners to start. I sat behind my name card at the long table set up for board members under the institutional fluorescent lights. The table faced rows of folding chairs set out for the owners who had demanded the meeting. Most of them were still unoccupied.

One by one, or in small groups of two or three, the owners of Britannia were straggling in and settling into the chairs.

They were, at the best of times, an inscrutable bunch. This evening, it was especially hard to read their expressions. As usual, and despite a history of owner complaints about being unable to hear at annual meetings, they were favouring the chairs at the back of the hall. This left a sedentary no man's land of empty chairs between the owners and the head table.

Barnstead's name card stood on the table as far away from mine as possible. Was this just a coincidence? I hadn't connected the dots immediately, the evening I had seen him surreptitiously departing from Alexandra's, but I had seen enough to catch my attention. And he had almost certainly seen me, although he had betrayed no sign of it.

It had taken a while for my suspicion to congeal because I had been absorbed in my own preoccupations. My course load for the coming term would require some real effort and the classes I had been assigned portended drudgery. Perhaps that was why my exhilaration at the termination of the suspension hearing had been short-lived. However, even before I met with Jasmine about my teaching duties, I had been experiencing a strange sense of deflation. Two colleagues I had shared the news with after meeting Jasmine seemed more excited than I was. I had begged off joining them for a celebratory drink on a lame excuse about family duties.

There hadn't been any family duties. Andy and Francine were getting ready to be airborne, heading to England for two weeks with her parents. I had already been missing them.

My thoughts were interrupted by the arrival of Philippe. He swept into Hall B an uncharacteristic two minutes before the meeting was scheduled to begin. He was decked out in a blindingly white summer suit. In combination with his signature Panama hat, it made him look as if he had just emerged from the drawing room of an antebellum cotton plantation or, possibly, a very esoteric literary salon.

Interestingly, he arrived alone. Then again, supporters might have detracted from his entrance. Possibly they would have distracted his neighbours from the flourish with which he deposited his hat on the chair beside the one he occupied, a flourish so grand that the hat threatened to become airborne. Typical Philippe.

Several owners took in Philippe's performance with bemused expressions. However, most appeared to focus on catching up with nearby neighbours. Others gazed phlegmatically in the direction of the head table. A look of disappointment flashed across Philippe's face before it reverted to the expression of grave and dignified concern it had worn as he entered the room.

"Ladies and gentlemen! It is now 7 p.m. and I would like to call this Special Meeting of the owners of Britannia Condominium to order."

It was David Schwartzman, our condominium lawyer.

"I have been asked to chair this meeting as an impartial third party because tonight's business involves owners who have expressed dissatisfaction with the board. Is that agreeable to people?"

Hearing no objections, Schwartzman declared that when the seven proxies received by the condo manager were included, the thirty owners present were enough to meet the quorum requirement of twenty-five percent of owners. The meeting could proceed with the requested business.

"Your agenda tonight consists of one item, with a second one as an option," Schwartzman continued. "The requisition for this meeting has been circulated to all owners and it requests a free and full discussion of the five items listed in that document. Owners have the option during discussion to suggest the resignation of one or more board members, but resignations were not requested for the agenda. This means it will be up to board members to accept any such suggestions or not. If any director chooses to resign, nominations can be made from the floor and voted upon tonight. Does anybody have any questions at this point?"

Schwartzman paused briefly. There were no questions.

"Okay, I'll take that as agreement with our agenda, so I'd like to invite Philippe Gibbon to present the concerns of owners and start off the discussion."

An expectant silence settled on the room. Eyes turned to Philippe.

"Philippe?" Schwartzman asked.

Philippe rose majestically from his chair. He turned to face the audience, one arm folded across his chest in a gesture I vaguely associated with portraits of Napoleon.

"As our lawyer has advised us," he said, "the letter demanded this meeting on behalf of owners so that a full and free discussion could happen, in the interest of our community. I believe that the letter presents the concerns of owners, fully and fairly, and on behalf of owners, I would like invite the board to respond to these concerns. It has not done that yet."

It is an anatomical impossibility to sit down with a flourish, but Philippe's descent onto his folding chair came close. Perhaps it was the suit.

Silence descended again. It became awkward. Bill, our property manager, leaned over to Schwartzman and whispered something.

"Sonya? Perhaps you could start us off with any comments you might have, on behalf of the board," Schwartzman said.

"We're here to listen to what owners have to say,"

Sonya replied. "It was owners that requested this meeting."

More whispering between Schartzman and Bill. Schwartzman looked worried.

"Sonya, if I may," Schwartzman said, "you could be very helpful by making a brief comment about the first item raised in the letter, the removal of potted plants from several balconies."

"The removal of the non-compliant potted plants has been completed," Sonya said. "The letter demands that this should be stopped but this is quite misleading. There is nothing to stop at this point. All board members, including Mr. Gibbon, voted in favour of this when it was proposed. As you all should be aware, Rule 38 prohibits the use of balconies for storage purposes. It also requires that they be kept in presentable condition at all times. We have been advised, again and again, that the board has a duty to enforce the rules and that is what we were doing with the potted plants."

"Is there anyone present who has concerns about this?" Schwartzman asked.

Again, silence.

Philippe rose to his feet.

"We are here tonight to help this community move forward and protest against the way this was done. I was removed as treasurer without due process, so I did not have any role in deciding if the plants needed to be removed. The people who signed the request for this meeting are only looking for accountability. If they can't get that, then we will have no choice except to demand the resignation of all the board members at the table!"

"Okay," Schwartzman said. "But you are getting ahead into the optional part of the meeting, Philippe. I suggest owners still need to discuss the list of demands in the letter."

A man in leather jacket stood at the back of the room. I didn't recognize him but Bill said, "Yes, Mr. Mazzarini."

"We're going in circles here," the man said. "As far as I'm concerned, where there's smoke, there's fire. So I think we need a new board, but how can we decide to ask board members to resign if we don't know if there is anybody to replace them? I am asking Mr. Gibbon, could you please tell us who is willing to sit on the board so we know where we are going here tonight."

Murmurs of approval arose from the audience and a red-faced woman began clapping vigorously.

"Clarissa Benson," Sonya whispered at the table. "Drinking again."

Eyes turned to Philippe. Philippe stared into the middle distance, a familiar blank expression on his face. It was exactly the same expression we had seen each month at board meetings, when he was asked to comment on the monthly financial report.

This time, unlike board meetings, Bill was not standing by with a financial update to bail Philippe out. Instead, silence persisted.

With evident reluctance, Philippe rose to his feet.

"Our purpose is to serve the interests of the community by having a free and full discussion," he declared. "I have had extensive consultations with owners and it was decided that this meeting should decide about nominations instead of us because… um… the whole community needs to identify the problems in order to serve our community by finding the right people for the board."

"Mr. Chairman!" a man in a lumberjack shirt called from the back row. "This is getting ridiculous! Philippe, this isn't what you told me last week! You told me you would have a slate of board members to propose and that's why I'm here tonight!"

Sensing impending disarray, I could no longer hold my tongue.

"David," I said. "I wonder if we should just go through the other demands in the letter, one by one, and get the views of owners. Sonya has responded to the first one. The second calls for a referendum on all aspects of the implementation of Rule 38. I don't see how this is possible because we don't know how it will be implemented until there are specific problems where the board might decide to implement it. The compromise I would suggest is that the board just hold a referendum on the rule itself: do owners approve of it or not?"

I waited expectantly for nods of approval from owners or signs of agreement from board members. They sat inert, looking at me with blank expressions. The same expressions I was accustomed to at board meetings.

"Andrew," Sonya said. "We have a standard procedure for rules that allows owners to call a special meeting when the board announces a new rule if they don't want it. So this rule has already been approved by owners because they didn't call for that meeting when Rule 38 was announced. A referendum would just duplicate this and cost us money."

The last thing the meeting needed was board members arguing in front of the owners. I adjusted my face into an expression of gratitude for Sonya's precious enlightenment and stayed silent.

"Mr. Chairman?" It was Mazzarini again. "I like the idea of going point by point. We don't want to be here all evening. So what about this idea of creating a Britannia Condominium Owners Advisory Committee? We need six volunteers for that. Philippe, what can you tell us on this one? Do you have any volunteers from your consultations?"

Again, from Philippe, the fixed stare into the middle distance. It was almost as if he were going into a self-induced trance.

"Okay," said Mazzarini. "Let's get moving on this one. You want volunteers? I'm willing. Who else?"

Yet again, an expectant silence. Yet again, a silence that rapidly became awkward.

This time, it was Barnstead who saved the day. "Thanks, Sergio," he said. "It looks like Crestview Court has the activists here tonight. If people agree, the board could pick up on this at its next meeting and use our newsletter to look for volunteers. Why don't we leave this one for now?"

"Mr. Chairman?" It was Hornby. I hadn't spotted him in the room. A wistful hope that he was not present had taken shape within me. He had to be the person responsible for the complaint in the letter about redacted minutes. Of the five demands in the letter, this was possibly the one that made the least sense, although there was intense competition. Hornby had never explained how explanations of redacted information could, somehow, keep the redacted information confidential.

"I have already raised the issue of board minutes numerous times at our AGMs," Hornby began. "However, we have seen no change and no response to critical accountability issues that I have been informing owners about. As we know, owners can obtain copies of the minutes of our monthly board meetings, but important information is redacted on the grounds that this is confidential. However, we are in the position of having to accept this explanation purely on faith. We have no basis for determining whether the information is confidential or not. And the minutes provide no explanation that might help us to be confident that information we need to know is not being concealed."

"In the interest of time on an evening when most of us are tired from a full day's work, Mr. Hornby," Schwartzman intervened, "could you please get to your point as quickly as possible?"

"Yes, of course," Hornby said. "I was making my point before you interrupted, sir. I know that I have raised these points at AGMs, so I would hope that they are not news to owners. However, my point is that nothing has been done about them. Board minutes are not the most exciting reading but they are a vital accountability tool in a condominium corporation. We need to remember that the condominium board is accountable to all owners. I hope I do not need to remind owners that in my day job, I'm an accountant. I have been an accountant for thirty-two years and I know something about accountability. As I try to tell owners at our AGM's, the minutes of the board meetings are a central tool for achieving that accountability—"

"I'm very sorry to interrupt here," a woman in a bright red pantsuit said, loudly enough to bring Hornby to a stop. "Céline Dupras, number 68 here, Mr. Chairman. Time is passing very rapidly and I don't think we're getting to the issue that brought most of us out tonight. We have a letter saying there seems to be a problem on the condo board, but most of us don't really know what's going on and we just want things to get sorted out. So could we deal with the issue of resignations, if we need to, before we get caught up in this one?"

"Thank you, Céline," Schwartzman said. "Mr. Hornby, Ms. Dupras has a point. Are there any specific problems that you could tell us about, that we could perhaps resolve without delaying other discussion here tonight?"

As Schwartzman had spoken, Sonya's mouth gradually compressed into a line of tight-lipped rage. The lawyer's compromise was sensible, but he was placing himself in peril. Sonya did the redacting at Britannia and had apparently been doing it for many years. It was generally assumed that she had professional instruction about how to do it but, not surprisingly, there seemed to be no record of this. And now, Céline Dupras, plainly a woman not to be trifled with, was glowering at Schwartzman as well.

"Yes," said Hornby. "As a matter of fact, I was coming to precisely that before I was interrupted again. Here is a line from our minutes of two months ago: 'Moved by Andrew Walmer: That Creepy Critters Animal Service be contracted to remove the [redacted] from [redacted].' Now what are we to make of that? How are we to hold Andrew, or the board, accountable for whatever it was they decided to do? We simply have no idea what's going on. Andrew, what can you tell us? Without, of course, revealing any confidential information. And Sonya, how do we know that each of these redactions should be confidential?

"Well," I said. "At a typical meeting, we often make routine motions that authorize the property manager to arrange work responding to an owner's problem and I'm guessing that's what this was. I'm afraid I don't actually remember what it might have been, beyond that but—"

"We have definite guidelines for redacting," Sonya cut me off. "They reflect professional advice because, as you know, the Condominium Act requires that we do not disclose confidential material. So these redactions reflect legal advice we have been advised about."

"Yes, I understand that," said Hornby. "But I come back to these specific redactions. How do I know the information was confidential?"

"I don't know what you are suggesting," Sonya snapped. "We can put a note in each redaction saying confidential information was redacted. Would that satisfy you?"

Attempting to head off an altercation, Bill intervened:

"Charlene, could you pull up the e-file of those minutes? If owners agree, as a neutral party I could examine the unredacted version and try to describe each redaction in a way that might make it more understandable."

"I don't think this is necessary," Sonya sputtered.

The owners watched impassively. Charlene, who was present to take the minutes of the special meeting, entered a few keystrokes on her laptop and presented it to Bill.

"Okay," he said. "So I'm just finding that line in the minutes... Okay, here we go. So the line reads 'Moved by Andrew: that Creepy Critters Animal Service be contracted to remove the [redacted]'… uh… Sonya, I'm sorry, but

I think I have to disclose this. I have an obligation to disclose requested information to owners unless it's confidential. The word 'chipmunks' is what was redacted here. I think I have to disclose that. A contractor was being engaged to remove chipmunks from an address where they were damaging the building."

Sonya's face was now white with fury. "As far as I'm concerned, this was confidential! Any owner who is observant would know where there are chipmunk problems at certain homes, so they could easily put two and two together if they read these minutes and figure out which residence was involved."

"I can't agree with that one," said Hornby. "Chipmunks aren't confidential. The Condominium Act doesn't make us responsible for protecting the privacy of chipmunks."

Chuckles echoed in the room.

Sonya was not chuckling. She looked murderous.

"And the second redaction," Bill said, hastening to firmer ground, "is the owner's address. The Condominium Act clearly prohibits disclosure of individual owner names and addresses, so that is why it would have been redacted."

"Well, I'm not satisfied," said Hornby. "But if explanations along these lines could be included in the minutes, then at least we'd know where to ask further questions. Perhaps, since it is getting late, that is where we could leave this..."

"Explanations will need to be a board decision," Sonya said, her hands clenched white on the table. "We need to start being efficient here and move on!"

"Mr. Chairman?" It was Hank Van Vliet, one of the victims of Sonya's plant genocide. My heart sank. Now we were in for it, just when people were getting tired and wanting to go home.

"We're here because of what happened to the plants on some of our balconies. But I think most of us have other things to do tonight, and now Sonya is saying it's all finished anyway. So I hope the board gets our message. We think things went too far this time. That's all I have to say."

"Thank you, Mr. Van Vliet," Schwartzman said. "Does anyone else have anything to add, or perhaps a board member would like to respond?"

Board members remained mute. The room was silent. Several owners had surreptitiously departed during Hornby's oration about the minutes.

"Well, that looks like it will do for the discussion part of this meeting," Schwartzman said. "Do I have any calls for resignation that would trigger the optional discussion involving resignations and nominations from the floor?"

"Mr. Chairman?" It was Amelia Oscroft, who lived near the board office. "There seemed to be a medical emergency the other week at the board office and I see Letty Bishop isn't present tonight. Could someone tell us what is happening with her?"

"There is no official board vacancy right now," Sonya responded. "I do not have a written resignation and I haven't received any documentation about the medical incident. However, it's not too soon for people to be thinking about volunteering. The board will be reaching out to owners if a volunteer is needed."

"I like to volunteer." It was Mrs. Svensson. She had been concealed behind a very large woman wearing a purple blouse. "I'm Ingrid Svennson and I talk to Andrew about your board. I am happy to be on it if you need somebody." She sat down.

"Thank you, Mrs. Svensson," Schwartzman said. "The board will monitor this situation and be in touch. Would anybody else like to express interest at this point, or raise any other comments?"

Schwartzman waited briefly and then, with a look of relief, declared the meeting adjourned.

Sonya plainly did not share the general relief. Her hands were sill clenched and the angry line remained where her mouth could normally be seen. As Bill organized the clean-up and Charlene packed up her equipment, Sonya hustled board members into a small conference room next door to Hall B. The expression on her face did not encourage resistance.

"We need to talk about what happened here tonight but, frankly, I'm in no mood to talk right now. This was completely shameful! I've heard enough about board minutes to last a lifetime and frankly that was insubordination, what Bill did. Completely unacceptable and we can't let it go this time! And not a word of thanks from anybody! Not even a peep from any of those people sitting in those chairs about the work we have been doing. The time we have been spending! I've really just about had it. And now we have that Svensson woman to deal with, standing up like that in front of everybody when her husband was just a pervert. What would that say about the board, to remind people of that? It's embarrassing to everyone."

"We hear you, Sonya," I said. "We're all tired and it's been a very stressful night. But really, the owners ratified this board because they had a chance to call for resignations and they didn't. So that's something and you deserve the credit. If we need to reach out to Mrs. Svensson, I'm sure we can deal with that."

"He was a pervert!" Doreen said. "Just a nasty little pervert showing off to those poor girls in that bathing suit. She was married to him for years and we have no idea what was going on over there. We can't have anybody like her on the board. I agree with Sonya!"

"I'm sure Mrs. Svennson won't make trouble for anybody," Henry said. "I think Andrew's right and we should leave all this to another day. And thank you, Sonya, on behalf of the rest of us for getting us through tonight. You're a real heroine!"

Under the cover of Henry's diplomacy, I thanked

Sonya and made for the door. I'm betting that others didn't linger either.

I walked home brooding about the meeting. *How many of those signatures on Philippe's letter were from people who had even read it,* I wondered. Most of the people at the meeting had seemed to have no idea what it was about, much less a basis for deciding what do do. It was hardly surprising that the meeting had floundered. Our condo was supposed to be a miniature democracy. But how do you make democracy work when most people aren't even paying enough attention to know what they don't know? I would give this challenge to my students. It wasn't just about condos.

Chapter Twelve

I Finally Ask Her

"It's just jet lag," I wanted to yell. "You're amazing to be out there pitching at all!"

I had arrived late for Andy's game and at a bad time. As I took my seat, he burned in one of his fastballs, slightly wild. It took out another Amanda. This was the fourth Amanda of the season, counting the one he had hit at the demonstration game in May. I knew her name was Amanda because that was what the agitated woman sitting beside me was calling out.

"Amanda! Amanda!" I heard. "Are you okay?"

The injured Amanda was an unusually large and sturdy-looking girl, but when the ball hit her on the left thigh, she doubled over in pain immediately.

It was more than a little awkward. Support for Andy would not have gone down well with my neighbour. She was now out of her seat and hurrying to the visiting team benches. Nor would it have been well received by the other parents, watching anxiously. What is it about these Amandas? It seemed to be almost karmic. *Maybe there are a lot of Amandas in Andy's age group,* I thought. *Or maybe softball has a special attraction for them.*

Coach Greb did not look happy. He conferred briefly with the other coach after Amanda had been helped to the bench. Then he signalled in the direction of the Bears' bench. A tall and very athletic-looking boy jogged to the pitching mound. This was Jarrod Watson. Jarrod had been emerging steadily as the star pitcher of the Bears. After the game they had played before Andy had gone to London, he had grudgingly acknowledged this. Everybody on the team liked Jarrod because he was supremely modest. Also because he was supremely good, with an exceptional variety of strong pitches for a 12-year-old.

Coach Greb stepped over to Andy and gave him a consoling pat on the back before Andy walked back to his team bench, shoulders slumped in dejection.

I sat in the bleachers, feeling helpless, watching Andy's

slow walk away from his dream. Tomorrow, he might feel different. Right then, despair was what it would feel like. This was the agonizing side of being a parent, when you feel the suffering of your child and realize the vulnerability of that young life, the vulnerability we all still remember. You would do anything to protect your child from these moments but, already, there is less and less you can do.

With the injured Amanda on the bench, the game resumed at the peaceful cadence of softball. My mind wandered to the past two weeks, when Francine and I had fallen into a rhythm of daily video calls across the Atlantic that felt very natural. I hoped she felt that way too. Perhaps because she was free from the demands of the university and her other work, she had seemed less aware of time and schedules, more immediately involved with Andy and her parents. I sensed her realization that her time with her parents no longer stretched indefinitely into the future. Each day, she was making the most of it, creating happy memories for them as well as herself and her son.

The day before they had flown home, they had all toured Blenheim Palace on a sun-drenched Oxfordshire day. Francine reported that Andy had delighted his grandparents with what seemed to be a precocious interest in the history of the occupants, the Marlboroughs and related Churchills.

"Do you think that living in this house might have made them feel special?" he had asked. "And maybe

Winston would come here for his visits to kind of recharge that feeling or something."

Advanced thoughts for an 11-year-old that plainly delighted his grandfather. Somewhat improbably, Grandpa Antoine had become absorbed in the history of the great British country houses since retiring from a 40-year career with TfL, the Transport for London Authority. He had started as a London bus driver and ended as a successful senior manager.

"You're a very perceptive young man," Francine proudly told me her father had said. "Winston's visits were unusually frequent during the most difficult days of the war."

During our conversations, Francine and I were no longer distracted by my need for advice about my suspension hearing. However, as her holiday began, there had been several lengthy discussions about what had happened.

"I need to tell you something about Gina," I had said, determined to have no more secrets.

"Actually, we each need to tell each other something," she had responded, her voice amused. "Remember? "

"I'm sorry I didn't tell you this earlier," I said. "Things happened so fast at the hearing and I hadn't expected you to take over as my legal counsel. I ended up putting you in a very difficult position. If you had known what I need to tell you, you would have had to disclose it at the hearing. Or at least it would have been awkward, if… well, if things had gone differently."

I stopped floundering and told Francine about seeing Gina on the bench by the bridge the week before the hearing, and the conversation we had had.

"Frankly," Francine said, "I thought her explanation for seeking me out, that she knew about my work, was a bit lame. But in the circumstances, I didn't press her about it."

Francine had put Gina in touch with Natalia Rifkin in the biology department, knowing that she had been through everything Gina was experiencing. An internationally known researcher in genetics, Natalia had restored Gina's confidence in herself and her ability to decide her future. Gina had paid Francine another visit, to thank her and let her know what a difference her suggestion had made.

"So, she didn't give any advance warning about wanting to drop the complaint?" I said.

I had been worrying about this ever since the hearing day. Had I affected Gina's decision, just by going over to her on the bridge? If I had, then I needed to do something. But what?

"Not in so many words," Francine said. "She sounded like a different person, much more self-confident. I felt she was making her own decisions and that they would be good ones. Good for everyone. It is also possible, Andrew, that I let myself be guided by what Sophia Lansdorf said at the end of your hearing: sometimes there are things we don't want to know."

"Go Bears Go! All the way! Go, Go, Go!" The Bears' cheer resounded around me and I realized the game had wound to a conclusion. The Bears had been down before I had drifted off to my recollections. Now they had squeezed out a victory. Jarrod's pitching was likely the reason and the team was now clustered jubilantly around him, back-slapping and high-fiving each other. Andy was right in there, a smile on his face, back-slapping with the best of them. My 11-year-old could swallow his private grief, join his team in celebrating, and give Jarrod his due. This was Francine's influence. I was grateful for it.

As Andy began to pack up his gear, I headed down to the Bears' bench. Coach Greb intercepted me before I got there.

"Mr. Walmer," he said. "Good to see you. Can we chat for a minute?"

It wasn't really a question so I didn't need to agree.

"I guess you saw what happened out there. I'm taking Andy off pitching for a while," he said. "He has some real talent that we're going to work on. But at this age, they can get pretty erratic while the growth spurt is happening, you know. I can't be putting players at risk and I'm sure you understand that. Andy does. He's a good kid, Andy."

"Yes, I saw the accident and I hope the girl is okay," I said. "He just got off the plane from England last night and I bet jet lag had something to do with it."

"This time maybe," he said. "I know you've been

working with him and that's great. It's a great way of bonding. Maybe work on some of his other skills along with the pitching, okay?"

"Yes, for sure. We'll do that, and thanks for everything you're doing for the team."

Greb departed. Andy approached me, lugging his equipment bag.

"Hey," I said. "You did your best. You made your Dad proud out there, Andy. Baseball has its speed-bumps, just like life. But you picked yourself up and I was really proud of the way joined in with the team to celebrate with Jarrod."

"Thanks, Dad," he said. "I really don't know what happened this time. My arm just kind of went the wrong way. I checked with Amanda and she's okay, so that's good. Coach Greb is taking me off the mound for a while, but I'm hoping I can make a comeback."

"That's the spirit," I said. "Whatever happens, you're a good team player and a great Bear. So, shake time?"

"Awesome," he said.

Our journey to Francine's was interrupted by two stops: the customary chocolate shake stop at the Dairy Queen and a second stop to pick up the pizza I had ordered.

When we got to the house, Andy continued on to his room. I hesitated at the doorway, not quite sure about walking in. When I did, I found Francine sound asleep on the living room couch. Jet lag was affecting her more than Andy.

I sat in the living room, watching her. She was beautiful to me. It wasn't primarily because of the way she looked, although I had always thought she was spectacular. It was more because of what I knew about her, the barriers in life she had overcome, and how she had overcome them, always with her wonderful grace. I had never met anyone who combined the analytical mind of a lawyer with her capacity for empathy, including an understanding of why people might create the barriers she worked to remove. Everything she did seemed effortless, but I knew about her hours of work, her dedication, her quiet determination.

I realized she had woken and was looking at me. There was a smile in her eyes.

"Andrew," she said, her voice husky with sleep. "I hope I haven't been keeping you from your pizza for long." Her smile was now on her face.

"Actually, no," I said. "I…" I found myself fumbling for words. She rose from the couch. I stepped towards her. I found myself reaching out for her. Her arms went around me and we held each other. It was only a fleeting moment. I didn't say anything to interrupt it and she wasn't saying anything either. Simultaneously, we realized we hadn't been greeting each other this way for a long time and suddenly felt the awkwardness of it. Still wordless, we stepped apart.

"I have to warn you, things didn't go that well today," I said in an undertone as we headed for the kitchen. "Greb has taken Andy off pitching for a while." I turned to the hall leading to Andy's room.

"Andy!" I called. "Pizza's on!"

I arranged the pizza and a caesar salad on the table while Francine laid out plates and tableware along with our customary wine. Andy shuffled into the room, putting on a brave face that didn't conceal the puffiness around his eyes. As we sat down, Francine and I both eyed him, wondering how to gently offer parental consolation. We were also exchanging glances, but they were skidding away from each other. Our moment in the living room still hovered, creating what felt like a kind of shyness.

"So, Andy," Francine said. "Dad let me know what happened today but, really, you were playing through jet lag and we think you're amazing to even be able to do that. You know, I haven't been able to do anything all day, just walk around in a kind of fog. So you're way ahead of me."

"Mom's right," I said. "Try not to let it get to you. We all have bad days, but part of growing up is learning what we can from them and then picking ourselves up and moving on."

My eyes went to Francine's as I said this. Our eyes were not skidding away this time. A kind of watershed had been crossed. We were both absorbing that.

"You know what?" I said. "Medical professionals now

say there's one thing that can cure jet lag and speed-bumps at baseball at the same time. Pizza! You just have to make sure you eat enough of it. So let's dig in!"

And we did. Francine and I enjoyed the resilience of our son. It was visible with his first generous bite of the Hawaiian-style pizza, his favourite. He ate with single-mindedness. We could see, with each mouthful, a return of the optimism that is so natural to the young.

"We have a lot to tell Dad," Francine said. "You had so much fun with Grandpa and Grandma."

"We do?" Andy said, looking sly. "Even with you and Dad talking all the time when you thought I was in bed?"

Francine caught my eye and we burst out laughing. Andy might have been laughing too if he hadn't been stuffing his mouth with pizza.

"What about the day we went punting?" Francine said. "He doesn't know about that yet."

The story emerged, Francine and Andy giggling and interrupting each other. I was already aware that in retirement Grandpa Antoine had decided to take up a growing number of activities in a category that he persisted in calling "athletics." Originally, to compensate for his sedentary work, Grandpa had formed a habit of early morning walks on Hampstead Heath. The townhouse that he and Grandma had gradually bought, with the help of a large mortgage and a succession of boarders, was a short walk from the park. After retiring, Grandpa had incorporated a daily swim in the Hampstead ponds. Initially, these had been limited to the summer months, but more recently, Grandpa had become an avid year-round swimmer, insisting that swimming in frigid water was beneficial to his blood.

Francine and Andy had discovered that skulling, canoeing, and punting had been added to Grandpa's list of "athletics." An afternoon of punting on the Regent's canal in East London was made virtually mandatory early in their visit.

"We should have seen a warning sign when Grandma said she wouldn't be joining us and gave him a very pointed look," Francine said. A former nurse and very active woman with a growing collection of medals in her seniors' category of marathon running, Grandma Antoine would normally have been eager to embrace any proposal for activity.

As the punting expedition got underway, the reason for Grandma's reluctance soon became apparent. Beneath his benevolent exterior, Grandpa Antoine concealed a strong competitive instinct directed, especially, at the large punts loaded with tourists that congested the canal between Mile End and Old Ford Lock. He asserted priority wherever collisions seemed imminent and seemed to take special pleasure in advancing upon the slower tourist punts from behind and passing them at close quarters, regally ignoring the stares of captive tourists.

"It was so fun!" was Andy's verdict. "He was just like you that day at Krazy Karts, Dad. Well, maybe not that bad. And when we got away from all the boats, he showed me how to use the pole. And he only had to grab it once!"

"Well, only once," said Francine, laughing. "But don't forget that he stopped you from falling into the Thames at least twice. Twice, Andy! That would really have given the tourists something for their cameras!"

From there, the conversation moved to other memories of the trip. Francine's parents were extraordinary people. They had emigrated from Jamaica to Britain in the late sixties and worked with single-minded determination to create opportunities for their children. Eventually, Francine had gone to Cambridge as a scholarship student and her brother became CEO of an automotive parts supplier in the midlands. Somehow, on top of exhausting jobs, the parents had managed to buy and extensively renovate a second townhouse in nearby Camden Town that now provided them with a rental income. Grandpa Antoine, in addition to his "athletics," found time for delving into the history of aristocratic families and their houses, and was active in a range of heritage architectural societies. Grandma, never to be outdone, still ran marathons at the age of 68 and had gotten involved local politics and advocacy for recent immigrants.

Andy managed to consume a second helping of chocolate ice cream before the convergence of a large dinner and jet lag had their predictable result. After an extended yawn, he said goodnight to each of us and headed to his room. We watched him go, enjoying his enthusiasm about the trip and obvious attachment to Grandma and Grandpa.

When Andy had gone, Francine and I sat in silence. The moment in the living room still hovered. If I sat there with her and let it go by, it might not come again. For months I had been anticipating this moment, and dreading it because I still had no idea what to say.

I opened my mouth and started talking anyway. "Francine, I need you to know that when we held each other tonight, it was such a moment of happiness for me that I just can't let it go by. I've never stopped loving you and I miss you terribly. I miss you in my life, and I want you back. I want us to be back in the life we had before. I would already have told you this but I've been terrified it would just bring everything back and cause us more pain."

"Andrew," she said. "I have never stopped loving you either. I think we both know our feelings haven't changed that much. But to start with, I really only need you to tell me one thing. Why did you do it?"

"I really have done my best to be honest about that," I said. "It was the most terrible mistake I've ever made. I don't think a day has gone by when I haven't felt sadness about it, since we sat here and cried together about what we were losing. It has made me question everything about my life, Francine, and I'm still doing that. To me, explaining the affair seems like the simple part, in a way."

"No," she said. "I didn't mean the affair. I understand it was an impulsive thing, for both of you, I suspect. I mean, why did you tell me, Andrew? Why did you feel you had to tell me, when you knew me well enough to have a pretty good idea of how I'd react? This is the part we need to talk about, before I can feel the way I used to, like I really understand you completely. I need to know we aren't going to hurt each other again."

When she saw I was at a loss for an answer, she continued. "Let me explain myself better… I know we've both been doing a lot of thinking. When people love each other and something like this happens, it goes beyond the affair. It feels like a disintegration of your life and you begin to question your judgment about everything. As you said, you almost begin to wonder who you are—"

"Francine," I interrupted. "I don't think I can stand this! I don't think I can stand hearing that I put you though this. You're the last person who should be subjecting yourself to that kind of evisceration. I am just so completely sorry—"

"Okay," she said, smiling. "My turn to interrupt here. You're the most compassionate man I've ever met, but it sometimes makes you impulsive. Which is something I love about you, if you don't know. But let me finish this. Yes, I did my share of crying at the beginning. I guess we both did. But then I realized this was an opportunity to grow in self-knowledge and maybe even make myself a better human being.

"When people face the unexpected and are dealing with a lot of stress, they automatically reach for the self-concept that they have created over the years, and the values they see themselves as championing. You might call this kind of our default guidance system. As the cognitive psychologists are telling us, this system often gives us the explanations for what we are doing after the fact. Who was it who described the conscious mind as a kind of spin doctor, following along behind us and cooking up rationalizations for what we do after we've gone ahead and done them?"

"I think it might have been Steven Pinker," I said. "But don't let me interrupt you."

"Okay," she said. "I won't, but I'm starting to really feel the jet lag, or maybe it's the pizza, so I'll keep to the short version. We're going to need time for this anyway, Andrew. Enough time to get it right."

"Yes," I said. "There was a time when we knew each other completely. It would be wonderful to get that back, regardless of what we end up doing."

"I started asking myself why I decided we needed to separate," she said. "When we did it, I felt I virtually had no choice. I had fought so hard for women's rights over the years and worked so hard to persuade so many women to value themselves enough to insist on zero tolerance. I felt I couldn't do anything else. I think the conversations we

were having while I was at Mom and Dad's made me realize how connected we still are, after three years. In a peculiar way, the fact that we were talking at a distance, on
computer screens, seemed to help with this. When Mom
and Dad were doing things with Andy, I began to take long
walks on Hampstead Heath. Eventually, I was asking myself if my conscious reasons were really why I had insisted
we separate. At the time, I just did it. I just told you we
couldn't stay together and, being Andrew, you respected
that. But I began to wonder what I had actually been feeling. I think what I was feeling was pure anger, just being
terribly disappointed in you for not being the person I had
believed you were, and just wanting to hurt you. To punish
you, essentially.

"Being the star law professor and champion of reason,
I immediately repressed all those feelings, you know? Professor Francine Antoine couldn't possibly be so visceral.
And my internal spin doctor was right there waiting, ready
to make me feel like the virtuous defender of women's
rights that I had worked so hard to be, ready to keep on
proving myself to anybody who was watching."

"But you had every right," I objected. "You're the
women of steel when it comes to your principles, Francine.
It's one of the things that I admire about you so deeply, it
makes you absolutely fearless. And I—"

"Yes, I hear you," she said. "You're right, I do have
these commitments. But my question was whether they

were why I was doing what I was doing, at that time. I don't think they were. Not the complete story, at least. I don't think I was even living up to my beliefs about my principles and how to uphold them, and this is where you've been more influential than you might think. I was forgetting your favourite saying, or at least one of them. The one from your favourite completely opaque German philosopher."

"Hegel?" I said.

"No. Come on. What has anything I've said got to do with owls flying at twilight? No, it's the quote from Kant you are always trying to drum into your students: *From the crooked timber of humanity, never was a straight thing made.*

"This is a beautiful quote. It always reminds me to think about the people, their humanity. Remember your principles and be faithful to them, but never forget the people they are being applied to, the consequences to lives, how deeply we feel things. People have done so much violence to one another when they forget this. And I think we forgot it, Andrew. Or at least I did."

She understood it perfectly. There has never been a principle that does not collide, sooner or later, with the beating heart of a human being. We need to uphold our principles but we cannot allow ourselves to uphold them blindly.

She was telling me that she could do this, think about the human beings as well as her principles. She would do it for us. For me and with me, we could find a way to do it together. I felt a wave of hope. It was a wave of emotion that I didn't know what to do with. I hate it when emotions bubble up like that and I just wanted to get away somewhere by myself. But I couldn't just get up and run while Francine was talking.

Francine was looking at me. Kindly. Smiling.

"Andrew," she said. "You're forgetting that I know you. You need some private time and I need you to really think about my question. And I need more jet lag recovery. Let's plan to keep talking. I'm so glad we're doing this. But let's give it a rest for tonight, okay?"

I had forgotten how perceptive Francine could be. And I didn't trust myself to try and tell her how grateful I was, how happy about what she had been saying.

"Yes, you're right," I said. "Francine, you've been completely amazing to do this in the middle of jet lag. I'll call you tomorrow and see how you're feeling. And I can keep bringing food over, you wouldn't believe how long I can keep doing that."

We stood up and I took her in my arms again, just for long enough so I would have the feeling of her against me to drive back to the condo with. I left her standing there. Standing with such a sweet smile on her face.

I drove home, fragments of our conversation running through my mind. She was asking me why had I told her. I had been telling myself it was simple honesty, but I hadn't thought about it in the way that she had been doing about her own motives. I needed to. I had been thinking about everything else: my life, my career, my theatre work, the affair; I had begun to wonder about all my choices. Even my efforts to keep the condominium board functioning and moderate its folly. Why was I doing anything? Who was I, actually? Did the real Andrew Walmer have any resemblance to the person I had persuaded myself I was?

Francine and Andy were the real things in my life. This was what I still knew. Francine seemed to be the only completely authentic choice I had ever made. The rest had begun to seem like amiable drifting. I was ready to do anything to keep them. Answering Francine's disturbing question was where I needed to start.

Chapter Thirteen
Blind-Sided by Bungalow-Buying

I don't remember much about driving back to Britannia. I was completely distracted, rerunning Francine's words in my mind.

Francine had questioned herself so deeply and fearlessly. It was almost as if she had interrogated herself in a personal courtroom. She hadn't stopped until she had definite conclusions, decisions about herself.

My efforts at introspection seemed feeble by comparison, like so much of my life. I had arrived at uncertainty and confusion about everything, with no conclusions about doing anything different. I hadn't asked myself the question she had left me with. It hadn't even occurred to me.

I had always prided myself on my honesty. I may not always tell the truth, but I like to think I don't fool myself about what it is. I had told myself that I couldn't live in secret with something as serious as an affair with one of our longtime friends. But why couldn't I? Why had I told her, especially since the affair had been over? Francine had scraped away spin doctor explanations and somehow found her way back to her real motives. I needed to do the same.

I had agreed with Monique that Francine should never know. And then, somehow, there I was at our kitchen table, blurting it out. The only feeling I remembered having before I did this was overwhelming guilt that had built up steadily during the affair. I felt worse and worse about what had happened, even after it stopped. Francine was so undeserving of what I had done; I could hardly look her in the eye. I had felt completely trapped. So I just sat down and told her. Something had to change and I couldn't think of anything else.

Francine had asked how I could do this when I must have known how she would react. Try as I might, I couldn't remember thinking about that at all. The feeling of guilt and hopelessness had been overwhelming. That was what I remembered.

So it had really been all about Andrew. Me and my feelings, me and my guilt. It had not occurred to me that our marriage could actually come apart over this. Or over anything. I expected something very painful, terribly painful to us both. But then a kind of absolution would happen. After all, the affair was already in the past, the receding past. I didn't consciously think this out, it was more that it never occurred to me that it wouldn't be this way.

It had really been all about me and making the guilt go away. That was what I would have to tell her.

I pulled into my driveway but I couldn't get out of the Jeep. I sat there, feeling exhausted. Exhausted and ashamed.

Eventually, my attention returned to the present. I had a vague feeling that there was something amiss in the neighbourhood. I had driven to Britannia, all normal. I had driven through the condo entrance, all normal. I had driven along the lane… and now it came to me. Something had caught my eye. A lawn sign. Was it possible that a For Sale sign went up, just that evening?

I backed the Jeep out of the driveway and drove around the Crestview Court circle. All normal. But then, in the lane that entered the court, there it was. FOR SALE, the sign clearly said, on the lawn in front of number 2, ReMax Real Estate, Call Antonia Adjuczar. There was no doubt about it. Number 2 was up for sale. But this was Doreen's house. Sonya's friend, not to mention her ally on our troubled board. How could this be? There had been no sign of anything like this coming. It made no sense.

I eased the Jeep forward, turning from the entrance lane back onto Crestview Court. A sudden motion caught my eye. A man was moving from the doorway of number 6. Henry Barnstead. Henry Barnstead scuttling, just the way he had a few weeks ago from Alexandra's door. This time it wasn't Alexandra's. It was Mrs. Svensson's, and it was almost 10:30 p.m. An unusual time to be having an orientation meeting about possible condominium board work.

On the other hand, Henry was a busy man, without much free time during the day. He had probably seen Doreen's sign and realized our board was about to lose another director. Sonya and Doreen had clearly not liked the idea of Mrs. Svensson replacing Letty on the board, but there had been no firm decision. Now, with the board shrinking to its basic quorum of three, appointing a new director was urgent.

Henry moved quickly to the border of the laneway and began strolling, with elaborate casualness, towards his house. The same behaviour I had noticed at Alexandra's. I eased the Jeep alongside him and lowered my window.

"Henry," I said. "Nice evening for a stroll."

He looked startled but only momentarily. "Hi, Andrew. Yes, I've taken up walking in the evening when it's cooled down a bit. I was dropping some materials off with Ingrid since I guess we don't have much choice about getting her onto the board. You've seen your mail tonight, have you?"

"No," I said. "I'm just getting back from Francine's, but I saw the sign. That's sure a surprise. Do you know what's going on?"

"You better look in your mailbox," he said. "I sent you an email about it. I've got to run now because Jane was expecting me an hour ago. We need to talk, so why don't you come around tomorrow morning, anytime after 10."

Expecting him an hour ago. That didn't seem to make sense, for an evening stroll. But then again, how much of anything to do with Britannia made sense, even at the best of times?

Henry was already heading for his house. I needed to get to mine and find out what he'd been talking about. I aimed the Jeep for my driveway and accelerated to the 10 km/hour speed permitted since Sonya had laid down our traffic regulations. Actually, I might have gone a bit faster.

As I parked, I could see my mailbox. An envelope protruded from it. I locked the Jeep and headed towards my door. Closer to the mailbox, I could see that there were actually two envelopes.

Two envelopes? Doreen was resigning in duplicate? Even Philippe didn't think of that one. I grabbed the envelopes and went inside.

Envelope number one was from Doreen. The second

was from Sonya. I headed for my office, where I kept the condo files, opening Doreen's envelope first:

Dear Board Members,

I am resigning from the Britannia Condominium Board of Directors because I have just put my house up for sale. Some of you have probably seen the sign that went up today. If needed, I could continue on the board until my house sells.

Sonya and I have talked about this and she is going to write you to explain everything. Philippe and those owners shouldn't have made us have that special meeting. I don't see why I should be serving our community and trying to do things for them when that is how they act. I think Sonya was completely right to be so mad after that meeting.

I hope you keep going with Sonya's Britannia Beautification Campaign. It is exactly what is needed, and cleaning up the balconies was absolutely necessary. Something really needs to be done about the garbage cans that people are leaving out after pick-up. Sometimes they are out there for days!!

I guess you will be looking hard for new board members now. I don't go to the mailbox that often because I don't get that much mail, so I don't know that many people. Also, I really believe very strongly that Mrs. Svensson should not come onto the board. Think of the example that would give to other husbands.

Yours sincerely,
Doreen Nicol

Doreen had been Sonya's amanuensis for as long as I had been on the board. In normal circumstances, I wouldn't have been getting out the sackcloth and ashes about her resignation. But these were not normal times. There never seemed to be normal times on the Britannia Board.

The letter said that Sonya would explain everything. It looked like Doreen was resigning in a huff over the special meeting and I couldn't really blame her for that. But why did Sonya need to send us a letter to explain? More and more things that evening didn't make sense.

I opened the second envelope:

To: Directors of Britannia Condominium
From: Sonya

This memorandum provides my resignation in writing from the Board of Directors of Britannia Condominium, as required by Rule 2(a). My resignation takes place as of 12 p.m. today and I have deposited my keys in the office mailbox for Bill.

I am sending Board members a private and confidential email as a follow-up to this letter. Please note that it is for the Board's eyes only and not to be shared with other owners or the Property Manager.

Thank you for your attention.

Sonya Dietrich

I sat in my office chair. Stunned.

Stunned was putting it mildly. I had to make a conscious effort to keep breathing.

This was so completely uncharacteristic of Sonya that I wondered if it was fraudulent. Or perhaps some kind of joke. However, the signature was plainly Sonya's and Sonya never made jokes. Especially not about Britannia Condominium, which had been her obsessive focus in life for years.

Trying to keep Sonya from running amok and sending our biggest investment down the toilet had been my central reason for staying on the board. What would the board be like without her and her faithful acolyte? It was hard to imagine.

Yes, Sonya had plainly been furious about the special meeting. But Sonya had been furious before. Quite regularly in fact. Indignation about people disobeying our rules, if not full-blown fury, was a constituent part of her personality. The idea that she might someday voluntarily renounce Britannia had simply never entered my mind.

And what about the explanation that Doreen had promised? Sonya's letter didn't offer any. Just the facts. Sonya was going by the book and providing something that could be attached to our meeting minutes as an official record.

I needed to see what she had said in her email. I went to my office and opened my inbox. There it was:

PERSONAL AND CONFIDENTIAL

To: Board of Directors
From: President
Subject: Resignation

I am sending you this email on a confidential basis, as a private communication to follow up on my resignation letter.

As you know, I have been deeply offended by several of our owners recently, and their behaviour at the special meeting they demanded. On top of this, I believe that decisions are now needed about our Property Manager. In my opinion, he was directly insubordinate at that meeting and that is completely unacceptable. If I were continuing as President, replacing him would be the first item on my agenda. I have been through a change of Property Managers before. It is a huge amount of work on top of the duties of Board members and, especially, the President.

I have also received a number of personal messages from owners that are nothing but hate speech. I would take them to the police but I simply can't waste my time on this kind of thing. These messages are from people who have done nothing but complain, over the years, while I and other Board members have been donating our time to serving this community. I have devoted countless hours to my property inspections and reporting compliance issues to the Property Manager. For the past two years, I have been insisting on daily reports from him so that I can keep track of his activities. None of this is visible to owners and it may not be visible to you. We have been advised in the past about our roles and I have always taken my responsibilities as President of our Condominium with the utmost seriousness. This is important work for our community and I could never do it any other way.

With all of this in mind, I have been reflecting deeply on my future since the special meeting. I no longer have the motivation to do this work the way it needs to be done. I have concluded that it is time for me to pass my responsibilities on to others and move forward to new challenges. Serving the Britannia community has been an honour for me during the past ten years and I would like to thank you all for helping with this work.

Doreen has put her house up for sale. My sign has not been put up yet but I will also be leaving Britannia in the near future. As some of you may be aware, Doreen and I have grown close during our time on the Board and we have found a bungalow that we will be purchasing together. We are looking forward to making this bungalow a wonderful home for both of us. This will be a new phase of life for Doreen and me and I know we can count on your good wishes.

In the coming months, I am also looking forward to spending more time with my extended family. I have two young nieces who are now on the threshold of adolescence. Time is passing rapidly and I need to devote more of it to them at this critical period in their lives.

It will, of course, be up to the Board to appoint the next President. However, based on my experience over the years, I would strongly recommend Henry Barnstead for this role. Henry has been working with real dedication since joining us a few months ago. His knowledge of Britannia Condominium stretches back many years. As you may not know, he has been devoting evenings to building bridges with a number of our owners and reporting results to me on a regular basis. For example, he resolved the lilac issue with Alexandra Varga, at least for now. You can expect further information and other positive developments in the near future.

Very best wishes as you continue to serve our community and contribute to Britannia Condominium.

Yours Sincerely,
Sonya Dietrich

I sat staring at my computer screen. The more I looked at what Sonya had written, the more it seemed peculiar.

The tone of Sonya's email echoed the formal resignations of presidents of medium-sized countries or, at a minimum, CEO's of major corporations. But, after subtracting Sonya and Doreen, the board she was addressing now had only me and Barnstead on it; two people, unless Letty had risen from the dead. Sonya had always invested her role as president with great self-importance. It wasn't surprising that her resignation would reflect this. But as an email to two neighbours, it did seem somewhat inflated.

Tongues would already be wagging among people who

had seen Doreen's sign. They would be wagging at higher speed when Sonya's sign went up. So there was hardly anything in the email that called for her bold and underlined "PERSONAL AND CONFIDENTIAL" at the top of it. Her issues with Bill would be no surprise to anybody after the special meeting.

And what about the extended family she planned to spend more time with? Those two nieces had never been mentioned before. Did they have any idea of what would be happening to the remaining years of their childhood?

I sat there having irreverent thoughts. However, I could also feel my body beginning to clench with anxiety. Somewhere deep in my interior, awareness of implications was setting in.

My escape from the condo board was now completely blocked. I was trapped! Barnstead and I would soon be the only directors left. I had the same feeling in the pit of my stomach that I remembered from walking into a lake once on a soft muddy bottom and sinking in. Deeper and deeper. I remembered the feeling of panic. Of being swallowed up by something dark and bottomless where I wouldn't be able to breathe.

How was I ever going to get off the board? How?! The more I tried, the more I struggled, I just seemed to be sinking deeper and deeper. I couldn't simply resign because that would leave Barnstead stranded on it and I was the one who had talked him into joining in the first place. And there was my responsibility to my neighbours to think about too.

We were about to lose quorum! The place would be paralyzed if we couldn't find at least one board member immediately. I had just seen how owners could be about issues like chipmunks in the meeting minutes. I didn't want to find out what would happen if we messed up completely and major repairs that the owners were expecting came to a stop.

The prospect of being responsible for the collapse of Britannia Condominium Corporation made me feel ill. Any kind of responsibility for Britannia had always made me feel a bit queasy, but Sonya had always been there. Making sure Bill was dealing with the landscaping, sewer back-ups, and whatever else came along. My focus had been trying to put boundaries on Sonya. Now that was gone. I felt a growing sense of vertigo.

Furthermore, the Condo Act required us to have a president. Henry had only been on the board for two months. So that left me. If I couldn't persuade him to take it on, I would be well and truly stuck. Taking on the presidential role would be like shutting myself in the board office and throwing away the key. I would be responsible for a long list of projects and issues that I hadn't been paying attention to. If I took on the presidency, I couldn't turn around immediately and resign. I would need to find a replacement president. Unless I could persuade Henry, that would take months. Maybe years!

I shut down the computer and headed for bed. However, retreating under the covers brought no relief. I slept fitfully, migrating back and forth between my troubles and terrifying dreams. How could I tell Francine the truth about my selfishness and complete failure as a human being and still hope for any future with her? Would she finally see me for the pathetic piece of human wreckage I actually was? More immediately, how could we keep the condo board from collapsing, and how could I ever get off it? How could I make sure my investment was protected without becoming president, at least until Henry got up to speed? How could I ever get free?

How? How? How? My anxiety grew as my mind went around and around. I would lose Francine, and Andy too. I was going to end up alone. I would lose my job. I would not be blessed with an early death but would live on and on, a shrivelled husk of a man, fretting endlessly about plants on balconies and neighbourhood cats. Collapsing balconies. Loneliness. Angry cats...

I drifted in and out of troubled sleep.

After an interval, I awakened with a start, mouth dry and heart pounding. I had been trying to drive my Jeep around a laneway, initially like Crestview Court, but then becoming eerily white. White and smooth, it was the rim of a giant toilet and the Jeep was sliding inexorably into a heaving mass I knew was there but couldn't see. And, in the same impossibly compressed moment, there were garbage cans everywhere, and neighbours yelling. A cat was fastening itself onto my back. Its claws were digging into me and someone was yelling "Get him, Donald! Get the president!"

It was the claws that brought me fully awake.

My clock said 5:30 a.m. I decided to stay awake rather than brave further nocturnal horrors. I dragged myself out of bed and stumbled to the shower. The water brought a measure of calmness. My dreams were never prophetic—a consoling thought. I could be confident I wasn't going to end up being president.

I felt physically exhausted and unusually hungry. I thought of coffee and breakfast. Bacon and eggs. Those were my immediate needs and I set about meeting them.

An hour later, hunger sated and a second coffee in hand, I headed up to my study. A busy day awaited me, even without the meeting with Barnstead. I was scheduled to meet Jasmine and Anna Vasilakis, the grad student who would be teaching my parliamentary government seminar. I had agreed to help, in one of those conversations where saying no is not really an option. Besides, I liked Anna and I didn't want her to be a victim of my tangled relationship with the department. Later in the afternoon, I would be going to Francine's. She would still be jet-lagged but, knowing Francine, she would be well on her way to recovery after a good night's sleep.

I took the Condo Act and the Britannia by-laws off my

shelf and settled in to look closely at them. I remembered that the by-laws contained specific provisions about appointments. They were on the page after the one about resignations, dog-eared by wistful study.

In the dawning light of day, my situation didn't seem as grave as during the night. The board could continue to function as long as it had a quorum, defined as a majority of the members. We needed three directors present at a meeting to do the business of our five person board. Doreen had said she was resigning but that she would continue temporarily if there was a need. This had to mean she wasn't resigning immediately because, if she had actually resigned, she wouldn't have been able to continue. Also, she hadn't stated a specific time and date for her resignation, which was required by our Rule 2(a). Thank God for 2(a)! Doreen couldn't have resigned yet, even if she thought she had.

Barnstead might have figured this out on his own. In any case, it was possible for us to maintain quorum at the next meeting as long as we could persuade Doreen to attend for long enough to vote on appointing Ingrid Svensson. Ingrid would then give us our quorum of three and the board could continue to do business without relying on Doreen or Sonya.

If we lost our quorum, Rule 2(b) required a special meeting of owners to ratify emergency appointments that the Condo Act permitted a two-person board to make, or elect alternative directors. That would be a huge project, trying to get enough owners out to get this done after we had just held a special meeting that had wasted everybody's time. It could easily turn into "shame the volunteers" night, given some of the personalities that inhabited Britannia. It was also impossible to predict how it would end up. The outcome might be a board paralyzed by fighting over whether "chipmunks" should be in the minutes, or a board that would let our property fall apart in order to save money on monthly condo fees.

I hoped Barnstead might have some ideas about suitable directors. When I thought of who to ask, my mind was a complete blank. Mrs. Svensson had been the only arrow in my quiver and there was only one of her. If she came on, that would leave us as a three person board, capable of functioning, but two people short of full strength.

My thoughts were interrupted by my phone. I saw "Barnstead" in the ID window. I was glad to see his name. It meant I wasn't alone on what increasingly felt like a sinking ship.

"Morning, Andrew," he said. "I hope I haven't called too soon this morning."

"No, actually I was up kind of early today."

"Look, I'm calling because I have to go out this morning, so could we meet right away, or else postpone to tomorrow? For one thing, we need to start organizing and make sure we can get a quorum for our next meeting."

Shit, I thought. *Oh shit!* By "organizing" he was obviously saying we needed to find a president, probably just not wanting to hit me with that before he could persuade me. I needed to think fast.

I told him I'd be right over.

I don't remember much of what I was thinking as I headed to Henry's door. Shit figured prominently. Shit and panic about how to persuade Henry to be president.

Chapter Fourteen

Turning Points

I found Henry waiting for me in his kitchen, a pot of coffee on the table.

"Coffee?" he asked. "I made it extra strong because I can still taste that fish from last night."

Henry looked tired but strangely calm and contented. I wondered what else he might have had last night at Ingrid's, apart from her surströmming. After my night of turmoil, I wasn't in the mood for small talk.

"Thanks," I said. "I'm very pressed for time and you

are too, Henry, so I'm hoping we can crunch right into the issues here. I've been thinking about the president position since we no longer have one and I'm hoping we can settle that one first."

"No problem," he said affably.

"Yes," I said. "The president is going to have to be comfortable with what we do to keep the board afloat, including new directors."

"Right," he said.

"Okay," I cut in. "So let's crunch into this one then. I think you're the person who should do it. Your background in managing capital projects makes you the best person for this."

My strategy was to talk fast and keep talking, at least to stop him from saying "No" until I could give him my list of reasons. I just needed to not run out of breath.

"I'm still a relative newby here at Britannia and I really don't have a pool of people to draw on when it comes to getting people onto the board," I said. "In fact, Mrs. Svensson was really the only one and now I'm completely dry. And the other thing is, I remember when we were talking just after the board meeting and I was complaining about how our meetings seemed to go on and on with people wandering all over the place. You said you were used to chairing meetings and you'd have us out of there in an hour. Max, you said. And..."

I was gasping, I had no choice but to stop and inhale.

"Right," he said. "Like I'm saying, no problem. Sonya tagged me to do it in her letter and I'm fine with that. At least until things settle down a bit."

My lungs were now full and I was primed to continue with my arguments, including a promise to support him on the board for as long as I needed to. I don't know if my mouth would actually have formed the words for that one, but I was poised to try.

Instead, I breathed out. "Oh, that's great, Henry. I think I have a way to get us through this without another special meeting." And I outlined my thinking about Doreen, and why she could still come to meetings and vote.

"So we just need to make sure she comes to our next board meeting while she's still a director and she can vote to appoint Mrs. Svensson," I said. "And we need to make sure Mrs. Svensson will come onto the board, of course. Then we'll have some time to find more directors."

"Okay," he said. "You're the political scientist. I guess you can deal with that stuff."

It was the first time since I had gotten onto the board that a board member had acknowledged a political scientist might actually know something. I was momentarily shocked.

"Ingrid won't be a problem," he continued, with what could have been a slightly smug expression. "I'll phone her. But, Andrew, I can't face more of that fish. If she needs a visit, could you do that?"

"Okay," I said. I decided to hope that Henry could get it done over the phone and cross the surströmming bridge later if I needed to. Now was the time to solve the immediate problem and we were doing that.

"I'll call Doreen and explain why she still needs to come to the next meeting," I said. "I'll make sure she's available and willing. But there's still one problem. Doreen made it clear she doesn't want Ingrid on the board. What do we do about that?"

"Simple," he said. "We don't tell her. If she doesn't have somebody else, she'll have to support Ingrid at our meeting or be responsible for paralyzing the board."

It didn't look so simple to me but I needed to support my new president so he'd keep being president. I headed out the door, in plenty of time for my meeting with Jasmine and Anna. There was also time to phone Francine, to make sure that jet lag wasn't going to stop her from getting together later today. She picked up on the first ring and, yes, she would be waiting for me. Andy was spending the day with Anwar, so we would be able to talk without distraction.

"I'm trying to stay outside in natural light to help the jet lag," she said. "I've been craving Britannia Park since the middle of my time in London. Would you be okay with going there? We could even settle on one of the benches where we used to watch the sunsets."

"Yes, I'd like that," I said. That was an understatement. She was remembering us together on a bench. This told me she had been thinking about us. What we had lost. Like me. I didn't know what we'd decide, but at least we were going to be on the same side. Finally on the same side again.

The meeting with Jasmine and Anna turned out to be an easy one. It took less than half an hour. My inner cynic told me it had been easy because I was agreeing to do everything they asked me to do. However, my agreement was entirely voluntary. I was trying to build up my stock of diplomatic credit in the department or, more accurately, create some credit to lower my outstanding debts. Anna was going to be a good teacher and I was happy to help her along. I was also grateful that they treated me as if I had choices, asking with sincere expressions about each thing they wanted me to do. Some of them were even going to be interesting.

"Anna has absolutely no experience of actual politics and your course outline features a lecture on 'What is Politics?'" Jasmine said. "We're hoping you might be willing to do that one."

This was the lecture where I tried to give students an awareness of how difficult politics was, complex but also fascinating. Too many students seemed to think it was mostly about giving election speeches. I would tell them that the essence of politics was strong-minded people who often disagreed going into rooms of various sizes and knowing they had to come up with an agreement. Political parties that didn't succeed would face ruthless public criticism for being indecisive, probably followed by eventual humiliation when people voted. More broadly, governments faced the task of keeping 40 million people relatively content, which was demonstrably impossible.

Democratic theory promotes the idea that rational debate is a kind of competition of ideas where the best one emerges. In theory, this should enable persuasion and eventually produce general agreement, if not unanimity in that hypothetical room or even the big imaginary room called Canada. However, in reality, people don't often change their minds about the basic differences that fuel political debate. Our system of parliamentary government rests on a very questionable theory, I would tell my classes. Democratic practice works better than democratic theory, at least most of the time.

Last year, I used examples from the condo board in this lecture. Think about dog-lovers trying to coexist in the same building with people who are hypersensitive to noise and hate the sound of barking, I had suggested. Or landlords who rely on rental income to fund their retirement needing to reach agreement about the annual budget with people who want to think they belong in Downton Abbey, with an army of groundskeepers and tradesmen keeping everything immaculate and dusting the chandeliers every week. The students had engaged in a lively discussion about how any system could meet these challenges and I felt I had succeeded in making them think.

I had time to check my office mail before heading back home. There wasn't much. A green envelope caught my eye because it wasn't something official. The note inside was signed by Gina:

Dear Professor Walmer,

I heard about what you did at the suspension hearing and I want to thank you for that. It told me that you were as unhappy with the hearing process as I was. It made me feel that I wasn't the only one and I really appreciate that.

I am hoping you might be willing to meet for coffee and discuss my course work plans for this fall. Also, I would like to explain my behaviour in class that day. It was due to some new meds the doctor had put me on. I feel very bad about that and I strongly believe in trying to make things right as I go along.

Thank you for your support, including your suggestion about talking to Professor Antoine, which really helped me a lot.

Gina

This was a surprise and a delightful one. If I could do anything to help her on her way, of course I would.

I left the department and headed to meet Francine. Back at the condo, I traded my casuals for walking shoes. The Jeep started on the first try and I headed to what I still felt was my real home. I hoped I would feel that way after Francine heard what I had been discovering about myself.

"Hi," I said, as she met me by the door. "How are you doing? I hope you're okay with this today."

She was smiling and I felt a strong impulse to take her in my arms again right there. But you can't hug someone when you're also holding an aluminum screen door open. I made sure she was through the doorway before I let the door go, and by that time, she was heading for the Jeep.

"Slept like a log," she said. "I feel much better today and Andy seems to be completely back on his feet. The resilience of youth."

She filled me in on Andy's plans with Anwar for the day. Their focus on softball was expanding to, someday, buying a team. They had decided to be entrepreneurs and were designing a computer game. They were going to be working on a plot. Francine thought they might mean pilot.

"My brother took Andy to see his office in a black Aston Martin," she said. "I could see it made quite an impression."

Ah, the possibilities of life when you're 11, I thought, as we neared the beach. Parking the Jeep, I told Francine about my meeting at the department and Gina's note. "I'm glad she got in touch with you," Francine said. "I thought she might. She told me that she had the kind of experience in your class that she'd always hoped for in university. I think you need to hear that."

"That's great," I said. "But, Francine, I think we need to do the hard stuff first here today. The emotional stuff I always try to stay away from. As you said yesterday, we need to know and understand each other completely, the way we used to. I feel it's my responsibility to get us back there."

"I think we need to do this together," she said quietly, as we began strolling.

"Yes, you're right. But the more I've been thinking, I've been finding out I'm not the person I thought I was and I feel you need to know that. You wanted to know why I told you about the affair with Monique. I've thought a lot about that and my answer is that it was terribly selfish of me. Completely self-absorbed. I was feeling more and more guilt and it was weighing on me. Making me miserable whenever we were together. I just wanted the guilt to stop. It didn't occur to me that we would ever separate, although I knew you would be deeply hurt and disappointed."

"But you knew about my principles, Andrew. You knew about my advocacy for zero tolerance, it certainly wasn't a secret."

"Yes, I knew. But I simply couldn't stand the guilt any longer. I was feeling desperate. On some subconscious level that really disgusts me. I think I felt that if I confessed and honestly repented, I could get away with it. I wonder if you're right about my mother and the Catholic church leaving a lasting imprint on me. Somehow, confession would wipe the slate clean. I couldn't imagine that we'd ever be apart. I told myself that I was being courageous, living up to my core value of honesty. This made me feel like the moral person I have always wanted to be. But I'm not that person, Francine, and I wasn't then. I wasn't even honest with myself about what I was actually doing."

"Actually, Andrew, I'm not disgusted. I'm relieved. My great fear was that you were telling me because you knew I'd have to end our marriage and, maybe subconsciously, that was what you wanted to happen."

"No Francine," I said. "I..." We were standing on a sidewalk by the beach and I was having trouble controlling my feelings. "Could we walk down the beach and take a few breaths?" I asked.

The walking helped and I continued: "I couldn't imagine us being apart, and so I just assumed that, somehow, we wouldn't be. When you said we couldn't continue, I was stunned, and I felt a kind of numbness that I don't think has ever really gone away. I didn't know what to do. You were so certain and I realized I had already done so much damage. I couldn't think of anything but agreeing with you. As you probably remember, agreeing with whatever you said about how we should separate and what should happen next. It all seemed unreal to me and I just felt it couldn't be happening."

"I thought you were agreeing because that was the way you wanted it," she said. "So it made me sad, but it didn't seem surprising that you seemed so passive. When these fractures happen in relationships, they can reveal fault-lines that people might have been completely unaware of. The memory that kept haunting me was your story about your mother and the wallflowers. You know the one? About how she was the moral voice in your life and she had per-suaded you that you had a duty to dance with the wall-flowers at your school dances to make sure they had a good time like the other girls."

"Yes," I said. "I do remember."

"So you would do that, ask them to dance, but you didn't form any attachments to any of them and some of them were quite nasty. You were doing the right thing, An-drew, but just going through the motions. I wondered if that was how you felt about me, on some level. If I might be your wallflower, the Black girl you had a duty to rescue from racism..."

"No, Francine," I interrupted. "It was never like that. Never!"

I remembered the day we first met. It was one of the few things in my life that still felt absolutely real. It had been at a conference in London on relationships between law and public policy. I had wandered into a panel discussion on reconciling judicial discretion with the rule of law, and I hadn't been able to take my eyes away from a woman on the panel, her afro hair and red jacket such a contrast to the monochrome academics at the table. She had been dazzling, her contributions flawlessly lucid. I had been transfixed. I sat there anguished, knowing she was the kind of woman I could never summon the courage to approach.

Later that day, I had squeezed onto an elevator and discovered, to my terror, that I was facing her. She nodded in recognition and seemed to expect me to say something. I made a fumbling remark about something she had said in the seminar. Somehow, a conversation began. It continued while the elevator rose, and then continued back down to the bottom floor with neither of us noticing until the doors opened and we were facing the building lobby. That had been the first laugh we shared together.

"The elevator!" I said. "That ride is engraved on my memory as if it were yesterday. I was completely terrified but also desperately wanting to talk to you. I have never felt anything so completely in my life and I certainly wasn't thinking about any moral duty to wallflowers."

"Yes," she said, smiling. "The elevator. I was completely charmed by your terror, actually. Your terror and the way you were struggling to speak. I had been fending off politically ambitious law students, so very self-assured, who just wanted me as an adornment to their social consciences. And then of course there were the men who couldn't deal with my colour and the fact that I was a woman. There were plenty of them at Cambridge. You said something that made absolutely no sense to me, but when I got you to start talking, you were very perceptive and you seemed to forget where you were. We had a completely human connection, right from the beginning."

"You're the one thing in my life that seems completely real," I said. "You and Andy. I sometimes feel like you're the only part of my life I've ever really chosen. Since we separated, what has kept me going is the time I've been spending with you, and the feeling that as long as that was happening I hadn't lost you completely."

"I've always felt that with you, we could just be human beings," she said. "And you also have a lot of compassion for people. Maybe too much. And you're not complacent, I can't stand people who don't question themselves. And you're a wonderful parent for Andy, and—"

"Francine, please," I interrupted. "I don't deserve this. How could I have been so self-absorbed? Listening to that inner voice telling me that at least I had finally done the right thing and told the truth. I thought I deserved credit for that. Andrew Walmer might have destroyed his marriage, but at least his self-image was intact."

"I think you're being too hard on yourself," she said,

her voice gentle. "We both had our spin doctors going. They each told us we were doing the right thing. They each helped us to avoid seeing what we were actually doing. The important part of what we were doing, I mean. We lost sight of each other, Andrew. Ourselves too, we lost sight of our best selves."

"Francine," I said. "I..." But I was choking up. I covered that by taking her in my arms and holding her against me as if she were life itself.

"I'm never letting you go," I said.

We held each other by the water. I found her lips and we stayed locked together until we had to breathe. Then we did it again.

It was bliss. I could have stayed there forever. Francine in my arms. The water lapping softly on the sand. The sun shining. Summer sounds in the distance.

"Come on, Andrew," she said. "I'm taking you back and not letting you out. I'm taking you back to our home!"

She grabbed my hand and began pulling me back towards where we had parked.

We were both laughing by then. Laughing the way I remembered, from sheer delight in being together.

"What about the condo board, Andrew?" she said mischievously. "You have your wife and your job back. Are you still going to need the condo for distraction?"

The condo board. It hit me like a blow to stomach.

"Shit," I said. "Shit!"

I had completely forgotten about phoning Doreen. I had promised Henry I'd make sure she would come to our emergency meeting. Britannia's little government was depending on me to make sure we had a quorum. Our new president was depending on me. I was already letting him down.

What was happening to me?

Whatever it was, it felt kind of wonderful.

Chapter Fifteen

Mrs. Svensson Saves the Day

It wasn't a director's job but I did it on impulse. I had gone to the condo office before the meeting to check some files and there it was, a massive weed growing in the middle of the office flowerbed. Bill should have dealt with it, or the landscaping crew, but I didn't want such a conspicuous sign of negligence on display to any owner passing by.

That was why I was squatting under the board office window. I was pulling on the stem of the recalcitrant plant when I heard them through the window screen.

"...little Swedish cupcake," I heard. It was Henry's voice, sounding amorous.

"You beast!" I heard. It was Ingrid Svensson, giggling and sounding delighted.

The voices were followed by a rustling. Then what could have been heavy breathing, or possibly just urban noise.

I was in an awkward position, squatting under the window, appearing to be eaves-dropping. It would get a lot more awkward if either of them detected motion outside the window and came to close it. I hoped that Doreen wouldn't be coming to the meeting early.

First Alexandra, now Ingrid. My suspicions about Henry had been growing, but I hadn't really been thinking about them. Now they were confirmed beyond a reasonable doubt. Britannia was well-stocked with widows and divorcees. I wondered how many of them Henry was "working" with.

I didn't feel indignation, more a kind of envy. What was it about Henry, anyway? What did he have that other men, including me, apparently didn't? He was a middle-aged man, an early retiree in his mid-fifties, a dumpy little fellow who seemed completely nondescript. He was sociable, I had to give him that. He always seemed to be cheerful and, as I was finding out in our quorum crisis, completely unflappable. But the Lothario of Britannia?

Britannia's Rasputin? You never would have guessed. Maybe that was his secret.

Women. They were beyond comprehension. Especially Alexandra. Maybe it was some kind of craving for paternal attention or something. There was no telling.

Then again, who was I to be complaining? I was a beneficiary too, even more than Henry. Francine's story about being attracted to my terror in the elevator when we first met had been a new one, a new mystery. And the fact that she was taking me back, still caring about me after everything. A mystery. A miracle, even. There wasn't any understanding women but, whatever it was that made them tick, it was a godsend for men. A complete godsend for someone like me, something I would never forget to be thankful for.

Even so, Ingrid was still a surprise. However, as I thought further, her evening walks with Bobbi were hardly inconspicuous. Ingrid's abundance of curvaceous flesh, jiggling in its nordic whiteness against the minimal restraint of sundresses she liked to wear, attracting the eye even though the mind might be elsewhere. One could imagine possibilities. Evidently, Henry had done more than imagine them.

I crept along the board office wall and then around the corner of a nearby backyard fence. I would postpone the inquiry into office files I had been planning and keep an eye out for Doreen, in case she arrived prematurely. Her support for Ingrid was already uncertain. If Doreen caught her in flagrante with Henry it didn't need much imagination to predict what would happen to our quorum.

The community garden committee was on the agenda to present its final report to the board. Melissa Wagner, the coordinator, would be attending, if not others. Bill and Charlene would also be arriving to perform their regular duties.

Aside from being uncomfortable, my position was strategically bad. How would I intercept people without looking entirely foolish, if not demented, rushing out from behind a neighbourhood fence? I crept further along the fence until I got a safe distance away from the board office window and then moved to a nearby front step. It commanded a good view of the lanes running towards the board office. For any early arrivals, I would be just sitting there enjoying the evening before going into a stuffy room and oh, wait, could you stop for a minute? There's something I wanted to ask you before the meeting?

Minutes ticked by agreeably. Britannia, with its massive trees along the lanes, was not an unpleasant place to sit on an evening in July, at the height of summer.

The first to show was Charlene, at 6:55. Surely a safe time to enter the office, unless prudence had entirely given way to passions of the moment inside it. As she approached, Bill's Hyundai pulled into the laneway on its way to the parking area. I rose from the steps and caught up with Charlene. As we approached the door, I slowed her in order to point out, very loudly, where the offending weed had been.

Inside the board office, platonic serenity reigned. Henry and Ingrid sat facing each other across the boardroom table. Their faces were composed in expressions of gravity behind reading glasses. Files were open on the table in front of them.

"Oh. Hi, folks," Henry said, giving the impression that our arrival had jolted him out of deep concentration. "I've been working with Ingrid and she's doing a great job of getting up to speed. Bill, I'm sure you know each other. Charlene, you probably remember Ingrid Svensson from our special meeting, when she offered to help us out with the board if we needed it."

We greeted one another and found places at the table. There was a gentle tap on the door. Melissa could be seen through the screen.

"Hi, Melissa," Henry said. "Come right in and find a chair. We're just waiting for our third director so we have quorum and then we can get going."

There was a second tapping on the door as Melissa sat down. A very large florid-faced man peered in at us. It was Manfred Swalm, a second member of the community garden committee. I was impressed by his dedication but taken aback by the expression on his face. It was grim. As he came into the room, Melissa's normally sunny expression was replaced by stony hostility.

"Sorry for the intrusion," Manfred said. "But there's no way I'm letting Melissa represent our committee, the way things have gone. So I need to have time to speak tonight as well."

"I guess you're Manfred." Henry stood up and reached out to shake the man's hand. "I don't think we've met but I saw your name on the list for this committee. I'm sure the board would like to hear from everyone as soon as we get going."

Manfred sat down and silence descended on the table. Melissa glowered at Manfred. Manfred glowered at Melissa. Clearly we had a situation to deal with.

Perhaps as a distraction, Henry explained that he had volunteered to be the new president, since we'd lost Sonya. He wouldn't be president officially "...until we have our little festivities tonight. And Ingrid Svensson has agreed to be appointed to the board. So we'll need to make that official as well."

He went on to explain, for Manfred's benefit, that we were waiting for Doreen so we would have quorum. As we continued to wait, he began to reminisce about what she and Sonya had done for Britannia, over the years, and how they would be missed.

Still no Doreen.

"She did say she was coming, did she?" he said, looking at me.

"Yes, she seemed quite definite," I said. I had followed

Henry's plan and avoided mentioning Ingrid when I had called Doreen. Doreen had sounded out of breath and, to my relief, had not asked who she would need to vote for at the meeting.

As minutes continued to tick by, Henry began to fidget. "Let's not stand on formality," he finally said. "We're all here, basically, so I'd like to bring the meeting to order so we can get going."

Charlene looked at me anxiously.

"Henry," I said. "We can't really start the meeting without a quorum."

"I hate this procedure stuff," he said. "It's a pain in the ass and it just wastes everybody's time. We're just neighbours here and we're just trying to do what needs to be done, so isn't there anything we can do before Doreen gets here?"

"Well," I said. "Why don't we just hear the presentation from our community garden committee? If we need to make official decisions about it, we can always make them later when we have quorum. Then they can go onto the record in our minutes."

"Okay," he said. "So we can have a meeting as long as we don't call it a meeting, right? And we have everybody here who will be making any decisions about this. So, Melissa, I'd like to turn things over to you at this point, as chair of our gardening committee."

"Thank you, Henry," she said. "I brought a short

report with our recommendations, so I'll just summarize the main points for now. If you—"

"I'm sorry," Manfred said, loudly. "I can't sit here and have that woman pretend to represent the committee when she doesn't. She—"

"I'm not going to sit here and be interrupted like this," Melissa interjected, even more loudly. "Mr. Swalm is—"

"I am not!" he said.

"Order, order!" said Henry. "Could we please have order here! We want to hear what you both have to say, but we can't hear it if you're talking over each other. So Manfred, please let Melissa give us her presentation. Then I'll give the floor to you for as long as you need."

The garden committee members resumed glowering at each other.

"As I was trying to say," said Melissa. "I'm tabling a short report with our recommendations. The main point I need to make here is that I agreed to chair this committee because I wanted to give back to our community. I have really worked hard to represent the views of the community here and we feel strongly that any community garden on Britannia's property needs to be in line with the tone of our property, and—"

"I'm sorry!" Manfred burst out. "This is all lies! I'm tabling an objection—"

"You can't table an objection," Melissa shot back. "You don't have anything to table because you haven't written anything, so why can't you just be quiet!"

"Please!" Henry said. "If we can't have order here then we might as well all go home. Manfred, you have to let Melissa have her turn and then you'll get yours. Melissa?"

"Thank you," Melissa said, directing a gloating look at Manfred. "Britannia owners have very high standards, at least some of us do, and we feel strongly that vegetables do not belong on the public areas of our property. Britannia Condominium is not a farm, we're a heritage community, and our neighbours are not that type of people. So we think our community garden needs to reinforce this with the kind of flower gardens that you see on the streets around us. We are fortunate to have lots of very talented green thumbs here to do this. Our plan is for a coordinated group of planting beds that our gardeners would just love to contribute to and the details are all in our report. You can see that the individual gardens are colour-coordinated and we have lists of permitted plants for each one. So it's really going to be a very classy addition to our property. I'll leave it at that for now, but I'm happy to answer questions once you've had a chance to digest the proposal."

"Thank you, Melissa," Henry said. "Manfred, please go ahead now."

"What Melissa is telling you just isn't true," Manfred declared. "I only got onto this committee to make sure owners were represented and I've been talking to neighbours since day one. Many of us want vegetable gardens, especially now that prices are going through the roof at the grocery stores. So this garden needs to be practical. People should be treated like adults and allowed to grow what they want to grow. Including flowers if they want. We could raise some revenues for Britannia by leasing plots to some of the people who live on the streets around here. Melissa is just talking for a little in-group of old ladies who like flowers. The board shouldn't let them take over board decisions!"

"Thank you, Manfred," Henry said, although Manfred had been opening his mouth to continue. "I think we get the drift here. Plainly we're not getting a consensus report from your committee. So the board will need to take this on and work on next steps, maybe a survey of owners or something."

"I don't want to take up any more of the board's time," Melissa said. "But I don't want my name associated with anything that turns Britannia into a produce farm. And we already know our neighbours so I don't think we need to delay things with any kind of survey that could just be divisive."

"And I don't want my name associated with a bunch of elite snobs!" Manfred shouted. "I'm warning the board that owners feel very strongly about this and you could be facing some kind of owner revolt if you just go ahead with what Melissa is proposing."

As he said this, Manfred rose from his chair. "I don't have more time for this tonight so I'll say goodnight to you at this point and thank you for your attention," he said, and headed for the door.

He closed it with elaborate care.

"I won't take more of your time either," Melissa said. "Our report really says it best and, of course, I look forward to any questions you may have."

"Thank you, Melissa," Henry said. "The board will need to review your report and think about Manfred's input as well. We'll need to have some kind of follow-up. Once we get tonight's meeting going, we'll discuss next steps and I'll be in touch. I'd be happy to work on next steps with you and make sure that the work you've done gets used by the board."

"Thank you very much, Henry," Melissa said. "That sounds like a plan. I'll look forward to hearing from you."

Melissa gave us a warm smile that seemed (or was it just my imagination?) to linger in the direction of Henry. Then she departed.

"I'm going to phone Doreen," Henry said. "We can't stay here all night." He seemed to have her number in his phone.

"Hi, Doreen," we heard. "We're here at our meeting and wondering where you are."

"Oh. I see. Yes, we have been looking for people, but Mrs. Svensson is the only one we've been able to find and we need to do this tonight."

"Oh…"

"I'm sorry to hear that. You realize that we don't have a quorum at the moment so the board won't be able to do business."

"…I'm sorry you feel that way Doreen. Is there anything we can do to make this happen?"

"Oh."

He said goodbye and put his phone away.

"She's not coming."

We sat there looking at each other.

"Well, I guess we can't have an official meeting," I said. "We might as well let Charlene and Bill go home."

"Wait," Henry said. "I'm calling Sonya. I know her well enough to know that she isn't going to let us down." He got his phone out and entered something.

"Hi, Sonya," we heard. "Look, we have a problem here because Doreen said she would delay her resignation and come to our meeting so we'd have a quorum and appoint a new director. But now she can't come. So, Sonya, would you be willing to take back your resignation just so we can have a vote. Your resignation would go back in effect right afterwards…

"You would? Oh that's so good of you. I knew I could count on you. So we're voting to appoint a new director right now plus I'm willing to be president. Can I tell people you're voting 'yes' to that?…

"Great. Don't worry about it. Okay, thanks a lot! I

have to go now so we can get on with business…

"So," he said, turning to us. "As you heard, she was good enough to help us out here. Charlene, that means we can start our official meeting at the time of my phone call, because Sonya rescinded her resignation and that means we had a quorum and you heard her vote. Andrew can we have your vote as well? I'm voting 'Yes' to Ingrid, so that makes a majority."

"Henry, this isn't really very kosher," I ventured. "You can't really have a meeting with people on a phone unless it's agreed ahead of time, and you were chairing before you got elected president. And none of the rest of us could hear her on your phone. I didn't hear you actually tell her who she was voting on for director."

"Yes, we might be bending a few procedures a bit here," he said. "But we're all here to serve our community and people just want us to make sure the place gets looked after properly. We have at least one urgent item on the agenda, the paving contract for the parking areas. We're already late on that and if we don't get it decided, we may not even get it done this season."

"I understand," I said. "But what kind of a precedent are we setting here, Henry? We can't just ignore procedure whenever it's convenient. Governance is important! It protects all of us and makes sure accountability is maintained and boards don't abuse their power."

"Yeah, yeah, I know all that," he said. "But we're not

setting any precedents. We're just dealing with a situation that won't happen again and, besides, let's be real. This is a condo board, not the United Nations or something. Owners only pay attention if things get messed up. If we don't get the paving done, that will definitely get their attention and we won't like it."

As I raised my concerns about our vote, I hadn't detected much support from others. Henry was making an effort to be polite, but his fingers began to drum the table impatiently. Ingrid's expression reminded me of when I travelled in foreign countries and accidentally spoke English to people who didn't speak it. Charlene and Bill gazed stoically at the table.

"This is a board decision, of course," said Bill.

Bill had been quiet during our proceedings, his face fixed in its default expression of polite attentiveness.

"Andrew is right, strictly speaking," he continued. "But I have to advise you that there is a good chance the paving won't happen unless you make a decision tonight. If you don't put Mrs. Svensson on the board, it will take time to organize something with Sonya and notify people, and she might not be available at all. We're now in high vacation season, as you know, and the last time I talked to her, she was planning to be at a cottage while her house was listed. I'm off starting next week for three weeks, so my stand-in would have to try and coordinate something for you. It's just a very bad time of year for something like this to happen."

"Well, could we at least confirm what has happened by calling Sonya?" I said. "I'm completely confident in your call, Henry, but that would be confirmation for the record in case we have owners asking questions."

"If you want," he said, face impassive. "Here. I have her programmed in my phone." He handed it across the table.

I could hear her phone ring. And continue to ring. Then her voicemail clicked in.

"She's not picking up," I said.

"I'm not surprised," Henry said calmly. "She was rushing off somewhere so she's probably gone."

They were all looking at me expectantly.

"Well, okay," I said. "Okay. I guess we don't have much choice."

I needed to support our new president. Otherwise he might stop being president and walk out the door. But how could I ever stand in front of my political science classes again and talk about the importance of the rule of law?

What was happening to me? Whatever it was, the damn condo board was doing it. I had to get off that board! I really, really, had to get off.

"Ingrid, welcome to the board. I can give you this now," Bill said, handing the information package for the meeting across to her.

As my attention returned to the meeting, Henry was asking Bill to brief us on the paving contract.

"In terms of dollar amounts, it's the biggest decision you'll need to make this year," said Bill. "I've done the analysis that's in your meeting package. Are there any questions I can help with?"

I was struggling with shame about what I had just done and now new guilt stirred unpleasantly in my stomach. I had been completely preoccupied with everything that had been happening in my life and the meeting information package had only arrived a few days ago. Fortunately, we had Henry's capital projects experience to rely on.

I looked hopefully at Henry.

Henry was looking hopefully at me.

Ingrid was looking at the information package. She did not look hopeful at all.

"Um, Bill, perhaps you can just review the high points for us," Henry said.

"Well, it really comes down to relatively fine details," Bill said. "AtCo, as you can see, came in with the lowest bid by $45,000. They have a good reputation and my colleagues have had good results from them at other properties. Capital Paving is very competitive and they include a year's follow-up in their bid, with free repairs to any cracks that show up. Normally there wouldn't be any, but that's some extra protection. And Klein Roadworks has a stellar reputation around town, especially for the fine details like embedded drainage paths. That could pay off if you get heavy rainfalls. I don't have to tell you these are becoming more of a problem."

"So," said Henry. "What do you recommend?"

"Well, they're all good," said Bill,

"Yes, we can see that," said Henry. "But if you were the board, what would you choose?"

"Well," said Bill, reluctantly. "If you want a recommendation, I guess on balance I would recommend AtCo. But, really, you'd be fine with either of the others too."

"Does anybody have a problem with AtCo?" Henry asked. "If nobody does, I move we go with AtCo. Does somebody want to second that?"

I did. Ingrid voted in favour. Then we agreed on our next meeting time and Henry adjourned the meeting.

We were done.

Bill and Charlene packed up efficiently and quickly headed for their cars, almost as if they were escaping the scene of a crime. Henry and Ingrid gathered their papers and departed, making no obvious effort to wait for company.

I followed at a discreet distance, detouring down an alternative walking path so it wouldn't seem like I was following them.

The more I thought about the meeting, the more uncomfortable I felt. Henry had ostensibly had a conversation with Sonya and reported her vote for Ingrid, but how did we know he had reported it accurately? And he had chaired the vote for president when he wasn't even president yet. How did we even know he had been talking to Sonya? The whole thing could have been faked. The fact that she hadn't picked up mere minutes after he had claimed to be talking to her made me wonder.

But supposing it had been faked, what was I supposed to do now? It was over and we now had official minutes recording it. My vote for Ingrid would be in them along with everything else. If anything underhanded had gone on, I was complicit. If I decided to raise objections now, I would only look foolish. And besides, I had no proof of anything underhanded.

The only way to do something about it would be to raise my concerns with owners and get them to demand a special meeting where board issues could be threshed out. A special meeting where, predictably, I would be a target of criticism for disturbing the community and dragging everybody out to an unwanted meeting. Especially so soon after the special meeting fiasco that had just happened. I would need to explain to my procedural concerns to unhappy owners and, to do that, I would need to explain the importance of the rule of law. It wasn't hard to predict how Britannia owners would respond to these explanations. If a community gibbet could be constructed, I would end up hanging from it.

I was going to have to hold my peace. Hold my peace and hold my nose.

The only positive outcome I could see was an addition to the stock of anecdotes I could use for teaching the engineers. The course contained a segment on democracy and the role of elected representatives, but representation is a complex idea and hard to explain.

Melissa and Manfred had given me a real-world example of how politicians could disagree with one another and all be convinced they were representing the people. There wasn't any solid evidence of what owners wanted. Almost certainly, most owners weren't paying attention and didn't have an opinion. Just like regular politics most of the time. Even sophisticated opinion polls often varied widely, depending on the way the question was worded or how people were feeling about something else.

I headed for our bungalow and my reunited family, grateful to be able to turn my mind to other things.

PART FOUR: AUGUST

Chapter Sixteen

Two Meetings
and a Funeral

It was the doorbell. I had a vague sense that the ringing had been going on for a while. Who could it be on my doorstep at 10 a.m. on a Wednesday morning? I hurried to find out.

The figure at my door was vaguely familiar but I couldn't quite place her. However, that was also my clue. There was one neighbour that I chronically failed to recognize when I met her at the local supermarket. I had also walked past her once on a downtown street, oblivious to her presence even though it was illuminated by direct sunlight.

It had to be Jane, Henry Barnstead's wife. Her face was devoid of any obvious emotion or distinguishing feature, like the rest of her. The woman was an incitement to amnesia. I could only recognize her when she was in her familiar habitat: their house.

The intrusion was not welcome. I had been at my desk, coffee at hand, working on the course I would be giving next month. The Power Point heading in front of me read "Parliament." I had been puzzling about how to present Parliament to engineering students. If government is a large machine, I could ask them, what part would Parliament be? It was a dangerous question to ask a room full of engineers. I would need to be armed against suggestions involving hot air and toxic fumes, or worse.

I was trying to get as much as possible done in the morning because the day was going to be busy. Henry was bringing over two potential board members early in the afternoon. After that, there was Letty Bishop's funeral. I hadn't known her well and, based on what I had seen during the plant removals, I couldn't honestly wish her well in the afterlife. However, as one of the few remaining members of our board, I felt obliged to go. Owners needed to see a board presence. Henry and I could give them a sense of normalcy, especially important because news of further departures since Letty's death would be making the rounds.

"Oh, hi, Jane," I fumbled, opening the door. "I didn't… er… that is, I was all wrapped up in my work this morning..."

"Hi," she said, in her familiar neutral monotone. "Andrew, I need to talk to you. Can I come in?"

"Sure," I said. "Of course. I have a meeting a bit later on but sure, come on in. Can I get you a cup of coffee or something?"

"No thanks," she said.

We stepped to my living room and settled into the two armchairs that faced each other across my small coffee table.

"Andrew," she said, betraying no emotion. "How could you do this to me?"

"What?" I said. "I'm afraid I don't know what you mean?"

"How could you not know, Andrew? You got him onto the condo board and everything so I don't see how you couldn't know what's been going on?"

Her voice was still emotionless and her face seemed impassive. However, she now had my complete attention. I could see tears welling in her eyes. There was emotion there. Real human emotion. It just wasn't obvious.

"Jane," I said. "I can see that you are very troubled about something. I can see that. Please understand that I really don't know what it might be. You seem to be saying it's about Henry."

"It's like he has a..." she said, dabbing her eyes with a pink Kleenex that had materialized from a pocket. "It's not the first time, but I guess that was before you were here. He had to go for addiction treatment and it got under control. But then it got started up with that Alexandra woman, and now he's gone back to Ingrid again. And I don't know what else is going on, but I have friends here, and now they're seeing him at night and they're telling me things. It's the condo board that's setting him up with them, Andrew, and I don't see how you could be doing this!"

"Jane," I said. "I have to be honest with you. I might have had some suspicions. But with Henry, we're always focusing on board business and I would never have imagined… I just find this really shocking. I guess I didn't know about the past, or maybe I would have been more alert."

"Well, what are you going to do about it?" she said. "The condo board is just being like his pimp or something, Andrew. It's just completely disgusting and I'm not going to stand for it!"

Her voice had risen by several decibels. I realized this was unprecedented and immediately felt shame at this thought, with her sitting right across from me, but I couldn't help but notice.

"Jane, Jane," I said. "Of course I'm going to do everything I can. I can volunteer for some of the work he's been doing in the evenings but, right now, the only other person on the board is Ingrid, so this is going to be a problem. I will do whatever I can and I think we may have some other people coming onto the board very soon, so that could give me a stronger hand. I'm very sorry to hear this, Jane. I really am."

I felt terrible for the poor woman. If anything, her incapacity to express her feelings emphatically made it worse. The last thing I wanted was to be complicit in more human pain, pain of another suffering wife.

"I will do whatever I can to help," I told her. "You need to know that I have recently gotten back together with my wife, Francine, and I may not be living here for much longer. But for now, I'll make sure the board isn't contributing to Henry's… er… health issues."

"Thank you, Andrew, and I'm glad for you and your wife. I…" Tears welled up and began to run down her cheeks as she spoke. "Something's going to have to happen and I thought you needed to know," she said, rising to her feet.

I followed her to the door and watched her depart. She looked small and alone and I felt terrible. I had an impulse to rush out and put my arm around her but then realized that, no, this wouldn't solve her problems and no, it wouldn't solve my remaining ones either.

Heading back to my study, I realized I was feeling terrible out of guilt more than sympathy. I had seen the signals. I had even wondered about them. However, the truth was that I hadn't wanted to know. I had ignored what was happening until I had stumbled upon Henry and Ingrid at the board office.

I had avoided the obvious because I didn't want to get into conflict with Henry. Conflict with Henry might make him stop being the president. He might even leave the condo board entirely. We had just seen two volunteers go stomping off. I was the person who had gotten him involved. I had been telling myself I had a responsibility to keep the condo board from being disabled by conflict. It was part of my community service role as a director.

This thought made me skeptical immediately. My experience on the condo board was making me suspicious whenever I heard anyone mention community service or other high-minded obligations, even when the person was me. It was spin doctor language and I knew I wasn't really that altruistic. If I had to take on responsibilities from Henry, I would be digging myself in deeper on the condo board when I wanted escape. If conflict made Henry leave, then I would be left holding the bag yet again and I couldn't go on doing this, especially now that Francine and I were together. I needed to be honest, at least with myself. My conflict avoidance wasn't about community service. It was about me.

It was now almost lunchtime and Henry would be bringing his board volunteers over for me to meet them in the early afternoon. I needed to make a good impression, and make sure they agreed to join the board. If this happened, there was still a possibility I could try and help Jane without delaying my exit. New board members would provide a good rationale for sharing out some of the tasks that Henry had been doing. I could even take some of them for a month or so while things settled down. The plan that Francine and I had arrived at—for me to complete my move back to our home and put the condo up for sale in the early fall—could still be saved. It would all depend on how things went this afternoon.

In the meantime, I needed to focus on the course I would be giving the engineering students. Experience told me they would be a challenge. I didn't mind that, actually. I felt strongly that everybody needs to know how our system works. After all, engineers were voters too. And, you never knew, some of them might end up in politics one day. Or they might end up in volunteer organizations like condo boards where decision-making needed to follow basic procedures.

I hadn't told anyone in the department that I didn't mind teaching the engineers. If they wanted to think they were punishing me for my transgressions, I would get credit for bearing my burden without complaint. The engineers might learn something and I would have some fun experimenting with teaching strategies along the way.

However, no sooner had I sat down to work, my

thoughts began to drift. They drifted out my window to the beautiful August day and its sense of possibility, to the happiness that had come back into my life. I had returned that morning to my townhouse from our bungalow, where I was now living. I had been staying with Francine and Andy since the day Francine and I had taken our walk in Britannia Park.

I had my life back again.

I was still reliving that day, savouring it. When Francine had taken me back to our home, there had been a moment of shyness between us before I took her in my arms and she came to me, the way she always had, with eagerness. Afterwards, we lay beside each other for the longest time, completely silent, listening to muted sounds of a summer day unfolding beyond the window. We were slowly absorbing the feeling of being together, not wanting to lose another second of it.

Jane's visit had returned me to the world beyond my family. The world of the condominium, where things seemed to go from bad to worse despite my best efforts and where my hopes were endlessly dashed. However, two new board directors would mean that I could leave and not strand Henry and Ingrid without a quorum.

These and similar thoughts preoccupied me as I made my lunch, early so there would be time for Henry's visit and the funeral later that day. I had gotten fresh-baked sourdough rye bread on my way over to the condo and I had been looking forward to liverwurst sandwiches with my favourite Dijon mustard.

Lunch provided a welcome distraction but I couldn't dispel a vague sense of anxiety that Jane's visit had left me with. Surely a day that had begun with such promise would not derail my escape plans. Surely not again. The stars finally seemed to be aligning. However, the condo board had taught me that even astronomical alignments can be temporary. There are an infinite number of ways for the unpredictable to happen. That was why it was called the unpredictable.

Before long, the doorbell rescued me from increasingly morbid thoughts. The doorbell was having an unusually busy day. Henry was on the doorstep, his face betraying no sign of domestic turbulence. Two figures accompanied him, remarkably similar to each other.

"Andrew," Henry said heartily. "I'm sure you've seen the Gallardis at our AGMs but I don't know if you've ever met them. This is Dominique."

"Hi," I said, shaking Dominique's hand. "And you must be Dominic." I shook his hand as well. The hands were remarkably similar, strangely limp and somewhat cool.

"I'm delighted to have a chance to meet you," I said. "Come on in."

I had seen Dominique and her brother, Dominic, around the complex and at AGMs. They were hard to ignore. They seemed to be virtually identical. Several neighbours had taken to calling them "the two dominiques" and now we all did it.

Of course, there was a gender difference. That had to be assumed although it wasn't easy to detect. They were somewhat older than I was, probably in their early fifties, rail thin, and wearing black clothing that highlighted extremely white complexions they shared. I associated the whiteness of the dominiques with the funeral home they had inherited from their parents. It made me think of corpses.

The dominiques were almost never seen without each other, strolling the laneways accompanied by a large grey slow-moving dog. Someone had told me it was an Irish wolfhound and its stately pace was consistent with that exotic breed. There was something mysterious about the three of them, even slightly sinister, but they always seemed genuinely friendly to neighbours. At least the Gallardis were friendly. The dog was more aloof.

The Gallardis seemed keenly interested in the condominium, especially the landscaping. I had seen them come to a halt by flowerbeds or trees, engaging in conversations accompanied by emphatic gestures. The dog's interest in landscaping was more practical, frequently urinary.

Fortunately, rooms do not betray secrets, I thought, as Henry settled comfortably into the chair that had recently been occupied by Jane.

"The Gallardis have been kind enough to offer to come onto the condo board," Henry said. "They bring business experience that will be excellent for our condo and they have a special interest in landscaping as well."

"Thank you, Henry," Dominic said. "We have been very fortunate with our business and now we are able to step away a bit. We would like to give back to our community. Dominique and I, we really appreciate what our volunteers on the board have done over the years and we would be honoured to be able to help."

Dominic's voice was low and soothing, strangely resonant given his almost skeletal thinness. It was a voice designed for consolation. I imagined it bringing peace to troubled owners and turbulent AGMs. I could even feel it bringing peace to me.

"Yes," Dominique added. "We were wondering if the board needed volunteers, now that we have people helping us with our business. So, Henry, your call came at the perfect time for us. We understand that our role on the condo board would be to represent all owners and not just act on personal agendas. And we look forward to getting to know our neighbours better and helping make Britannia the community we all know it can be. We are really looking forward to this."

Her voice was a softer, more musical version of his, a more affirmative counter-point to Dominic's gravitas. I could imagine her reaching out to the bereaved, supporting Dominic's sympathy with a message of caring and healing. A soothing coda perhaps, as credit arrangements were gently finalized.

The two dominiques would bring healing to Britannia, a diplomatic resolution of divisions over community garden plans and the like. They were a heartening illustration of how first impressions can be misleading. They were warm-hearted people, not corpse-like in any way. I could feel, right in my living room, the beginning of an era of harmony at Britannia.

Not to mention an era of me not being on the condo board.

Henry's experience with capital projects would be complemented by the new culture the dominiques would bring. I wasn't sure what Ingrid would be adding yet, but she was a real trooper to be willing to come onto the board in the first place and, of course, she would help keep Henry there. My work would soon be done! I could leave the condo board with my head held high, looking my neighbours in the eye with honest optimism.

"...that need to be worked out," Henry was saying. I descended from my dream of condo harmony and tried to figure out what he'd been telling them.

"Of course, there are always issues like this," Dominic responded. "We work with people who are often under special stress and that sometimes brings out feelings that they may not even be aware of."

"But to us, this can be a wonderful opportunity," Dominique added. "We have seen divided families move forward when they realize that by pooling resources they can do something wonderful for their loved one. Helping people in need is what we're all about in our business and we have seen families come together in a wonderful way through the bereavement experience."

"It's great that you understand the challenges," said Henry. "Andrew, you've been quiet over there. What do you think?"

I still didn't know what they had been talking about, but I wasn't going to say anything to spoil the mood.

"I think this is a great day for our condo," I said. "I'd be tempted to say you're going to make Britannia great again, but I guess that line has been taken."

"Well, that's just terrific," Henry said. "We can carry on for the next couple of weeks with three on the board. That gives us our quorum in case Bill needs us to authorize anything. And then we can formally appoint you when we meet."

"We look forward to that," Dominique purred. "In the meantime, we're going to focus on getting to know our neighbours better and we already have some ideas about our landscaping."

"Excellent," Henry responded. "And now we only have an hour before Letty's funeral so we need to wrap this up. I've been running errands all morning and I haven't had lunch yet, so I have to get back for a quick one before Jane and I go. And Andrew, I'm assuming you'll be coming?"

"Yes," I said. "I think the two of us will be reassuring to owners, given the board turnover lately."

We said our goodbyes and they headed out the door. I had been wondering if I should give Henry some kind of alert about my visit from Jane that morning but there hadn't been an opportunity. Now he was strolling companionably down my walkway with the dominiques, his usual unflappable self. Best to leave things be, I decided. I wanted him and the dominiques to bond together. In combination, they were the future of Britannia's board.

I'm not keen on funerals at the best of times. I hoped this one wouldn't raise problems for the board. There was the mysterious interval after Letty had been taken out of the board office, but still allegedly a member of the board. Owners might quiz me about this. Or they might ask questions that would uncover the board's telephonic meeting with Sonya, which would be awkward, to say the least. Also, Henry was obviously planning to attend the funeral with Jane, but the state she had been in a few short hours ago made me wonder how well that was going to go.

I arrived at the Gallardi Funeral Home parking lot slightly late. There was plenty of room.

Inside the entrance, an immaculately dressed young woman greeted me and steered me towards a small chapel at the end of a hallway. The service proved to be uneventful, and surprisingly short. I wondered if perhaps there had been an abbreviated service option available at a discounted rate. As it concluded, mourners were advised that immediate family only would attend the interment and others were invited to a reception in an adjacent room.

At the reception, I positioned myself at a discreet distance from the sandwiches and drinks, close enough to be visible to anyone who might want to ask me something about the condo board but not so close as to interfere with grazing at the table. There were several plates of sandwiches, all with crusts carefully removed by members of the ladies auxiliary at Letty's church.

I took a ham sandwich. I ate slowly, to avoid having to stand there with nothing to do with my hands. I recognized several people from the condominium but no one that I actually knew. Several nodded in my direction but nobody appeared to be needful of my company, or information about the condo board. They stood in small clusters of two or three, chatting quietly. Having eaten my sandwich, I approached one of the couples that I recognized and introduced myself.

I explained that I was on the board of directors, where Letty had served until recently, and said she would certainly be missed. Did they happen to have any questions about the board, I asked. In particular, did they think the board was effectively representing owners?

They looked at me blankly.

"Board?" the man said. "I guess we don't know too much about that kind of thing… We have ants though. In the kitchen. We've had a lot of them showing up lately. Would you be able to do something about that?"

"They're bigger than the ants you see outside," his wife added. "Black ants, you know? Big ones. You don't suppose they might be carpenter ants, do you?"

I told them it wasn't really a condo responsibility since the ants were inside the dwelling. They regarded me impassively.

"I got ant traps at the hardware last year," I told them, suggesting that might help.

They nodded, chewing their sandwiches. They seemed to have no further conversational ambitions.

"Well, I guess I better get another sandwich," I said. Easing away from them, I went to a plate on the other side of the table. I took a sandwich and looked for another social opportunity.

Across the room, I saw a familiar face. It was Henk Van Vliet. He was eating a sandwich. He stood against the wall, looking wistfully at the doorway through which we had all entered. I made my way over to him.

"Henk," I said. "I'm glad to see you here today. I'm sure Letty's family will be grateful that her neighbours took the time to be here."

"I'm mainly here because the wife wanted to see her

bridge club," he said. "Look at them over there. All talking like a blue streak. They see each other each week so you'd think that would do it."

"Yes," I agreed. "I wonder what they talk about."

"Beats me," he said. "The wife didn't think much of Letty, after what happened with her plants. To tell you the truth, we're probably here just to make sure she doesn't rise from the dead or something."

I maintained my neutral board director expression. For about three seconds. Then I chuckled behind the sandwich. "Yes, Henk, I hear you," I said. "But she wasn't alone. I've sometimes wondered if Britannia might breed them, people like Letty. Or maybe it attracts them with some kind of strange magnetism. But Henk, I can tell you that things are actually moving in a very positive way on the board. I can't give you details, but I think the board is about to get a lot better."

"Oh?" he said. "I hope you're right. I've lived here now for twenty-one years and the board was about to get a lot better back when I moved in. It's been about to get a lot better ever since. I have to tell you, I'm not holding my breath."

Mrs. Van Vliet and her bridge club were now moving towards us, plainly intending to depart. I used them as cover to slide out the doorway, inconspicuously I hoped.

As I headed to the Jeep, the vague sense that something hadn't been right at the reception congealed into a definite thought.

It was Henry and Jane. They hadn't been there.

Only a couple of hours ago, Henry had stood in my doorway and said they would be there. But then they weren't. I didn't see how this could be good.

Chapter Seventeen

Sweet Unpredictable Life

"You can lead a whore to water but you can't make her think," Stanley said. It was his punch line and he eyed us expectantly.

However, the line made no sense. He had it wrong.

I had read the *Globe and Mail* that morning. Its review of a new Dorothy Parker biography provided delightful anecdotes, including her response to the challenge she faced one day at a table of journalists. Could she come up with an aphorism containing the word "horticulture"?

Never at a loss for words, Dorothy had fired back: "You can lead a whore-to-culture but you can't make her think."

Correction—my immediate impulse—would have embarrassed Stanley in front of his peers. The two at the table in the small conference room where he was accustomed to hold court were already chuckling. It was hard to tell if the subdued chuckles were sincere, or even actual chuckles instead of some form of geriatric respiratory problem. I decided not to disrupt their mid-afternoon social hour. Instead, I looked ostentatiously at my watch and muttered that I was late for an appointment.

I had arrived at the departmental office that afternoon with enough time to check my mailbox before having the meeting that Gina and I had arranged in the wake of my suspension hearing, as she departed for a summer break.

In order to get to my office, I had to venture down the hallway by the mail room. I saw that hallway as the departmental equivalent of a Potemkin village and normally avoided it. Along with administrative rooms, and the small conference room that had gradually been taken over by senior professors as a kind of lounge, were four large offices. Each office belonged to an elderly man dressed consistently in tweed. Each office door bore an imposing title, implying that the hallway marshalled a concentration of academic firepower that might have existed in former times. Collections of pipes, dating from the same era, occupied the desks in the offices. A faint odour of pipe smoke continued to emanate from them.

Stanley, or Professor G. Stanley Dunlop, Redpath Professor of Comparative Institutions, occupied the office nearest the conference room. His elevated status in the department dated from several decades ago, when he had published a lengthy and mind-numbing compilation of comparative information on legislatures. New arrivals in the department soon became aware that Stanley's father—Hartwell M. Dunlop—had been a towering figure in an earlier cohort of political scientists, authoring a text that had been ubiquitous in classrooms for decades. Perhaps because his father's prominence had eluded him, Stanley's role in the department was as a relentless critic of student grammar and syntax. It had propelled a number of them into other fields.

"By the way, Andrew, we were glad to hear that you got that trans person business sorted out," I heard as I was leaving the room. "Certainly not the kind of thing we need to have hanging over us these days, is it?"

I agreed it wasn't and fled. That hallway always left me wondering if I belonged in academia. The other hallways did this too. More and more of them were occupied by colleagues like Martin Bell, now strolling towards me carrying a poster likely destined for the departmental bulletin board. "STAY WOKE!" it read.

Martin cultivated an adulatory circle of student followers and rarely missed an opportunity to offer moral leadership to the department. Most recently, he had taken up the campaign against hurtful words in lectures and called upon us to check our white suburban privilege and avoid words like "ghetto," with their painful historical associations.

"Hey, man," he said. "I heard about your suspension hearing. We think you might be one of us after all." Martin had an instinctive talent for mutual reinforcement, reaching out and fostering the feeling of belonging that so many students craved.

"Thanks, Martin," I said. "We have a long way to go on these issues and I hope I can help. But I'm late to meet a student so I have to keep moving here."

"Take it easy, man," he said, moving down the hall. "We should talk sometime, hafta get some of these folks to wake up, right?"

I didn't crave acceptance into Martin's moral mission. Predictably, since I was a faculty member and potential rival, his embrace would be followed by a reference to the reason for the suspension hearing, reminding me of Martin's primacy on the departmental scale of progressive ethics.

His brand of crusading idealism was not for me. I had a problem with people who felt the need to call themselves "woke." The word seemed to be an all-about-me word, asserting a personal identity rather than anything about the world that needed to be built. It was a word for the very young, not middle-aged tenured professors cultivating promotions and popularity with students through ostentatious wokeness combined with flexible grading practices.

On the other hand, what had the campus been like before wokeness came along? There had been a handful of activists, but racial, sexual, and other minorities had been targets in a culture of pervasive prejudice, and sometimes a lot worse. Many of the people who now ranted indignantly about woke virtue-signalling had been there. What had they done? For most of them, it had been a time of comfortable inertia that amounted to complicity.

Gina was waiting on one of the folding chairs stationed in the hallway to my office, mute reminders of the lowly status of students in the university. She looked a great deal more relaxed than she had when we met by the bridge before the hearing.

As I opened my office door, she began to apologize, once again, for her outburst in class and started to explain the medical reasons that had contributed.

"Gina, please," I interrupted. "I'm ashamed that you even feel you need to apologize. My joke was insensitive and just plain ignorant. I was thinking only of myself and my teaching, and you jarred me out of my self-absorption. You should never have had to go through the stress that the whole complaint process created. I'm the one who should be apologizing. I feel terrible about what you went through and I am very sorry."

"Thank you," she said. "But it's okay. I realize that a process like that is needed. It wasn't what I needed, that's all. And the TFA Caucus people told me about what you said at the hearing so I already know you're not the enemy here."

"What about your proposal for sensitivity training?" I responded. "I haven't heard anything more about that."

"Actually, something good seems to be coming out of that proposal," she said. "I was talking to Marion Philbert this morning and it looks like the university is going ahead with a program and she's working with them on it."

"That's excellent news," I said.

"I'm not sure everybody in the Caucus is on the same page about you helping," she continued. "But Marion seems to be interested. She said she was going to contact you to see if you were serious about contributing."

"Wonderful," I responded. "I feel I should be doing something. I've been doing a lot of thinking about that joke, and about how culture change can happen. You obviously have too. I'm guessing we agree that society needs rights and enforcement, but they aren't enough and sometimes they aren't even the right tools. Moralizing at people and lecturing them isn't going to change what they think either. Or how people feel, which is really where the essential changes happen. I've been slowly learning this on a condo board. My lectures about the rights of owners have been producing blank expressions that are finally teaching me something."

She laughed. It was the first time I had heard her laugh. It was a heart-warming sound.

She segued to my parliamentary government class.

"Professor Walmer, I really learned a lot in that class. It motivated me to even think about getting involved in politics someday. Your jokes really did lodge things in our minds. Although, to be honest, some of us used to laugh about them because they were... er... sometimes a bit corny. But seriously... it was the content of that course. Your lecture on representation was awesome and it gave me the idea for what I want to do for my research project."

Gina would start her fourth year in the fall and had applied to do what the department calls its Independent Research Option. This involves study guided by a research advisor and presentation of a research report to a panel of three professors; a dry run for graduate studies.

"Professor Walmer, I want to look at trans person representation in some of the European legislatures. It's already beginning to happen in some of them," she said. "Would you be willing to be my advisor? Your course gave me a whole extra dimension for this, about the challenge of making all people in large impersonal societies feel represented."

There was real enthusiasm in her voice. There is nothing that makes a teacher happier. We don't mind flattery either.

"Of course. I'd be delighted to do that," I said. I

would need to make sure that the department would authorize this respite from my time with the engineers. I couldn't imagine there would be a problem, especially since the request would signal a rapprochement between an offended student and a professor.

Gina's work in the parliamentary government class had been first rate, especially for a third year student among many in their fourth year. We agreed to meet again as her work took shape.

After flipping through my mail and messages, I headed for home. Perhaps I wasn't simply the department's resident comedian after all. Students in that class, some of them at least, had been listening. And thinking about the issue close to my heart: how to make representative democracy work better.

Francine would be wrapping up her day's work and we could relax with a glass of wine. We had been talking about the shared future that we now had again. For me, these conversations still had a slightly miraculous quality. I couldn't get over the feeling that something bad was coming to right the balance.

First my affair with Monique and now my offensive joke in the classroom: I seemed to be getting away with both of them. True, I had confessed and done penance. But, somehow, that didn't seem enough. If I confided my feelings to Francine, I knew she would instantly ascribe them to my childhood in a rigidly Catholic family. She would probably be right. My feelings reflected conditioning in a distant past. But even if my apprehensions had no connection with the present, something bad could still be coming.

"There's something I've been meaning to tell you, Andrew," she said once we were settled on the couch, wine in hand. I felt my heart take a lurch. Could this be what I had been dreading? I didn't want any more surprises in my life. Not from her. Not from me either.

"I think I'm going to be appointed Dean of Law," she said.

"Francine, that is completely awesome! I can't begin to list all the ways this is awesome! Including what it says to students and what you will be able to do for that faculty."

I was delighted. Mainly for her, but maybe also because this wasn't the punishment I had been fearing.

"My work over the last few years has a lot to do with it," she said. "My way of coping was to focus on work and Andy. The work pay-off was that I've become a kind of publications powerhouse in the law faculty, on top of the outside work that has been getting the department some public attention. They aren't stupid. They know they can use this."

"Oh no," I said. "You haven't started yet and you're already sounding disillusioned."

"I hope to be at least a little bit disillusioned," she responded. "If you don't end up disillusioned from time to time, that probably means your standards aren't high enough. Right now, I think I'm simply being realistic. This is a transactional deal. I am sure some of my colleagues, in their calculating way, think that having a Black dean with an established track record on social justice issues is going to put a reassuring cloak of righteousness over the whole faculty. Give them a trump card in university politics and a licence not to change. But you know me… I've thought this through, and of course I've talked to people. The powers that be are assuming I'll view this as a career triumph and won't rock the boat too much. However, it will give me unusual leverage because the faculty can't afford having a newly appointed Black dean stomping off in highly public frustration after a few months. I know you have mixed feelings about woke campus politics, Andrew, and I agree it sometimes gets out of hand. But let's face it, this wouldn't be happening without those pressures. It's this environment that's giving me my leverage. It's a window of opportunity."

"If anybody can do it, it's you," I said. "You're exactly the kind of person the university needs. And not to disrespect the law faculty, but you're definitely the kind of person needed by that bunch.

"And more immediately, you're needed in the kitchen," I said, standing up. I was the designated chef that day. I had kebabs marinating in the fridge and ingredients marshalled for my signature gazpacho.

"Fine," she said, as we headed away from the living room. "I'm not the dean yet so I'm still willing to be involved in food preparation."

Andy was at Anwar's for a sleepover and I had planned a special meal. Now, with Francine's news, we had even more to celebrate.

In the kitchen, as we put together our meal, talk drifted back to my visit to the campus. I told her about my encounter with Stanley and the old guard who ran the department, and then meeting Martin in the hallway.

"I don't feel I belong there," I said. "There are a few like-minded colleagues, surviving by keeping their heads down. It's really the students who keep me going. Just one conversation like the one I had today with Gina makes an amazing difference."

"I think you're a born teacher, Andrew," she said. "But if you want to migrate to something else, you should do that. You're only 38, much too young to just be going through the motions."

"Yes, you're right," I said. "The last thing in the world I want is to end up like that."

"I think this should be the moment when you make a choice," she said. "I wonder if you feel like you've never really made one. You kind of washed into teaching about Parliament on a little departmental current, the way you describe it. I think you need to double down or else move on. What about shifting to teaching drama, maybe? Your first love, right? Before your parents manoeuvred you over to something that they thought would have a job at the end of it?"

"Well, that would be years trying to work on a Ph.D again," I said. "That would kill me. You'd end up living with a corpse and I've never thought you were into necrophilia."

She laughed. "Andrew, there might be other reasons why I find you so attractive."

She had my attention.

Now she was walking towards the bedroom, smiling over her shoulder.

I followed.

Later, as we lay beside each other, our conversation resumed.

"It's really the teaching that I like and teaching is teaching, whether it's drama or political science. But, you know, I've never really been driven by a sense of vocation. I think you're the one who has that. I have thought about other things sometimes. I don't think I have a sense of vo-cation for any of them either. I was even wondering about getting involved in politics a few years ago. I thought being on the condo board might be like a test run for this. I guess it was, in a way. A kind of microcosm of politics, working with all kinds of people you know? Well, I'm not the per-son to do this. I seem to have a talent for not influencing people and causing them to look at me as if I'd arrived from another planet or something. I'm beginning to think it wasn't an accident that took me to the political science department. It might have been the hand of God keeping me away from everything else."

She was laughing. She wasn't disagreeing.

"A lot of people don't have a sense of vocation," she said. "I think you're right that I'm someone who does. I simply love the law and I can't remember ever not feeling that way. So much of my life has been about overcoming barriers and the law has such a fundamental role in this. I feel as if it's part of who I am."

"Yes, I see that in you," I said. "I think you know and accept yourself in a way that I haven't found. But maybe I'm getting there. The longer I teach the parliamentary government course, the more interested I'm getting in it. There is the whole issue of representation, for example. We call our system representative democracy. We describe MPs as representing the people in Parliament, but what they actually do, especially in public, is represent their po-litical parties. The whole character of Parliament is almost completely different from the way it was when many of our ideas about it took shape a couple of hundred years ago. Then, each riding had a few hundred electors and MPs knew the people and the issues in a way that nobody else did. So MPs listened to each other in Parliament and what they said influenced decisions. Now, most of that is gone. The conditions that enabled it are gone too. But people who think traditional representation can be revived ignore this."

By now, we had made our way back to the kitchen, accompanied by wine. Francine poured us more. A sure sign of ebbing interest. I realized I had been getting carried away.

"Sorry," I said. "I'm lecturing."

"Yes, but that should tell you something."

"What?"

"That you like lecturing," she said, grinning.

"Oh.

"Actually, Francine, now that we're back together, I seem to be looking through a different lens at almost everything. And feeling different too. I can't explain it. I'm even looking forward to teaching the engineers."

Life, I thought. *Sweet unpredictable life.* It was a lot like gambling. You get a string of weak hands but there comes a time when your luck has to change. There was even a law of probability about this. Now was my time. I had Francine back, and Andy. I had my job back, mostly, with a gifted student I would help on her way.

Even on the condo board, at long last, things were finally working out. Once the dominiques were appointed, my path to freedom would be secure. All I needed to do was patiently await the next board meeting, now only a week away.

Chapter Eighteen

Catastrophe!

The diaries of natural disaster survivors often begin by describing in minute detail the final hours of normalcy, even an eerie calm, before the world of the diarist comes to an end.

That is how I remember the third Wednesday of August. It wasn't a natural disaster. It was entirely manmade. That only made it worse.

I was sitting comfortably at my desk, giving the property manager's information package a quick review before the board meeting and sipping a coffee. There was a calm, although it wasn't eerie. I even remember the coffee mug. It was an oversized cream-coloured mug with green trim, and "Be Present" inscribed on the side. "Be Engaged in What is Going on Right Now," it said. It was the wisdom of zen, exactly the right message for me, the serenity of it.

I didn't plan to break the news about my departure to the board for a few more weeks, until the new directors got more settled in. But I knew. The Britannia board meeting I was about to go to could well be my last. The current of life was gently sweeping me along to something new.

My phone buzzed beside me on the desk, so I picked up immediately.

"Andrew?" the voice said. "I'm really sorry to spring this on you like this, but I don't have any choice. I've put our house on the market this afternoon."

"What?" I said.

The voice was Barnstead's. He sounded agitated, bare-ly recognizable as Barnstead.

"We put our offer in on a bungalow yesterday and it's just been accepted," he said. "I'm coming to the meeting tonight so we can appoint the dominiques, but I have to get off the board as soon as possible."

"Henry, what's going on?" I managed.

"Andrew, it's basically move to a bungalow or lose my marriage, that's what I've been dealing with. Jane made that clear to me for a whole lot of reasons I can't go into.

She found the bungalow of her dreams last week and, like I say, I really didn't have a choice. So I can't be president, like we planned. I can't even stay on the board and that's going to have to get sorted out tonight too."

I was speechless.

Dreams are creations of the mind, without material substance. When they come crashing down, there is no audible sound. But in my mind, the sound was deafening, almost drowning out his voice. He seemed to be saying something about giving me a heads-up because I would need to be president, at least for a little while because the dominiques were so new. He was apologizing again. He was hanging up.

I sat at my desk trying to process what Henry had told me. He was leaving the board. I would be left there, along with two completely new directors and Ingrid Svennson. I would never be able to leave the condo board. I could feel it in my stomach. And how was I going to tell Francine?

First Sonya and Doreen, and now Henry. Bungalows! Bungalows were destroying my life!

"Be Present," the words on the coffee mug said. They swam before my eyes: "Be Engaged in What is Going on Right Now. Not Worrying About the Future or the Past." The cruelty of it, the cruelty of what was happening to me, gradually sank in. I didn't need a goddamn mug telling me to be in the moment. I was already there. Trapped! Completely trapped in the moment with no way out. I had never fully realized the cruelty of zen buddhism, a loathsome state of mind that just deluded people and destroyed them.

I had an impulse to smash the coffee mug.

I controlled myself.

There was coffee in it.

My board documents lay in front of me. I made a half-hearted attempt to assemble them and headed for the board office. Dragging myself across Crestview Court, I felt oppressed by the mute blocks of townhouses, my inescapable prison surrounding me.

I trudged across the strip of open land between Britannia's two residential circles. This was where Britannia's community garden could have been if residents had ever been able to agree on what they wanted. But Britannia's reality remained what it had always been. Reality was the desiccated grass, audibly crumbling under my feet, and colonies of aggressive dandelions; a graveyard of dreams.

My thoughts during this journey were not complex but they seemed to happen in slow motion. We couldn't ask either of the dominiques to take over as president when they were just being appointed to the board. That left Ingrid and me. I had trouble seeing Ingrid as president, but the more I thought of it, why not? She might rise to the occasion and I would certainly help. I would be willing to do a lot of helping in order to remain free to go ahead with my own plans. It could be empowering for her and a positive signal to owners about the role of women on our board. The more I thought of it, there was hope and an opportunity to do good too.

When I got to the boardroom, Ingrid and the dominiques were already there, introducing themselves to each other and to Bill and Charlene. They all seemed cheerful, even bubbly, excited about meeting new neighbours and anticipating a productive evening. Evidently I was the only one who had received the latest news from Henry.

Henry arrived, looking slightly pallid. He quietly took a chair.

"Evening folks," he said, after sitting down. "I see a quorum so I guess we can get started."

Charlene began taking minutes and Henry proposed that we start the meeting with director nominations. Receiving nods of agreement, he nominated Dominique Gallardi and Dominic Gallardi as board directors, to hold office until the next annual general meeting. We voted, unanimously. The board was now officially a five-person board again, ready for business. Bill's face showed relief at the prospective end of a period of turbulence and Charlene also looked pleased.

Henry looked rigidly at the table in front of him.

"Before we move to regular business," he said, "I need to raise another item here and I'm really very sorry I have to do this. Due to various circumstances, I need to resign because my wife and I have bought a bungalow. So we will be selling our home and moving in the near future. I need to tender my resignation here tonight, although I will be around for several weeks to help out, especially you folks, Dominique and Dominic. But Charlene, could you please record my resignation as of…" he looked at his watch, "…7:14 p.m. tonight, just so everything is completely precise."

The others looked at him with stunned expressions. Silence descended, and lengthened.

"Henry," Dominic finally said. "You're really surprising us here and we are sorry you will be leaving us so soon. Dominique and I will want to spend more time with you so we can get up to speed on what the board has been doing, but do you really need to formally resign right now? After all, you will be here while your house is on the market—"

"I'm really sorry," Henry cut in. "I have made some commitments and I have to keep them. I'm expected back at home immediately and I really have no choice but to do this. So, again, I'm really sorry, but I have to leave the meeting at this point."

He had arrived without the property manager's information package or other documents. He rose from his chair and hastened to the door.

During Henry's announcement and the exchange with Dominic, Ingrid's face had undergone a dramatic transformation, from stunned shock and unusual whiteness to rising colour.

"Henry," she cried out. "How could you do this? This isn't the way you promised! This isn't the way you promised at all!"

"I'm really terribly sorry," he responded. "I'm awfully sorry to everybody, but it's all about personal reasons and I really have to go."

He headed out the door. Quickly.

"I resign!" Ingrid shrieked. "Right now! I've completely had enough of everything! Especially men who just sweet talk me into doing what they want and then… and then… they go after my neighbour's daughters and everything! I'm not living here anymore! Goodnight everybody!"

Ingrid stormed out of the room.

The rest of us sat in lengthening silence, contemplating the abandoned papers where she had been sitting.

Ingrid Svennson really knew how to slam a door. I had to give her that.

"Well, this is impossible," Dominique said. "I don't see how we can be part of this… Dom?"

In panic, I interrupted.

"Dominique, I completely understand how you must feel. This is a complete shock to all of us. But could we all please just stop and take a deep breath here?"

I took one. I could see them doing likewise.

"We need to think about why we are here, and what our owners need us to do," I said. "I know you're here for the best possible reasons, to give back and serve your community. Owners like you are so important for our community, I can't overstate it. The reality is that, as of now, the three of us are a quorum of the board. So it can still do business and serve our owners. But if any of us drop off, we lose the quorum and the board will be paralyzed. I can't believe any of us want that."

"There is one urgent item of business," Bill stepped in skillfully. "I know you're all in a really stressful position here, but could I suggest you just take care of this at least? It shouldn't need a lot of discussion."

The dominiques exchanged glances. Neither of them moved to leave.

"It's item 3 in your package," Bill said. "Woody's Tree Care has reported back on the oak behind number 27 on Valleyview Circle. It has to come out. It's diseased and they are saying it's a safety hazard because it could come down anytime. You can see their report there in the package. But getting it out is going to be expensive because of the flowerbeds that Sonya wanted there last year. We'll either have to put those plants somewhere temporary or lose some expensive shrubs. So, anyway, that's going to be around $5,000 onto your landscaping budget, which is already spent, so we'll have to find money somewhere else."

"Okay," I said. "What do you recommend and can it be funded?"

"I definitely recommend removal," Bill said. "If it falls on a fence, or even a house, you're looking at serious costs. And if it fell on somebody walking on that pathway, you could end up in court. So, yes, we need to find the money and I'll make sure we do."

"What about a second estimate?" Dominique asked. "Memorial Gardens, where we do most of our interments, uses RS Arboriculture Services and they have a lot of experience with removals in areas where access is difficult."

I could see that the problem had captured her attention. She was no longer poised to leave. I just needed to keep that going.

"That's a great idea," I said. "This is the kind of knowledge that our board hasn't had, Dominique, so I would like to move that we authorize Bill to get an estimate from them as well."

Bill looked unhappy. "This could delay things," he said. "We've generally had very good service from Woody's."

"Let's move that Bill gets the estimate and then goes ahead and contracts with the lowest offer," Dominic said. "That will make sure something happens without delaying too much."

"That's an excellent strategy," I said. I could see that contributing to decisions like this was engaging them. I just needed to reinforce that feeling of accomplishment.

"Okay," Bill said. "But I think you need to have a

president to handle these votes. I should only be chairing while you get one."

"We have a lot of experience running a business," said Dominic. "I don't want to boast but it's a pretty successful one. We're actually number one in traditional burials. But since we're completely new on the board, Andrew, would you be willing to take it on for a few months until we could help you out?"

He was saying they were staying.

I would have heaved a sigh of relief, but I didn't want to show emotion, so I concentrated on diaphragm control. They needed to feel good about the board, and not think about leaving. Dominic seemed to be assuming one of them would take over as president in the near future. Normally, I would have wondered about this, from people that had just arrived on the board. However, it fit perfectly with the plans Francine and I had been making.

I smiled at them warmly.

"If you need me to be president, just until we get things sorted out, I don't mind doing that," I said.

I had to force myself to say this. There was no alternative. If I tried to put the finger on one of them to take over now, I would be ignoring what Dominic had just said and replacing their feeling of accomplishment with pressure.

"Looking ahead, your business experience will be a tremendous help if you're willing to let us benefit from that. We're already seeing this tonight and thank you for what you've done!"

Now I needed to get everybody out of there while we still had a positive note to leave on. I had planned to let them know, that evening, about the plans that Francine and I had made and signal that I would be departing from the board as soon as our house was sold. However, with the way things had gone, this was plainly not the time.

"Bill, unless you have something else that's urgent, I think we should call it a night. It's been a night of surprises and we all probably want to digest them."

"Andrew, I'm not sure how the minutes go here," Charlene piped up. "The board needs to nominate a president and vote on that, and then I'm not sure what you want to do about the tree."

This was embarrassing. I was the political scientist who was always reminding the board about procedure and now I was trampling roughshod over it.

"Thank you, Charlene," I said, making sure I was smiling. "Charlene keeps us on the straight and narrow, and yes, let's make sure our records show owners what is happening here tonight."

"Could you handle this part, Bill? Dominique or Dominic, would you like to nominate me so we can vote?"

Dominic did this. The dominiques voted in favour with me abstaining. I explained that my abstention would avoid the appearance of a conflict of interest. The dominiques looked puzzled but Bill nodded. It could have been approval or it could have been a nervous twitch.

In my new capacity as president, I convened a vote on the tree removal and the board duly authorized Bill to go ahead and deal with it.

"Do you want to do anything about new board members?" Bill asked. "Another one would give the board a margin of safety. In case somebody can't attend a meeting or something."

Again, I felt embarrassment. I had the feeling that my brain was succumbing to some kind of condo-induced narcolepsy and thoughts that should have been immediate were only arriving late, if at all. I caught Dominique glancing significantly at Dominic.

"Why yes, Bill," I said. "Of course, and thank you for reminding us. Bill is perfectly right. However, I have to tell you that I've been drawing blanks lately in conversations with owners about this and I don't really have anyone to propose right now. Finding people willing to do this has been a chronic problem since I joined the board."

The memory of my most recent attempt was still fresh in my mind. I had met Van Vliet walking his dog and told him the board might be looking for new directors soon. It was a chance to beef up owner representation, I said, and make the board more responsive and transparent.

"Yeah right," he had responded. "I did time on the board ten years ago. Sorry, but you couldn't pay me enough to do that again. Too many people all puffed up about themselves and not thinking about what they're doing to the rest of us. If you want my advice, Andrew, people aren't going to know what you're talking about with all that transparency and everything. I know I don't. If I were you, I'd just stick to basic issues like trying to get our fees down."

"...talking to people as we do our walk-throughs," Dominique was saying. "We've actually found a lot of enthusiasm out there about some of the landscaping ideas that work so well in our business."

"Yes," said Dominic. "I suggest we carry on for a week or two since a lot of people are away at this time of year. Then maybe we could get together with a few of them. The way you and Henry did with us, Andrew. We think that was a good way to do it. And don't worry. We're very optimistic about Britannia and we're sure we can find some good people."

On that positive note, the meeting wound up. We would meet at the call of the chair, maybe sooner than normal if that would sort out board membership and get the board back on track.

I strolled to the parking lot. I still felt the way I had during the last half of the board meeting: anaesthetized. As the meeting concluded, I had been feeling a vague sense of relief. But, really, there was no reason to be relieved.

Earlier in the week, Francine and I had discussed our

game-plan for handling my departure announcement tonight. She would be waiting in our living room, back from a series of meetings about her appointment as dean. Looking forward to my report about how my resignation had gone. Instead, I would be telling her that I was the new president.

It was going to take some explaining. Some very careful explaining indeed.

Chapter Nineteen

A Cultural Interlude

"Look at those colours," I said. "See if you can focus on just looking at them."

I was doing my best imitation of the docents who instructed groups about art at the National Gallery. Andy and Anwar were following me. We had arrived in front of two massive abstracts that adorned a wall in the Contemporary Canadian room.

The early afternoon crowd was thin and the view was unobstructed. Each painting was a block of brilliant colour, one orange and one red. There was a vertical stripe of black down the centre of each canvas.

I was completely unqualified to instruct young minds about abstract art and had only been conscripted at the last minute. Ayesha—Anwar's mother—and Francine had decided that the boys needed something in their lives beyond baseball and video games, and Ayesha had planned to take them on the gallery outing. Then she had been called to the hospital to perform an emergency surgery. Francine had been tied up with meetings. I had ended up leading Andy and Anwar through the rooms, straining to find some way of presenting the art to boys who had been muttering in the back seat about "girly-girl stuff."

"Now, think about how they make you feel," I said.

"They don't make me feel anything," Andy replied. "They have more colours at the paint store and they even have a lot of brighter ones."

"How do they make you feel, Mr. Walmer?" Anwar said, a mischievous glint in his eye.

I could see that they were onto me. It wasn't going to be an easy afternoon. I was going to have to outflank them with a bold move that might put us on a different footing.

After the abstracts there was a gap on the wall and, close to the floor, an electrical plug. I stopped in front of it.

"Just look at that," I said, raising my voice. "What does it say to you, boys? Just think about what the artist is trying to tell you."

"Dad!" Andy said, as a nearby couple paused and waited attentively. "It's a wall plug, Dad! What are you trying to do to us?"

"But that's just it," I said. "It looks exactly like a wall plug. So the artist knew that people would feel embarrassed to stop and look at it. You can see that people don't stop and look at those abstracts either because they probably feel embarrassed about stopping, you know? I think she is challenging us to be brave enough to stop, but she's also saying that you can't get away from electricity, even in an art gallery, so it's really a comment about modern life too."

"Daaaad!" Andy said. "You're embarrassing us! Look at that man, he's listening to you and he's laughing at us."

"Yes, Andy," I said. "He gets it. There is tremendous humour in this piece because it doesn't even look like art. So it completely threatens the expectations people have when they come to an art gallery. It's brilliant, the way it has these layers of meaning. We need to sit on the bench here and spend some time with this."

Two young men, possibly university students, had now come to a stop near the couple. They were watching us, looking bemused. I could see a security guard hovering anxiously in a doorway behind them.

The boys and I settled on the bench. The couple and the young men lingered, then moved along.

"Okay guys," I said, speaking more quietly. "I did that to show you that a lot of people who come here really don't know much about art. Like those people who stopped. And that includes me, to be honest. What I want you to take from this is that the paintings here could mean almost anything. We just have to figure out what the artist is trying to say. Why don't you go around the room and just take a little bit of time with each of them. Talk about why you think the artist might have painted them and what they might have been trying to show people, and make sure you remember some of the artists' names. I'll wait here and read what the gallery people have to say about these paintings in the meantime, so we can talk about that on the way home."

The boys moved off around the room. I flipped through the catalogue sitting on the bench. I didn't see anything that was going to help me deal with the boys. My thoughts drifted back to the previous evening, when I had headed home after the condo board meeting.

Francine had been waiting for me in the living room, winding down after a day of meetings with a glass of wine.

"You're not looking happy," she said, as I entered the room. "Get yourself a glass and come and talk to me."

I did, filling the glass. Then I joined her on the couch.

"I can't believe what happened tonight. I just can't believe it. Barnstead quit and then Ingrid stormed out and now I'm the president. I'm the goddamn president! I don't know what to do."

Her reaction took me by surprise. She sat for a moment looking at me. Her mouth began to twitch. She was trying not to laugh and then couldn't suppress it. My wife was laughing at me.

"Look, Francine," I said. "This really isn't funny. I'm trapped there! If I just quit, the dominiques won't have quorum, and I can't do that to them. We just got them onto the board and we gave them the impression everything was okay. But if I have to stay on the board, then we can't sell the townhouse, and our whole plan just goes down the toilet."

By then she was laughing uncontrollably. Her laughter was infectious. Soon I was laughing. I couldn't actually see anything to laugh at, but laughing with Francine was good. At least it made me feel more relaxed. I felt that, probably, she hadn't really taken my message in. She was very preoccupied these days with meetings about becoming dean. I decided I would just let my news seep in and then we could talk about it later.

We drank our wine and she brought me up to date on the internal politics of the Law Faculty. They seemed to be quite bizarre. *Not so different from a condo board,* I thought, except the Law Faculty didn't deal with potted plants. My last memory of the evening was lying in bed and detecting a distinct tremor running through the mattress. It was Francine. She was still laughing.

I hadn't been laughing. I also hadn't been sleeping.

"What is this telling us?" I heard.

It was Andy, his voice raised to docent volume the way I had done. He and Anwar had retraced their steps and were now positioned in front of the electrical plug again. They were not looking in my direction. Instead, they were surreptitiously eyeing two girls who had been soberly contemplating the abstracts and were now moving past the boys. The girls were self-consciously elegant in school uniforms, their gallery visit perhaps part of a summer arts program at the private school whose discreet crest was on the uniforms.

The girls did not slacken their pace as they passed the boys or acknowledge them in any way. Their faces radiated frigid indifference, laced with contempt. I was reminded, poignantly, of what it had been like to be Andy's age. Girls acquired, seemingly overnight, mysterious attractions along with an effortless capacity for scathing rejection that could defeat the social skills of any boy.

"Hey, guys," I said, facing two dejected faces. "Don't worry about those girls. You don't need snobs in your life. Why don't we adjourn for milkshakes and then I'll quiz you on what you saw so you can remember some artists' names and impress your moms. Deal?"

That was what we did.

Fuelled by milkshakes, cheerful chatter emanated from the back seat of the Jeep. Baseball seemed to have displaced the world of the arts.

Back home, the boys headed to Andy's room and the

sounds of a video game, accompanied by cries of "Get him! Get him!" could soon be heard.

Francine and I settled into our customary places on the living room couch. After chatting about the gallery visit and hearing about progress, such as it was, in her discussions with colleagues, I returned to condo board issues that Francine would now have had a chance to digest. It was a subject that Francine was beginning to greet with exaggerated solicitude. Or with giggling.

"The whole thing is ridiculous," I said. "I knew Henry had to resign because he called me and told me before the meeting. But I had hoped Ingrid would take over as president. I thought she might find it empowering, actually, and I was going to help her. But then she just exploded. I already told you about Jane's visit, so I guess we know why Henry was resigning and what the explosion was about. I'm pretty sure one of the dominiques will be willing to take over as president quite soon but, for now, I seem to be the last president standing and we have to find some new directors for the board too."

"Andrew," she said. "I think you're probably the only person over there who takes this all so seriously. We've had this conversation before. I think it's the political scientist in you. You see that the condo has powers under the Condo Act, you see that the board is its governing body and gets elected by the owners. So you think of it as kind of a miniature government. And you want it to work like a healthy democratic government. You've been trying to make that happen ever since you got there. But you need to put this in perspective. I bet most of your neighbours aren't paying attention and just want their property looked after. You have a property manager doing that, so if the board flounders around for a while, the sky isn't going to come crashing down."

"I hear you," I said. "But if a small group of neighbours can't run things competently in their immediate government, what hope can we have for the larger world? Democracy and human rights are under threat everywhere, and keeping them alive is a continuous battle. Around the world, conflicts are happening, and each conflict represents a failure of politics, which is really the only alternative to fighting we've got."

"Andrew, you're making the future of world peace depend on you and your condo board here. This is where you need perspective. I don't think there is some magical solution that can be tested on the condo board and then put into practice in all the bigger governments. Whatever the solution is, it has to be developed within each government in response to the problems that government faces. Small volunteer organizations struggle with problems that aren't so obvious elsewhere. Like people not paying attention and not wanting to get involved. That's a problem you've been talking to me about since you started on that board but, in the bigger governments, there is fierce competition to get elected. And the competition makes people pay attention, at least at election time."

"Yes," I responded. "There are differences, but some of them are really just differences of degree. There can be fierce competition within the political parties and at election time. But it's among a small group of activists. One of the problems we've talked about in my class is the massive number of extremely qualified people who would never dream of going into politics and who aren't part of that competition. Look at today's political leaders and compare them to some of the very impressive leaders of the past. Could it be that we're seeing the consequences of a shrinking potential leadership pool? I sometimes wonder if this problem might be getting worse. But coming back to your first point, I think small volunteer organizations can be part of the solution. Alexis de Tocqueville saw this almost two hundred years ago in America. He recognized that the small councils of local government were the schools where people learned democratic practice and habits that they could take into legislative politics."

"Okay," she said. "You're putting on your political science hat and putting me at a disadvantage here. We could discuss all this for a long time, but I think we need to flip the conversation and focus on your immediate practical question. What do you do? You need to start with what you actually want to do."

Want. She had emphasized the word.

"There is more of your personality than you would likely admit that is still the obedient young man doing the right thing by asking the wallflowers to dance, Andrew. Now you're trying to make the Britannia Condominium wallflower happy. This might be noble, but I think you need to figure out what would make Andrew happy here."

"Well, when you put it that way, I…"

I had spent the last two years wanting to get off the board and also wanting to somehow control Sonya and make things right. There seemed to be two directions there. I had to admit it.

"Andrew, what do you actually enjoy doing? If you don't really enjoy the board then I think you should get off it. But if you do enjoy it, then we should find a way for you to continue. Even if we have to keep the townhouse and rent it out to students or something, so you could still be on the board as an owner."

Now I was completely floored. She was saying I could live in our bungalow and also stay on the condo board. This was a thought that hadn't occurred to me. I needed to process it.

It took about three seconds.

"Francine, don't do this to me!" I said. "I hate being on the board. I hate the meetings, I hate the complete absence of procedure unless I make a fuss about it, I hate the sheer incompetence, I hate the issues. I'm at the point that if anybody says something about messy backyards or potted plants to me, they better hope I'm not packing a gun. And most of all, I hate the fact that when I try to explain things to people, they just sit there looking at me as if I've dropped into the room from Mars or something.

I'm even starting to hate most of the people I have to deal with. They might be well-intentioned, whatever that means, but when they piously declare that they are only there to serve their community, it's starting to make me hate them. When they do that, I just know in my heart that they're going to come up with some crack-brained idea and the board is going to force it on everybody. I'm not a hater, Francine, honest. I've always thought of myself as an extrovert. But the condo board is turning me into an extrovert who hates people!"

I had to stop for breath. I didn't know where this was coming from. But it felt good to get it out.

Francine regarded me with what looked like a kind of love. Maybe it was pity. She had also started giggling.

"Would I be right that you don't like being on the condo board?"

She was now laughing and had to pause.

"Andrew, you're really saying that Britannia Condominium is your wallflower from hell," she said. "The one who never took baths and kept telling you you were stupid, and stomping on your feet when you tried to dance."

"Okay, okay," I said. "I'm not in denial about this. It's just that I don't agree. Really, I think you might be overdoing the wallflower thing. Yes, my mother was a champion for them, but I'm a grown man, you know? Anyway, yes, I have to get off the condo board. I can't disagree with that. It's really about how I do it, that's all. I just need to give the dominiques a little bit of time. I feel I owe them that, and me moving is going to be one more thing they weren't warned about back when they agreed to join the board. I don't want to do something sudden that might scare them off. They said they could find some new directors to replace Henry and Ingrid and I'll try to help. We could do a nice smooth hand-over at the next meeting, and by then, I'll have somebody to suggest for my own replacement too."

"I'd like to propose a toast," she said, lifting her glass. "To Andrew Walmer's freedom!"

We clinked glasses and drank.

It was one of those magic moments; we were smiling into each other's eyes and looking to the future. Our future together. I had a future again and it wasn't on the condo board.

"Awesome!" we heard from Andy's room. "We never made it to level four before!"

"Next time we just have to figure out how to stay there." It was Anwar, and they were coming to the living room.

"Looks like the animals need to be fed," I said. "They can impress you with their newfound knowledge of the arts while I put things together."

I headed to the kitchen to serve up the chicken tetrazz-ini I had prepared that morning.

In contrast to the beckoning future, in the present there is rarely a sky without at least a tiny cloud. As I headed to the kitchen, I wondered how I was going to break the news about my departure to the dominiques. How would they take it, so soon after joining?

What would they do?

Chapter Twenty

Off?

We no longer believe in purgatory, but nobody questions camping.

I lay there in our tent at Land O' Lakes Campground, still wakeful with my watch saying 3 a.m. I was thinking that camping, like purgatory, combines the worst features of being dead and staying alive. The main difference is that camping doesn't involve theology. This is a point in favour of camping. There aren't many others.

As a younger man, I had liked camping. At least that

was the way I remembered it. That nostalgia had inspired me with the idea of a camping trip with Andy back when I had bought the Jeep. Once Francine and I had reunited, planning had become a lot simpler and, finally, the trip had happened.

The Land O'Lakes Campground, with its population of loud families and tottering seniors, fell somewhat short of the wilderness camping experience I had envisioned.

On the positive side, it had bathrooms.

Andy and I were there because, the morning of our departure, the ominous noise I had been hearing from the Jeep had become a very loud ominous noise while the Jeep, now loaded with camping equipment, remained stationary in the driveway. This had resulted in our late departure in Francine's faithful Volvo and the need for a more accessible destination. However, the trip was still an opportunity for some father-son bonding before Andy's teenage years set in and I got wrapped up in teaching again.

Andy had seemed indifferent to the scaling back of plans. He wouldn't admit it, but I had the impression that the timing of the trip had been the most important factor for him. His eyes had taken on a noticeable gleam when he realized that the trip would prevent him from joining Anwar and his mother on a follow-up trip to the National Gallery.

"Sorry, buddy," I had heard a gloating voice declare from his bedroom.

Once Francine had been reassured she could stay at home, she had been enthusiastic about the trip too. I was expected to return in a state of internal peace, she told me, and would no longer be permitted to talk obsessively about the condo board.

I had adapted easily to the scaling back of plans because the prospect of wilderness camping had already begun to seem daunting. On top of that, I was still processing what had happened on the condo board during the final week of August.

Along with a succession of mosquitoes, that was what had been keeping me awake.

I struggled to get out of the body bag I had been trying to sleep in so I could journey to the bathroom. I had been lying there for four futile hours. For at least three of those hours, something had been digging into my lower back through a gradually deflating air mattress. No matter where I moved, whatever it was kept digging. It had remained oppressively hot for the first half of the night and mosquitoes had arrived with exquisite timing, each waiting for sleep to approach before hovering loudly near my ear.

When I returned to our campsite, now fully awake, I decided to avoid disturbing Andy by trying to get back into the tent. We had a full day of canoeing planned and I didn't want to be dealing with a cranky 11-year-old.

I got a blanket from the car and settled into a folding chair beside our proprietary picnic table. The darkness of night was gradually giving way to misty light and the scent of trees pervaded the air. The campground was peaceful. I had a lot to be thankful for. My son and I had done some real bonding yesterday, waiting for fish to materialize in the vicinity of our lines.

Andy had never said much in response to the improvised explanations Francine and I had given him, but my departure from our family home had affected him deeply.

"Hey, Dad," he had said, out of the blue as we ate sandwiches. "I'm really glad that you're back and you and Mom are, you know, good again."

"I'm really glad too," I said. "Mom and I were both very sad about what happened. I think that made it harder for us to talk with each other about it. We were both afraid of what the other person might say. But now we've gotten past that. We understand each other better. Ourselves too. Mom and I both love you a lot and that really helped us. The times you and I had together, with me coming back to the house afterwards, that helped us to keep seeing each other and realize that we needed to be together. So I guess we owe you, Andy. Just don't expect us to pay you in cash or anything."

I was trying to keep it light. Mainly because I could feel myself getting emotional. But I had realized there was more I needed to say. I needed to answer the question he hadn't asked.

"Seriously, Andy, the last few weeks, now that I've

moved back, Mom and I realize we still love each other very much, maybe even more than before. They've been the happiest time in my life. I don't think there is very much in life that is absolutely completely certain, Andy, but I can't imagine Mom and I will ever not be together. And being your full-time Dad again. I think we did pretty well when I was part-time, but I can't tell you how glad I am about that too."

"Okay," he had said. "Me too."

We had been sitting in the boat, gently rocking on the water, and companionably disposing of cherries that I had packed for a dessert. I felt an understanding between us. A very good feeling.

As the dawn light slowly brought the campsite trees into focus, my thoughts returned to my troubled night, haunted by the condo board. The condo had become a perpetual cloud on my horizon when, everywhere else in my world, there was wonderful sunshine. Yet again, just last week, the board had reminded me of a basic reality in all kinds of politics: there is simply no predicting what other people will think or do. They might look like you, talk like you, and wear clothes from the same stores you shop at, but then, when they open their mouths, you are sometimes confronted with completely alien beings, not like you at all. It left me wondering if we could hope to ever live together on the same planet without perpetual conflict.

After the last board meeting, the dominiques had

found two volunteers for the board. However, my relief about this diminished considerably when I found myself in the Gallardi living room sitting across from Melissa Wagner, whose highly totalitarian community garden proposals still awaited a decision from the board. Beside her sat a pleasant looking man I had not previously met. Wilson Chang was introduced by Melissa as one of the most effective contributors to the community garden committee. Melissa's enthusiasm affected me like a warning siren. However, the dominiques were smiling happily. Who was I to upset the apple cart, especially when I was about to get off it?

The new board members had wanted a special meeting as soon as possible to appoint directors and get on with business. That fit with the plans Francine and I had been making. I didn't want to break my news to new volunteers before they were even appointed to the board, but a special meeting before the end of August would give me the opportunity to explain why I needed to resign. We could also work out a transition plan for handing over the president position to one of the dominiques.

The special meeting had happened the evening before Andy and I left on our camping trip. The new appointments and routine business from the property manager were eagerly disposed of. There was an electricity in the air, almost the feeling of an evangelical revival meeting.

The electricity became noticeably more intense when

we got to the item Dominic had asked Bill to add to the agenda: "Reviving the Britannia Beautification Campaign." I had been surprised he was aware of Sonya's campaign, but it turned out he and Dominique were long-time converts.

Dominic was the first to speak and his voice was resonant, almost hypnotic. He and Dominique had shared life-changing experiences over the years in their business. They had witnessed how memorial gardens, immaculate and lovingly tended, brought peace to anguished mourners and provided them a continuing place of connection with loved ones. A caring board could give Britannia this wonderful gift.

Melissa and Wilson listened with rapt attention.

I listened with rapt attention too. But my rapt attention wasn't enthusiasm. It was growing horror. Dominic's concluding words were still branded on my mind:

"We have come together with our walk-throughs, Andrew, and we're sorry you haven't been able to share in this. We feel the Britannia Beautification campaign is an inspiring idea that can bring our community together in a wonderful way. The trouble that came up over the summer was because previous boards have never really gotten the campaign off the ground. We, as the new board, need to double-down and give people results they can see and experience in their daily lives here at Britannia!"

"Thank you for that, Dom," Dominique responded. "We're all absolutely on the same page here and, Andrew, you've already been working with Sonya Dietrich on this so we know you'll be with us too."

She went on to say that it was late in the season to try and start major changes to our grounds, but a perfect time to start planning for them. Melissa had come up with something that could be organized right away and done while late summer weather continued. She smiled encouragingly at Melissa.

What Melissa proposed was also branded on my mind. My mind had received a lot of branding that night.

"Yes," Melissa had said. "It's wonderful that a group of like-minded people has finally come together on the condo board and I'm really excited about what we're going to be able to do. As we all know, squirrels have taken a heavy toll on our property every year. They damage our buildings and there has been terrible destruction in some of the planting beds. This is a problem we can tackle right here tonight."

Two radiant faces eyed Melissa across the board table. Wilson was less demonstrative but he nodded politely.

"Many of our neighbours have bird feeders in their backyards and the squirrels are getting food out of them. This is bringing squirrels to Britannia from outside our property and we need to bring it to a stop. We already have a rule about this that says all bird feeders must be squirrel-proof and that means we have a legal obligation to enforce it. So I think a notice needs to go out requiring owners to take responsibility for this and we should follow up with a board… what do they call it? Isn't it a squat team or something?"

"Maybe swat team," Wilson offered. "Like in the police shows?"

"Yes," Melissa beamed. "Thanks, Wilson, that's what I was groping for. If owners don't deal with non-compliant bird feeders, then those feeders need to be removed. So why don't we settle that tonight? That's what I'd like to propose."

The dominiques were nodding approvingly. So was Wilson.

The boardroom swam briefly before my eyes. Could I be hearing right?

The idea of a SWAT team of directors marching into people's yards to remove offending bird feeders set a new benchmark in the Britannia boardroom, for sheer outlandishness. And God, in His wisdom, knew there was intense competition.

God also had a sadistic sense of humour. I was the president who would be officially responsible for this. I was ending up as president of the condo equivalent of North Korea!

Direct criticism of Melissa's idea would only provoke conflict. The others were so obviously enthusiastic. I needed to make sure they stayed happy and motivated. Above all, I needed them to not go stampeding off to buy bungalows and stay on the board long enough for me to get off it.

I decided to keep things light and rely on humour.

"Thank you, Melissa," I said. "I wonder how the team would determine whether the feeders are squirrel-proof or not? I think I know somebody with a pet squirrel, so maybe the team could borrow it and take it around with them. It could be Britannia's official bird-feeder test squirrel."

I waited for laughter.

There wasn't any. Instead, four faces regarded me approvingly across the table.

"Thank you, Andrew," Melissa said. "Yes, why don't we do that? That would mean we had the same test for everybody because that squirrel wouldn't be biased, so people would feel everything was fair."

My memory of exactly what happened after that remains vague. Eventually, I called for a motion and somebody made one. People voted on it. It passed.

I knew I couldn't close the meeting before at least warning them that I would soon need to resign. The latest bout of condo madness made this even more urgent, for the sake of my sanity.

"Before we adjourn," I said, "I have something I need to tell you, and I'm sorry that I have to do this tonight."

In the days leading up to the meeting, I had scripted out my announcement very carefully. It was a delicate moment, with two completely new directors just appointed and the dominiques basically new as well. I needed to make every effort not to discourage them and make things as easy as possible for whichever dominique might take on the president's role.

I emphasized that my formal resignation didn't have to happen immediately and I would work with the new president on the transition over several months, or longer if needed. After all, the process of selling our townhouse would take time. I told them how bad I felt about doing this so early in the life of what was, in effect, a new board, and how sorry I was to be losing the opportunity to work with them. I hoped they would understand my new circumstances, reuniting with Francine after three years of painful separation. Even after I moved, I would be living in the same neighbourhood and would certainly be available to provide whatever advice was needed and help in every possible way.

As I spoke, I watched anxiously for reactions. They weren't obvious. Dominique had begun doodling in the margin of the information package. Melissa's attention had strayed to documents in her file. Dominic seemed to be checking phone messages. Wilson, at least, remained po-litely attentive.

As my speech drew to a conclusion, board members regarded me with the expression I had seen so often on faces in the Britannia boardroom over the years. I still couldn't tell what people were thinking.

I braced for the worst. Surely the new directors would understand that I had not somehow lured them onto the board under false pretences. And I was doing everything I could to keep things running smoothly.

"Well, Andrew, that is quite a surprise," said Dominic, after a pause. "I'm very happy for you, and I'm sure we all are."

"I'm very happy for you too," Dominique added, her voice calm. "We all are and thank you so much for sharing your news with us."

"I guess we also have some news that should be part of this discussion," Dominic said. "Andrew, we're still comfortable with one of us taking over as president, as we were planning, but we're probably going to need a couple of months. We have an unexpected situation at the home that we have to deal with."

"Yes," Dominique continued. "We aren't going to be able to step away from the home as soon as we thought because the man who was moving into a partnership role, one of our best people, is no longer with us. We're like a second family at the home and this is very sad for us. Arthur Jolson had been with us for at least ten years and he was a key part of our plan to shift away from day-to-day involvement."

"It's not just the business aspect," Dominic said. "We need to be supporting our employees through this. It was very upsetting for them, the way it happened. They thought he was testing one of our new models and when he wasn't moving, they were joking about him sleeping on the job and playing tricks to wake him up. So, they are quite traumatized and we need to support them."

"You often hear that doctors don't take care of their own health because it doesn't occur to them that they can get sick," Dominique added.

"Well, I guess we have something a little bit like this in our business. People assume that we'll just go on and on forever, helping others. So the loss of Arthur has really hit people. We're all realizing that we are mortal and some of our people are having a very hard time dealing with this."

"I can't speak for Wilson," Melissa said, "but you certainly have our sympathies and, Andrew, of course we'll help you with things in the meantime."

Wilson was nodding and appeared about to speak.

"Yes, thank you for that." It was Dominque. "And thank you, Andrew, for being willing to carry on for now while we deal with things. We'll be supportive as well and, really, this will only be a month or two, at the very most."

The remainder of the meeting passed in a blur.

Something may have happened. Maybe nothing. After the meeting adjourned, the four new directors began chatting enthusiastically together. I told them I had family duties and left them to it.

I hoped they wouldn't be working themselves up about my resignation announcement. After closing the door, I hovered near the open window, listening intently. The only words I heard distinctly came from Dominic.

"...bird feeder behind #23," he was saying...

"Dad?"

"Dad!"

It was Andy. His voice was loud and about two feet from my right ear.

"What are you doing out here? Why are you staring like that? Why weren't you answering? Can we get some breakfast? I'm starved!"

"Oh," I said. "Right. Sorry, Andy, I was just thinking. Off in my own little world, you know?"

Warm sunlight was now streaming into the campsite. It was no longer early. My watch said 8:30 a.m. I wondered how five hours could have gone by since I got up in the night. Perhaps I had dozed, sitting there in a comfortable chair.

"What were you thinking about, Dad?"

Andy settled onto the picnic table, fully dressed and obviously ready for the day.

"Oh, you know," I said. "Just stuff. I didn't have that great a sleep, so I came out here. It wasn't too bad, nice and quiet actually. So what do you say about going over to O'Grady's instead of roughing it in the campground kitchen? That will speed us up and I can't have you starving now, can I?"

The day was beginning for Andy, not just me. I

remembered what it was like at his age, when life was immediate, without adult preoccupations. Camping could just be camping and waking up hungry was what you thought about until you tasted breakfast.

A day with Dad could be something to remember, but Dad needed to stop drifting away in private thoughts.

"So," I said. "Let's go!"

At the mention of O'Grady's, I had seen an anticipatory gleam in his eye. Yesterday, we had discovered that O'Grady's made an excellent chocolate milkshake.

We got there in time to snag the last remaining table. I remained impassive when Andy, eyeing me speculatively, added the chocolate shake to his breakfast menu. I also remained impassive when he produced his phone, which had been off limits during camping. After all, today was going to be Andy's day. And besides, he had a valid technical argument since we were sitting in a restaurant, not camping exactly.

While Andy communed with his phone, I reached for a copy of the *Ottawa Citizen* that had been left on the chair beside me. The world seemed pleasantly far away as I began casually flipping through it. More and more, the world resembled a giant condo board where bizarre characters passionately declared their attachment to noble causes and produced a steady stream of improbable events. Somehow it all seemed to work, most of the time. At least that was the way I felt sitting there in the comfort of a room full of sun-drenched vacationers enjoying O'Grady's succulent breakfasts.

On page three of Local News, my contentment came to an abrupt end. The headline read: "Local Activist to Run for Council." Beneath the headline, I read:

Local community activist Philippe Gibbon announced on Monday that he will run for municipal council in November. Gibbon is the first of several candidates expected to throw their hats into the ring in coming weeks.

Touting his extensive community experience, including the donation of "endless hours of time" as a volunteer board director at Britannia Condominium, Gibbon had declared:

We need fresh ideas on Council! I'm passionate about community service and my track record since moving to Britannia ward five years ago speaks for itself. I feel that it's my time to start giving back and I want to bring a new vision to Council. We need to start with a comprehensive beautification campaign that will make our city a destination of choice for tourism, business, and residents.

Sharon Corbeil, apparently a long-time resident although I had never met or seen her on the attendance list for our AGMs, was quoted:

Mr. Gibbon really made waves in our condo over the summer. I think he's exactly the type of leader we need on our Council.

There was more in the article. I couldn't bring myself to read it.

The plate of buckwheat pancakes I had ordered

arrived in front of me. I sat looking at it. Whenever I finally processed the events in my life, more events never failed to arrive. There seemed to be no end to them. And now, in municipal politics, the condo board would continue to haunt me.

"Dad!" I heard. "You're doing it again. You look like you're on drugs or something."

"Sorry, Andy," I said. "Sorry! I just read something in the paper about the condo board, I mean about politics, and it made me worried."

"The condo board got into the newspaper?" Andy interjected. "Are you in there, Dad? Man, that would be so cool!"

"No, Andy, we're not famous yet," I responded. "A man who used to be on the condo board is now getting into city politics. Basically, the city is run by a group of people who get elected to a kind of big condo board called the municipal council. What's worrying me is that he was a terrible board member. He never did anything and then he got the owners all worked up and tried to get them to put in a different board. So now I'm worried that he's going to cause trouble for the whole city. You know I teach about this kind of thing, right?" I reminded him. "Politics is really about people making decisions together. So it's important to have the right kind of people doing it, people who are good at understanding each other, especially when they disagree. Politics is the only way we have to solve problems together without some kind of violence. So when I see things going wrong in politics, like this man from the condo board getting into it, it makes me worried."

Andy seemed to be thinking between slurps of his milkshake.

"If it's so important, why don't you do it, Dad?"

I didn't have a ready answer. I forked a large piece of pancake into my mouth.

"That's a good one," I finally managed. "You know, Andy, I think the person who really should do it is your mom. She's very busy with some exciting things at her work right now, but I think in a few years she should go into politics. Maybe we should try and persuade her."

"Okay," he said. "But Dad, I'm only an 11-year-old, you know, and I came here to fish. You're doing too much talking."

"Right," I said. "Let's do one thing at a time. Today, let's catch some fish. Then let's see what we can do about the world when we get back home."

"Sounds good," he said.

I signalled for the bill. As we waited, Andy had another question. It made me wish I still had my pancakes for distraction.

"I thought you were going to be off that condo board," he said, "but at home, I heard you telling Mom that you're the president. So what's going on, Dad? Are you off it or not?"

"Well, it's complicated, Andy," I said. "I'm technically still on the board because people over there need me to help out, but they know I'm going to be quitting. So, I'm more or less off, practically speaking, except that I'm president because the person who's going to be president has a problem at work, so they don't have time to be president right now. But since I've moved back with you and Mom, other people are taking on most of the work, so I'm not really that involved in the board anymore. At least, I'm mostly not going to be that involved, except now the neighbours are going to be blaming me for some ridiculous things the board is doing..."

"So what are you saying, Dad?" he asked. "You're saying that you're off it. Mostly. Right?"

"Yes," I said. "I guess that's more or less it, for now at least. Off it, mostly, seems to be where I've ended up."

Acknowledgements

Writing is a solitary activity, but I am grateful to members of the Canadian Authors Association's Tuesday Ottawa Writers Circle, and coordinator/font of editorial wisdom, Arlene Sommerton-Smith, for their encouragement and thoughtful criticism. I am also grateful to Alanna Rusnak, publisher at Chicken House Press, for perceptive editorial comments and excellent support throughout the publishing process. Writing is a sedentary activity as well as a solitary one, so credit also goes to LF Products PTE, somewhere in China, where my office chair was made.

About the Author

Jack Stilborn showed early promise with a comic story that made a cousin laugh so hard she threw up. He was then deflected by life. Careers included part-time academic (political science); intergovernmental affairs advisor (Ontario government) and research analyst (Parliament). Outside work, he has raised three children with spouse Linda and enjoys eclectic reading, volunteer work, cycling, kayaking (no white water please) and cross-country skiing. Following a period of writing about parliamentary government, he returned to fiction with a short story that received Honourable Mention in the 2024 Alice Munro Short Story Contest, and this, his debut novel. His short stories also appear in literary magazines such as *Blank Spaces*.

Check out Jack's website: jackstilborn.com

Discussion Questions

These questions are provided to stimulate discussion in book clubs, but individual readers may find them useful too. The questions are organized with warm-up questions up front, to start conversations. Later questions go deeper, for those who want to go there.

Warm-ups

1. Which characters in this story do you like, and why? Who do you dislike?

2. Do you need to like characters in a story to find it engaging?

3. Which character would you most like to have lunch with? What would you ask them? How do you imagine they might answer?

4. What does the title of the novel say to you? Did you find that it made sense after you read the story?

5. What did you like best about the book? What did you like least?

Andrew and Francine

1. At the beginning of the story, we meet a confident Andrew who believes he can read people and situations. Does he? Can he? Who does he read right and who does he misread? Is Francine realistic about Andrew?

2. Andrew is a bit of a bumbler, but feels he has moments of courage. What are they? What would explain these moments?

3. Andrew values honesty "at least in the important things," but he tells himself there aren't that many important things, so "it's not a problem." Is this a joke or could he have a point? Do social relations (or politics) require little white lies from time to time?

4. Francine suspects that Andrew is obsessed with the condo board because he is looking for distraction from things he doesn't want to think about. Andrew believes he's on the condo board to help his neighbours and make the board work better. Who's right? What does Andrew accomplish on the board? In our own lives, how can we figure out why we do things?

5. After Francine confides that she let her principles over-rule her heart in their relationship, Andrew realizes he needs to think about his own deeper motives. What does he conclude? About his feelings for Francine? About his affair? Based on what the novel tells us, has he figured himself out or is he still telling himself stories?

6. Francine is extremely accomplished and wise. What attracts her to Andrew? Why does she accept him back? Would you?

Politics and Government

1. Andrew asks: if we can't make small organizations work properly, what hope can there be for the big ones (i.e governments)? Does he have a point? Or is it possible that we need to make the big organizations work properly in order to support the small ones? Or, could it be both?

2. What does the story tell us about politics? What are the similarities between condo board politics and politics on municipal councils or legislatures? What are the differences?

3. The public meeting held by the condo board quickly falls apart. Why? Are there realistic solutions that a condo

board could apply? Do any of these solutions apply more broadly, to democratic politics?

4. The condo board frequently bogs down on minutiae, but then its biggest decision (about an expensive paving contract) is passed in seconds. Have you seen this happen in other political settings?

5. Andrew tells his students that you have to understand drama in order to understand politics and politicians. True?

General

1. At various points in the story, people tell themselves that their intentions are good and avoid thinking about how their actions affect others? What are some examples? Is there any way to escape this "tyranny of good intentions"? Do any of the characters find a way?

2. What does the story tell us about human relationships? Why did Andrew and Francine separate, and what enabled them to restore their marriage? Is their marriage truly repaired, or is there trouble on the horizon? What challenges will they need to face?

3. In Chapter 12, Francine reminds Andrew of his favourite quote: "From the crooked timber of humanity, never was a straight thing made." He feels she has understood this and tells himself that sooner or later, every moral principle collides "with the beating heart of a human being." What sense are we to make of this conversation? What should a person do when important principles like honesty threaten to cause human pain? If we abandon principles whenever they hurt someone, then do we really have principles?

4. Humanism is a style of thinking that focuses on people rather than abstract principles, seeking a joyful world where people live happy lives. Principles can always be questioned if they seem to be doing harm. Which characters seem to be humanists? Which don't? Does this approach make things better, or worse?

Other

1. How do you feel about the way the novel treats minorities? For example, Francine is Black but, aside from an early hint (her dark skin) we don't find this out definitely until well into the story. Are other minorities present, even more inconspicuously? Is this a good thing?

2. Gina is a trans person and says she doesn't want to be an "issue," just a human being like everyone else. What does this say to you? If you are a trans person, do you relate to this? How do you treat trans persons in your own life? Does this mean Gina shouldn't be seen as somehow a representative of trans people (as Andrew treats her at times)?

3. Doreen and Sonya establish a relationship, but there is no direct evidence that it is sexual. Do you assume it is? Does this assumption reflect contemporary Western culture, or are there other reasons for it?

4. In the campground, Andy asks Andrew if he's back in the family for good. Is this the question an eleven-year-old would ask? What about 'why did you do it, Dad?' Would an eleven-year-old have asked that one?